Shadow of a Promise

A Vow

Patricia Marlett

Published in the United States of America
Published by High Tower Publications

First Edition 2009 ISBN: 978-0-615-41264-1
Second Edition 2017 ISBN: 978-0-9854059-9-1

High Tower Publications
2 Samuel 22:3

Shadow of a Promise

A Vow

The Story of Sophie

Acknowledgement

I will always, and forevermore, acknowledge and give thanks to God. I honor, praise and give the glory to my heavenly Father; for it is by His grace, that I am blessed. He is my inspiration and with the gift He has bestowed upon me, I write in His honor to glorify His name.

Also, much appreciation to my husband, Mark, for his unwavering love, support and dedication to making my dream come true. You are my rock, I love you.

Dedication

This book is dedicated to Christina, Caleb, and Caden;
my daughter and grandsons. You are my joy.

*To all the special Sisters
and especially Twins*

Chapter 1

"Push."

"Good. Now take a deep breath and push again."

"I can't."

"Yes, you can. Come on, don't quit on me now."

"I can do this, I can do this," she chanted between gasps for air.

"Looking good, we're almost there."

"I'm never doing this again."

"Of course not, we all say that with the first."

"No, I really mean it!"

"Here we go, give me one more big push."

Sophie held so tightly to her sister's hands both of their knuckles turned white. Sabrina was standing at the head of the delivery table with her face close, whispering words of encouragement.

"You're doing great, sis. Give us one more, and we'll be done," Brie told her, affirmatively.

"Alright, I can do it one more time."

No matter the agony, she intended to achieve her self-imposed goal of natural childbirth. Inhaling a big gulp of air while still holding onto her sister's hands as a lifeline, Sophie pushed with all her remaining strength. Suddenly, the room became very quiet and no one moved, as silently one and then another, slipped from her womb and that's when the commotion began. There was harmonious sound of babies wailing while nurses scrambled around, and yet again, the mid-wife telling her to push once more. Damp with sweat and fatigued from the ordeal, Sophie looked upward and smiled at her twin.

"Oh, Sophie, you did it. You have two beautiful babies," Sabrina said, watching the nurses take them to be quickly checked over and returned to their mother.

"Did I have girls? My twins have to be girls."

Sophie emphasized weakly still focused on her sister. She knew ultrasounds weren't always reliable. Sophie wanted to hear it said aloud.

"Yes, they are girls and you will be holding them shortly. They are getting ready for your introduction."

Sophie closed her eyes exhausted yet thrilled having giving birth to twins. She had yet to let go of her sister's hands as Sabrina leaned down and kissed her on the forehead.

"Now the fun begins," Brie whispered, teasingly.

Sophie smiled, waiting patiently for her babies. Nurses were carefully bundling each in a pink blanket and snuggled one on either side of Sophie as she wrapped her arms around her newborns. Tears filled her eyes when she set sight on her precious babies watching the little one on her right let out a perfect symmetrical yawn.

"Brie, look at that. She's going to be my feisty one, already opening her mouth," Sophie said in awe.

"Congratulations, sis. Which one is Faith and which is Grace?" Sabrina asked as she gently touched both babies' forehead.

"This is Grace on my right and Faith here on my left."

Grace was the one who gave her own introduction when she opened her tiny mouth to yawn.

"I'm going to get David. It's time for your husband to experience your special delivery," Brie said, winking at her sister before making her way to the door.

David was a handsome, slender man with his light brown hair trimmed neat and gorgeous blue eyes a woman could drown in. She always thought it was David's eyes that first attracted Sophie to him back in college when they met.

With a quick glance over her shoulder before leaving the room, Sabrina watched her sister talking to her babies. It was a priceless moment to see her twin holding her own twins. They arrived five hours prior to the *Regional Women Medical Center* located adjacent to the *Orlando Regional Hospital*, servicing the medical treatment and care of women only. Sophie chose this facility specifically because they allowed natural birthing but were equipped with an operating room should an unexpected emergency arise.

David and Sophie, as teachers, lived a comfortable life in a nice suburb of Orlando. They met in college when David was a senior, and Sophie and her sister were in their junior year. Two weeks after Sophie and Sabrina graduated, she became Mrs. David McKinley. Enjoying a few years in her profession before beginning a family, Sophie waited to have her first child.

Sabrina found David pacing in the empty waiting room ignoring the television mounted to the wall displaying advertisements of hospital entities. As David could not handle the sight of blood, and no persuasion on Sophie's part was going to convince him to be her Lamaze coach, the duty was relinquished to his sister-in-law. Watching her approach, he practically pounced on her.

"Congratulations, David. You're a daddy of two girls and your family is waiting for you," Sabrina said as she walked up and gave him a big hug.

With tears in his eyes, he smiled, and they held hands as she led him back through the doubled-doors and down a long corridor into Sophie's room. Cautiously, he stepped forward toward the bed bending down to kiss his wife.

"Oh Sophie, honey, what have we here?" he asked, beaming at the babies.

"Meet your little girls. This is Faith on my left and Grace

on my right. Girls this is your daddy," Sophie said, making the official introductions.

David gently slid his right hand under the pink blanket of Faith and slipped her into his arms while sitting on the edge of the bed. He glanced at Sophie and then Faith stole his attention when she seemed to have smiled at her daddy.

"Did you see that? She smiled at me," David proclaimed with a big grin on his face.

"I'm sure she did," Sophie agreed, looking down at Grace.

When Sophie first discovered she was expecting twins, she wasn't sure what names would be best for them. She and David exchanged ideas for weeks, but couldn't agree on what to call the girls. Sophie presented the question to her sister during one of their many phone conversations, and without hesitation, Sabrina blurted out Faith and Grace. At first, Sophie wasn't sure about her sister's suggestion, but eventually mellowed to the names when David agreed to liking them. Now five months since that conversation, the introductions have begun.

"I think Grace is going to be our mischief-maker," Sophie told her husband as he played with the tiny fingers on Faith's left hand.

"Why do you say that?"

"She was the first one to speak, sort of. She opened her mouth and let out this big yawn as soon as she was handed to me. Look, there she goes again," Sophie declared, laughing as she angled Grace toward David.

"And based on this, you think she will be the little troublemaker between the two of them. Maybe she is already bored with this new world she has been thrust into."

David couldn't help but tease his wife.

"I don't think so. Time to switch, you can't show any favoritism. Give Faith back to me and take Grace."

Sabrina remained away from the scene taking place at the bed, standing near the window allowing Sophie and David time to become acquainted with their new family members. It was emotional for her watching them hold these little babies they had created. She thought of Ben, her fiance, realizing that establishing her photography business, *Snaps by Sabrina,* when she first relocated to Asheville and continuing to travel as a freelance photographer for the magazine, *Nature on the Run,* inadvertently took precedence in her life. At that time, very little thought was given to marriage.

And there was also the endeavor with *Passionate Promises* that no one truly knew the depth of her involvement. With Ben equally busy with the new addition of a greenhouse to the family-owned business, *Cooper Christmas Tree Farm,* he wasn't compelled to press Sabrina. They both knew it would happen when work-related events settled in their lives. Thus, it became an unspoken mutual decision to hold off on their wedding plans.

However, now Brie questioned why she thought anything could be more important than marrying the man she loved. He was the only man she had ever cared about and had fallen for him the first time she looked into his dark brown eyes. It was like swimming in chocolate, metaphorically speaking. He wore his dark brownish-black hair longer than the norm, touching his shirt collar, which against his tanned skin gave him a very masculine and overall rugged appeal. Ben's six-feet towered over her petite five-feet, five-inch height, but that didn't hamper their attractiveness to one another.

Seeing David and Sophie with their infants, Brie experienced first hand what she was missing and it made her incredibly sad that she had waited. Time had slipped away and there wasn't anything she could do about that, but she could do something about her future. When she returned home, her first priority was to talk with Ben about planning a wedding; starting their life together and having their own family.

Chapter 2

Sabrina was motivated to move to Asheville, North Carolina following the sudden, unexplainable death of her beloved Aunt Millie, her last remaining relative other than her sister. Inheriting her aunt's two-story rustic English Tudor home in the foothills, and a surprising legacy of *Passionate Promises*, she settled comfortably into the country estate. It was the first time Sabrina took charge of her destiny, making decisions that directed her future rather than simply following instructions, being sent on assignments to various locations across the country as a photojournalist.

Having been with the magazine for more than ten years, she felt comfortable freelancing, opting to pursue her now well-established private photography business. Between the two, Sabrina is in constant demand as she continues to enjoy photographing animals in their natural habitat and remains amazed when invitations arrive to display her photographs in select museums. It is her documented work through the magazine that brings institutions and businesses seeking her.

When she moved into the house, leaving her condominium in Florida available for visits with her sister, Brie immediately began reconstructing some of the rooms with the insight to create a studio. The first thing Sabrina accomplished was turning the formal dining room into a general workroom. Utilizing the large, walnut table allowed her ample space to place her finished photographs for selection, matting, and framing. Next, she decided to take the laundry room located off the kitchen and made a few changes converting it into a dark-room for developing film, wanting the flexibility between chemical processing and computerized software programs.

With the completion of these two rooms, Sabrina then changed the living room into a commercial studio painting the walls a robin-blue and strategically placing several of her personal prints on one wall, while arranging framed portraits on the remaining wall space. Brie designed the studio with a Victorian flair, using French provincial pieces to create a settee along the front windowed area, making a picturesque setting with a view of the outdoors through the panes as a natural backdrop.

On the opposite wall was a low bench covered with a soft, pale-gray velour fabric used as the main seat for her clients. Behind it hung a large, roll-down slide of various backdrops to give the impression you were at the beach, on a snow covered mountain or nestled in a bundle of autumn leaves. There were also backgrounds appropriate for infants and children. To the right was a huge, white-canopied umbrella for deflecting the light in the room. Most often Sabrina was requested to capture her audience at locations of their discretion; however, when that wasn't possible, her studio was the alternative. There were still individuals who preferred their pictures be taken in a professional setting.

In the front foyer as you entered the house, was a small traditional Cherry-wood desk and chair for the reception area. Strategically placed on top was a flat-screen computer monitor, telephone and appointment book. Business cards and brochures were set on the corner of the table. A small, discrete sign was placed in the yard near the entrance. With this arrangement, Brie had incorporated the front of the house into a professional studio with the back section and second floor remaining private quarters. It worked out perfectly.

In one of her preliminary assignments, Sabrina visited a

nursing home photographing the residents and matted, framed, and hung the results along the walls at the home. The project became an instant success leading Brie to expand on the idea whereby she quickly picked up clientele. From the moment she had captured the candid expressions of the residents at *Weston Nursing Home*, Brie's life took a detour initiated by the desire to continue with her aunt's legacy. She enjoyed the freedom of being in charge which was never a consideration before having worked solely for the magazine.

Now things were about to change again. She wanted to marry Bennaird Cooper. They met during Brie's holiday sabbatical in Asheville and fell completely in love in the two short weeks they spent together. Ben often told her their instant attraction was because they were soul mates. Sabrina thought that was very romantic and had long ago believed it to be true. He was loyal in his love for her, waiting patiently for the day she would become his wife.

Remaining near the window, Sabrina was focused on Sophie and David being mesmerized by these two tiny beings. It was fascinating to observe the transformation in her sister as a nurturing nature overcame Sophie when she looked at her babies. Sophie looked up making eye contact with her twin.

"Brie, come over here and hold them. You haven't been officially introduced to your nieces yet."

Sabrina walked over to the bedside near David and gently took Grace from his arms as he handed the infant to her. He then reclaimed Faith. Brie walked to the opposite side of the bed and cuddled Grace placing the baby's face near her cheek. Brie whispered in her ear causing Grace to make an indistinguishable sound.

"What was that Grace just did? See, I told you she was going to be the vocal one," Sophie declared.

"Oh, she is definitely special just like Faith."

"Of course, they are special; they're mine."

Sabrina held her breath and nuzzled Grace's miniature nose, and again, she reacted.

"I can't believe this. What are you doing to make her do that?"

"I'm not doing anything but tickling her nose," Sabrina replied, looking down at the bundle in her arms.

"What did you whisper in her ear that made Grace react that way?" Sophie asked as she watched the interaction between them.

Sophie knew intuitively something was surely occurring between her sister and her daughter. At first, she thought perhaps it was her imagination, but as she continued to observe them there was no denying it. Grace responded every time Brie whispered to her, something not possible for newborns less than two hours old. At least, not the baby sounds she was hearing. For the first time with her sister, Sophie felt jealousy rise up within her and couldn't control the emotions that were emerging from deep within. She didn't like what she was seeing. Unmistakably, Brie had a connection with Grace and not understanding what was happening didn't help.

"I told her she was very special," Brie replied, keeping the answer vague.

"Why don't you swap with David?"

She intended to prove to herself this certainly wouldn't happen with Faith. Sabrina walked around the foot of the bed and came up beside David. She gently laid Grace on the bed and took Faith from his arms. With the baby cuddled against her breast, she walked back to the opposite side whispering in Faith's ear just as she had done with Grace. Faith quickly acknowledged her aunt. Sophie turned her attention from making sure David handled Grace properly to see her sister smiling at Faith. Giving equal attention to both babies, Sabrina tickled her nose. Like Grace, Faith made an audible reply.

Sophie stared at Sabrina watching intently to the visible response Faith showed to her aunt's playful handling. She didn't understand what she was witnessing. How was it when she held her babies they lay quiet, and yet, when Brie held them they became vocal? *They are too young to respond to another human being in this manner,* Sophie thought. She didn't want to be jealous, but it gave her a bad feeling to see her babies responding to her sister. It wasn't right. She was their mother and they should be aware of her touch, her soft whispers. Hiding her reaction from Sabrina, Sophie turned her head focusing her attention on David who was talking softly to a sleeping Grace.

Two nurses entered the room to claim the newborns informing them they were being taken to the nursery for an examination by their pediatrician; however, assured Sophie they would be bathed and returned shortly in their portable bassinets. Sabrina and David relinquished the infants and with the babies gone, the room became very quiet. Brie sensed her sister's distress, but offered words would not give her peace of mind. Deciding it best to leave for awhile, Sabrina announced she was going to the cafeteria for an early dinner.

"I'm going to the cafeteria. Do you want anything?"

"Could you bring a Sprite with a cup of ice?" Sophie asked.

"Will do, and David, how about you?"

"I'll take a cup of coffee."

"Okay, that's one soda and one coffee. It may be an hour before I'm back."

"That's fine, we aren't going anywhere," David replied.

Sophie and David needed this time alone. Suddenly three was a crowd. Brie left the room walking toward the elevator that would take her to the first floor. She wanted to call Ben and give him the good news of two new additions to the family. There were other topics she wanted to discuss with him, but best to wait until she returned home.

Chapter 3

Brie requested the special of meatloaf taking her tray to a table near a window. Lingering, she watched the hospital staff slowly trail in for dinner along with plain-clothed individuals taking breaks. After disposing of her tray, she walked out the automatic sliding-glass door to a small patio and sat down on a white, metal bench punching the number to Ben's cell phone. After five rings, he answered.

"Hello, Ben Cooper."

"Hello to you, Ben Cooper."

"Love, how are you? How is everything in Florida?"

"I'm an aunt," Brie declared, proudly.

"Congratulations, when did this happen?"

She took a quick glance at her watch.

"About four hours ago. This is the first opportunity I've had to call you."

"How are Sophie and the babies?"

Ben knew she was having twins.

"She had girls and Sophie is doing great. I wish you were here to see them. They are so tiny."

"One day it will be our turn, and I hope we have twins."

He loved children and wanted at least four and if they came packaged in twos that would be even better. This wasn't their first conversation regarding children aware the probability of twins for Sabrina was the same.

"How long will you be staying?"

"I'll be here about three more weeks until their check-up with the pediatrician."

"Give Sophie my best wishes and a kiss for the babies. One day, I'll officially be their uncle."

"That's right. I didn't think of that."

"So did Sophie really name them Faith and Grace like you suggested?"

"Absolutely, and they actually have personalities to match their names."

"How do you figure that? I would think they are too young to show any personality yet."

"Oh, an aunt just knows these things."

"Of course. How silly of me to forget that important bit of information."

"I've got to get back to the room, but I'll keep you posted on things here."

"I'm thinking of you, always."

"I love you too, Ben."

Shoving her cell phone into her jeans pocket, Brie was still smiling as she stepped back into the cafeteria to get the drinks. Upon entering the room, she noticed the girls had been returned and were sleeping in separate bassinets near Sophie's bed. She quietly placed the tray on the nearby table and poured the Sprite into a cup of ice handing it to Sophie. Reaching across the bed, she gave David the cup of coffee.

"When did they return the girls?"

"Just a couple of minutes before you walked in," Sophie replied.

Brie stood by the babies, admiring them. *What an awesome gift,* she thought. She wasn't the least bit envious, but rather accepting the reality that she was getting older, and should seriously think about starting her own family. It was something she was very much ready to do and knew Ben would be elated to set a date.

"Aren't they wonderful, Brie?"

"Oh, indeed they are."

"It's your turn. You and Ben need to get married so you can have your set of twins."

"Funny, you should say that. I was just thinking the same thing. When I get back home, I'm going to talk to him."

"Finally! I was beginning to think you would never get married. You'll make Ben a very happy man."

"And I'll be a happy woman."

"Yes, you will be. I can't wait for you to share this experience. Remember, we do everything together, so you need to get things rolling."

The three of them talked late into the evening. Sophie was showing signs of fatigue, so David and Sabrina decided to leave, letting her get some rest. When the babies woke up hungry, she would be awake also.

Brie was staying at their house instead of typically at her condominium on Cocoa Beach for the convenience of being with Sophie whenever she went into labor. At this late hour, Sabrina was glad she didn't have that drive to her own home.

Chapter 4

Sophie and her babies were released from the *Regional Women Medical Center* three days later. David had already secured two matching pink infant carriers in the backseat of their SUV. It was strange to Sabrina to see his vehicle toting baby gear, but this was the new role of her sister and brother-in-law. They were parents now and life was going to be different for them.

Making several trips to the vehicle parked in the front circular driveway of the building, Sabrina helped David load up all the essentials they had collected in the short time of his wife's stay. Bringing Sophie out in a wheelchair, the customary routine, she held both babies, one in each arm. David took Faith and placed her in the small carrier and then Grace, talking to them in the process. Then he helped his wife step up into the passenger seat while Sabrina sat in the back next to the infants. He pulled out into traffic anxious to get his family home.

When they knew they were having girls, Sophie couldn't wait to make the second bedroom a nursery with the third bedroom used as a guest room. She wanted the nursery to be very simple with no specific theme, choosing to decorate with soft pink eyelet valances on the windows which already had white plantation blinds, and matching bumper sets on the two white wooden cribs. The beds were placed on adjacent walls so the girls would be close and above each was displayed their name in large, white antique-style lettering. The mattresses had tiny checkerboard pink sheets. Also, a high-back white rocker was situated in the far corner of the room with a mauve-colored fabric back and seat cushion tied around the spindles. The changing table was against the opposite wall from the cribs completely stocked with all the necessary supplies, and a solid pink diaper bag hung from the side. A tall narrow dresser was positioned next to the changing table.

Sabrina made several trips to Orlando to help Sophie shop and decorate. She and David took a weekend and painted the walls a sheer pink hue leaving the baseboards, window sills and closet door white. Everything in the room was pink and white including two twin teddy bears for the girls, white fluffy fur with pink bows. They had a great time preparing the room for the arrival of Faith and Grace.

As Sabrina watched her nieces sleeping, completely unaware they were being transported to their new home, she wondered how Sophie and David were going to tell them apart. They didn't have any distinguishing characteristics with the exception of Grace's vocal abilities.

"Sophie, how will you and David tell your girls apart? I know a mother knows these things, instinctively, but when they are so completely identical it makes you wonder," Brie asked, sensitive to her sister's new motherhood.

"You're right. I'll know my girls, but you have a point. David may not be able to if I'm not there to tell him. How did our parents know with us? Do you remember, Brie?"

"Perhaps they used little name anklets. Most of the family never could figure out which of us they were in the presence of. We sure had fun with the pranks we played," Sabrina commented, reminiscing about their childhood.

"I guess it will be my turn someday, but I'll be ready when my girls try it. I like the idea of the anklets."

David didn't interject his own thoughts. Whatever made Sophie feel comfortable about her babies was fine with him. Secretly, he wondered about this very thing but had no intention of admitting he may not be able to identify his girls.

This easily solved the dilemma for him without the embarrassment.

"Brie, before you leave, I want to make a trip to a jewelry store and order them."

Sophie wasn't completely confident she wouldn't have a problem and was thankful the hospital's plastic identification band was still wrapped around their ankles. There was so much to learn about being a new mother. She had no intention of admitting the uncertainty she felt.

"Alright, we can do that once you have rested."

Sabrina believed her sister would easily adapt to motherhood. There may be days when she might feel over-whelmed, especially with two babies, but Brie was positive Sophie could handle it. Arriving home, they settled the twins into their respective cribs before David and Sabrina hauled everything into the house. Sophie sat on the sofa in the living room instructing where to place the items. Once things were put away, David offered to make a lunch of chicken salad sandwiches. He preferred to work in the kitchen alone, so Sabrina accompanied her sister in the living room.

"It seems like yesterday when we sat on this very sofa and talked about my excursions with the magazine. Now, we sit with two babies sleeping in the next room. Things are changing again for us, sis. You're going to be a wonderful mother. Don't ever doubt yourself," Sabrina told her, knowing her sister needed reassurance.

"Thanks, Brie. I'm going to do my best."

David walked in with a tray holding three plates already prepared and iced tea glasses. Putting it on the table in front of the sofa, Sabrina reached for one placing it carefully on her lap.

"Thank you, David. This looks good," Brie stated, before biting into the sandwich.

"There's plenty if you want more."

He handed a plate to his wife who used a pillow on her lap for a tabletop. David took the chair opposite the sofa and they ate while the babies slept.

"This is good chicken salad. You'll have to give me your recipe."

"I'll jot it down. It's easy to make; only takes celery, sweet pickles and a pinch of paprika to season it."

David enjoyed cooking which made him the chef around their house. It was a chore Sophie gladly relinquished to her husband, not being partial to planning and preparing meals.

It wasn't long before the quietness was interrupted by the sound of a crying baby. Sophie and David looked at one another in bewilderment, simultaneously realizing one of the twins was awake.

"Do you want me to take a look?" Sabrina asked.

"Sure, go ahead."

Brie stood up placing her empty plate back on the tray and went to check on the twins. When she entered their bedroom, it was Faith who was crying. She was lying on her back with her eyes closed when Sabrina walked up to her crib and gently placed her hand on her chest.

"Hey, little one, what's got you crying?"

Brie spoke softly to the infant. Faith immediately stopped when she heard Sabrina's voice and let out an audible baby sound.

"I know, sweetheart, but go back to sleep."

Instantly, Faith quieted and fell asleep. As Sabrina turned to leave, she saw Sophie standing in the doorway, watching.

"She's sleeping," Sabrina told her when Sophie walked into the room, verifying that Faith was okay.

They went back to the living room and reclaimed their positions on the sofa.

"Who was it?" David asked.

"It was Faith, but she went back to sleep," Sophie told her husband.

"What do you suppose woke her?"

"I don't know, but she's okay now."

Sophie directed her attention to her sister. She wanted to know what Brie said to Faith to calm her.

"Brie, how did you stop her crying?"

"I simply told her to go back to sleep."

"What did you mean when you told Faith 'I know, sweetheart'?"

"It was just baby talk."

David spoke up, interrupting the conversation, to see if anyone wanted another sandwich as he gathered the plates before returning to the kitchen.

"None for me, but thanks," Brie replied.

"No more for me, either."

"Alright, then. I'm eating the last of the chicken salad," he told them.

They were silent for a moment. Sophie wasn't accepting Brie's easy explanation and was trying hard not to be jealous when she saw her sister with her babies. It seemed they *listened* and *talked* to Brie which didn't make any sense. And yet, Sophie knew that's exactly what was happening. She saw it with her own eyes.

There was one way to know if their reaction was limited to Brie solely and that was to put it to the ultimate test. When the girls woke up they would be hungry, and she would be breastfeeding them. Sophie didn't have much luck in the hospital when the nurse helped acquaint them to their mother's breast, but she was told to keep trying and they would learn to latch on. She would bond with her babies and this was a beginning, something Sabrina couldn't do for them. *Thank goodness I have this,* she hoped, again, feeling the jealousy guiding her emotions.

Chapter 5

Sabrina didn't know how she was going to get through the next three weeks with Sophie's close scrutiny. Living in the same house with Faith and Grace would certainly stress her imagination to prevent an upheaval with her own twin. Brie was astutely aware of Sophie's mood swings. Being very mindful of her postpartum emotional rollercoaster, she treaded lightly to not disturb this balance. At times, it can be daunting to have such a mirrored closeness to another human, even down to the psyche of their existence. Identical outward appearances can be deceiving when deep within lies the difference between them and the sameness.

They had never kept secrets from each other which intensified the guilt Sabrina felt for having done so. However, at the time events began to unfold, changing her life forever, she knew Sophie would not be receptive to what she would eventually need to share with her. Now two years later, Brie was still apprehensive exposing such an anomaly.

"Sophie, you should get some rest while the girls are sleeping. I'll get you when they wake up," Sabrina suggested.

"Okay, I think I will."

She walked down the hallway to her bedroom feeling more fatigued from the birthing than she had expected. Maybe she wasn't going to bounce back as quickly as she thought. Sabrina went to check on the babies once more and retrieved the monitor that was sitting on top of the white dresser, turning on the dual units and placing one in the far corner of each crib. Taking the base into the kitchen and putting it on the table, she observed David wiping down the countertops when she walked in.

"Sophie went to take a nap. Anything I can help you with?" Brie asked.

"No, nothing at the moment, but got any ideas for dinner? I probably should plan out the weekly menu."

David took paper and pen from a drawer and sat down at the small kitchen table. Sabrina joined him.

"Since you'll be working, tell me what meals you want prepared each day, I can do that while I'm here."

"Sounds like a plan. If you'll start the preparations, I'll finish when I get home, but only if you have the time. Sophie and the babies are the first priority."

"Of course."

They sat for nearly an hour making two lists; one for the meals, and the second for grocery items needed. They agreed it best to keep the menu simple deciding on spaghetti and meatballs with a Caesar salad for dinner that evening. He took out a two-pound package of ground sirloin from the freezer and checked the refrigerator's vegetable bin for fresh lettuce. That's when they heard the noise. David turned to see Sabrina walking out of the kitchen, and he followed behind her.

When she entered the babies' room, both were crying. She walked over to Faith's crib and gently picked her up, placing Faith upward against her shoulder. Brie turned toward Grace's crib to see David doing the same. Sabrina leaned her face toward Faith's ear and whispered to her. She immediately stopped crying. David saw what Brie had done and copied her technique, but it didn't work. Grace continued to exercise her vocal cords.

"Let's switch since Faith has calmed down," Sabrina told him.

Brie laid Faith on the changing table, so she could take

Grace. David picked up Faith holding her against his shoulder, and she remained completely content. As soon as Brie enveloped Grace in her arms, she ceased wailing. Brie stood in place gently swaying back and forth, humming softly to both babies, knowing they responded to her voice.

"Wow, how did you do that?" David asked in amazement.

"They just wanted some attention."

"I was giving Grace plenty of attention, but she didn't stop crying for me. Don't tell me this is going to be a female thing. Are my girls going to cry every time I hold them?"

Sabrina saw the worried expression on her brother-in-law's face. She would have laughed at the absurdity had it not been that she didn't want to offend him. He was taking this situation too seriously.

"David, trust me, this is not a female thing. Your girls will know you are their daddy, and I have a suspicion you are going to spoil them," she told him, deflecting her obvious ability to comfort the infants.

"You bet I am. I can't wait for them to know their daddy."

"Oh, no you don't. There will be no spoiling these girls," Sophie declared from the doorway.

"Hi, honey, did we wake you?"

"No, you didn't, but Faith and Grace did. Maybe they were crying because they're hungry. Let me have Grace first, and I'll feed them," Sophie said, walking over to the rocking chair to prepare for the infant.

Sabrina stepped in front of Sophie and placed Grace in her lap. Accepting this was bonding time between mother and infant, and also a very intimate moment for David, she left the room excusing herself to make a phone call. She went to the guest bedroom to retrieve the cell phone from her purse and walked out the front door to call Ben. She needed to give Sophie and David privacy, and besides, she really wanted to make a call.

"Hello, Ben Cooper."

"Hi, Ben, what are you doing?"

"I'm standing in a maze of Christmas trees."

"What for?"

"To make sure they are still growing on schedule."

"Of course. I should know that, right?"

"True, it's my trade, and as my wife you'll need to know these things. When you can't find your husband, always look for him in the trees."

"I'll have to remember that."

This was the usual bantering they shared. Each had a sense of humor, and typically, it was Ben who always initiated it. He couldn't get enough of teasing Sabrina and discovered she gave back as good as she got. It was one of the many things he loved about her.

"How are Faith and Grace?"

"Adorable. We brought them home today, but Sophie hasn't had a chance to begin a routine. I'm sure she'll start planning her days soon."

"Why do babies need routines, anyway? They let you know what they want, when they want it, and how they want it."

"I didn't know you were such an expert on children. The first time one of ours starts crying in the middle of the night, he'll be all yours to deal with."

"You said *he*, so we are having boys. Hey, works for me."

"Alright, Mr. Wise Guy, your day is coming."

"I can hardly wait. I think we need to talk about a wedding. This isn't something I want to discuss over the phone, but give it some thought, and we can talk about it when you return home," he stated.

"That's interesting; you should bring up the subject. I have been thinking the same thing and agree we should start planning."

"Wow, I didn't expect this reaction from you. What has changed your mind?"

"Faith and Grace. I want children. We should be married with our own family, and would be right now, if I hadn't kept procrastinating," Sabrina told him, wishing she was saying this to him in person.

"That's in the past. We both were dealing with a lot of changes. Let's concentrate on our future, so think about a date and when you get back, we'll sit down and put some plans together."

"Sounds good. Do you have any preference to the month?"

"No, not as long as we get married soon. I have a better idea, let's elope. That would certainly speed things up," he said, teasing her again.

"I don't think so. How do you feel about a Christmas wedding since we met during the holidays? It's less than six months. Is that too long for you to wait?"

"Yes, but I'll manage. I like the idea of a holiday wedding. Our anniversary will always remind me when you came by the farm for a tree."

"That should be the date. The day Bella introduced us."

"It would be an appropriate anniversary date, for sure," he agreed.

"It just seems so romantic to marry on the very day we met. I think we have our wedding day," Sabrina announced.

"Unless you remember the exact date, I'll need to take a look at my records."

"You'll have to check."

"I'll have it the next time we talk. Thank you, love."

"You've waited two years, so I should be thanking you for your patience."

"I love you, and would wait forever."

"Love you, too. I'll call again in a couple of days."

Tucking her cell phone away, Brie stayed outside roaming around the yard inspecting the flowerbeds when she heard the front door open. David rushed out looking flustered.

"Brie, can you help Sophie with the babies? She is having trouble, and all three are crying."

She followed David into the house, hearing the wailing infants from the entrance, and went straight down the hall to the babies' room where Sophie was sitting in the rocking chair holding Faith, crying along with her.

"Oh, Sophie, it'll be okay. What can I do to help you?"

Sophie looked up at her sister with a tear-streaked face.

"They are hungry, but won't latch on," Sophie explained through her sniffles.

"First you have to be calm. They can sense your tension, and it can cause them to be on edge. Let me have Faith, and I'll put her in the crib for a moment. You have to be relaxed, so go take a break and get something to drink and after a few minutes, we'll start again."

Sophie, at a complete loss, did as she was told and left the room. Walking through the living room, she passed her husband sitting on the sofa, making her way to the kitchen. David followed her.

"Sit down, and I'll make you a glass of iced tea," he gently instructed.

Sophie felt embarrassed that she couldn't breastfeed her babies. *Why is it not working for me? What am I doing wrong,* she questioned herself.

David put the glass on the table in front of her and sat down.

"Sophie, everything will be alright. After all, this is only our first day with the babies. We have a lot to learn together about being parents," he said, trying to reassure his wife.

"I know that, but they won't take to my breast, David. You don't know how that makes me feel," she said, bursting into tears.

He stood up pulling Sophie from the chair, hugging her close, sensitive to how she was feeling. Once she had regained control, they went into the living room and cuddled together on the sofa. David wrapped his arm around her shoulder pulling her against his body as Sophie nestled into his side. He secretly enjoyed holding his wife in his arms wanting to console her. Until they established a schedule with their newborns, he didn't want his wife overly stressed anymore than a situation would normally create.

They both realized the house was quiet, there were no crying babies. It didn't sit well with Sophie that Brie could handle the twins so effortlessly. She was their mother and they should be responding to her, but they weren't, and that was a devastating blow. It put her on edge, and the nasty feeling of jealousy was crawling up her spine and overcoming her senses once again.

Chapter 6

Sabrina placed Grace alongside Faith in her crib, and lying together, they had stopped crying, listening intently to their aunt's voice. It put a smile on her face. *Oh, how I want my own babies,* she thought.

"I know you are hungry and your mama will feed you soon. Behave while I get her," Brie spoke softly to them.

Sabrina left the twins to find Sophie curled up on the sofa with David. She hated to disturb her sister but knew the babies needed to be fed.

"Sophie, the girls are ready whenever you are."

"Okay, I'll give it another try. I hope it works this time," she replied, without enthusiasm.

She walked back to their room with David and Brie following. Sophie looked at her babies with their soft cap of blonde hair and blue eyes, and fell deeper in love with them. *Surely, it must have been like this for our mom,* she thought. The short break settled her nerves and Sophie felt calmer, ready to feed her babies.

"It has crossed my mind that the twins look just like us when we were babies with their blonde hair. Except, I don't think we were born with blue eyes or else they changed color as we got older. Brie, wouldn't it be great if the girls favored our golden-amber eyes and wheat-blonde hair. There would be four of us!" she exclaimed, thrilled with the prospect.

"Now there's a thought. Four beautiful blondes and to think you all are my girls," David answered, not taking his eyes off the infants.

"That is very interesting, two miniature replicas. David would be delighted if his girls looked like their mother," Brie replied, turning toward him with a smile.

"Whenever you are ready, I'll bring one of them to you, and we'll see if we can get these little ones to eat."

Sophie settled comfortably in the rocking chair hoping this time she would be breastfeeding her babies. She desperately wanted this, and each attempt that wasn't successful added to her frustration. Sabrina took Faith first and handed her to Sophie, but when Brie turned to leave the room, Sophie called her back.

"Brie, don't go. I may need your help."

Sophie wanted to do this on her own, but after the previous failure, she wasn't prepared to undergo the twins' rejection a second time. It was David who opted to leave the women alone to handle this issue.

"Honey, if you don't mind, I'm leaving you women alone. I'm totally outnumbered and have no expertise to be helpful."

"That's okay. Let me figure this out first. We'll have plenty of time to enjoy the experience together later."

Sophie took Faith and cuddled her close turning her tiny body inward. As Faith rested in the curve of her mother's arm, Sophie gently held the back of Faith's head helping her locate the milk supply. Faith opened her mouth rubbing her lips back and forth on her mother's breast, but not clamping down and latching onto the protruding nipple.

"I don't get it. She's right there but won't latch on. This is what she did earlier," Sophie said, watching Faith.

Standing in front of Sophie, Sabrina placed her right hand over her sister's as she continued to hold Faith's head. With her left index finger, Brie gently rubbed Faith's cheek from the temple downward to the corner of her mouth with slow light strokes. Faith closed her mouth around the succulent spout and began sucking. Brie continued to stroke a few more times before removing her finger from Faith's face.

"Oh my gosh, she's doing it. How did you do that?"

More concerned that her baby was actually nursing, Sophie purposefully overlooked the fact that it was her sister who instructed Faith.

"I think I read about it somewhere," Sabrina replied, carefully.

"Well, it worked. Do you think we'll have to rub their cheek every time they need to eat?"

"No, I wouldn't think so. They should know instinctively how to get their meal."

Sophie was dealing with an expected imbalance in hormones causing her emotions to fluctuate sporadically. Anything Brie could do to keep her stabilized would be most beneficial to her sister and the babies.

Faith filled her belly and was temporarily placed on the changing table while Sabrina took Grace for her turn. Brie performed the same routine with Grace; however, she caught on quicker locating what she wanted. Brie took Faith in her arms to be burped and was already asleep before being placed in her crib, settling in without making a sound.

Turning around, Brie watched her sister with Grace. There was a surreal expression on Sophie's face as she focused intently on her nursing infant. When Grace detached, Sophie turned her around and she fell asleep while being gently patted on the back. Grace was placed in her crib with Sophie and Brie lingering for a moment before leaving the room. Sophie felt more relaxed having experienced her first true breastfeeding session. It did wonders to boost her confidence.

They entered the kitchen to find David preparing a Caesar salad in a large bowl while spaghetti and meatballs simmered on the stove. The aroma of garlic bread baking in the oven filled the air. It made Brie's stomach growl.

"Dinner will be ready in ten minutes," David announced.

"It smells delicious. I'll set the table and make some tea.

Sophie, I think you should sit down and get off your feet," Sabrina suggested.

Brie maneuvered around the kitchen staying out of David's way. He handled the large pot placing it in the center of the table on a trivet, and they sat down to an Italian meal from David's special recipe.

"David, you could make a fortune with your own restaurant. Your cooking is superb," Brie told him.

"Thanks. I do enjoy it, but if I had to cook under supply and demand conditions, it would take the joy out of the experience. In my own kitchen, it relaxes me and takes my mind off my day job."

"Well, you could always consider it a backup career."

"There you go, I suppose I could."

"Sophie, you're one lucky lady having your own personal chef."

"I know, and I'm thankful every day," she replied, smiling at her husband.

"There you go again, praising the man," David said with a grin on his face.

It made him uncomfortable receiving compliments. When dinner was finished, he ushered his wife into the living room to relax on the sofa. Brie helped clean the kitchen and then went to check on the babies while David brewed a fresh pot of coffee. They settled in the living room and chatted for awhile.

"First thing in the morning, I'll take the list and go to the grocery store, so if either of you have anything to add, let me know," David spoke up.

"I'll do a light cleaning of the house and the laundry. Sophie, your job is to rest," Brie told her, outlining her own plans.

"I won't argue with that idea because I know once you go home, I'm on my own. How long do you think the babies will sleep?"

"Probably until they get hungry again, maybe a few more hours," Brie told her.

"Honey, I'm going do the homework schedule for next week," David stated, excusing himself.

"Sure, go ahead. We're just sitting here until the babies wake up."

David took his coffee mug to the guest bedroom where he had a desktop computer. Sophie and Sabrina remained on the sofa in their respective corners enjoying the quietness in the house.

"Brie, you handle the twins as though you have done it for awhile. It comes so easy for you," Sophie told her.

She wasn't going to allow her bout with jealousy to get in the way of expressing sincere thoughts toward motherhood. That wouldn't be fair to her sister.

"Holding my nieces has given me a strong desire to have my own."

"I can't wait until you do. Just think, our children will grow up together, but you better marry Ben and start soon, or my little ones will be too old for your babies."

"Ben and I have officially set a wedding date."

"What! When did this happen?"

"Today. We were talking earlier on the phone, and Ben brought up marriage and we set a date."

"So when is it?"

Sophie had doubts her sister would ever get around to marrying Ben. After all, they had been together for two years with no official talk of a wedding. This was fabulous news.

"Well, it will be a Christmas wedding, and the actual date is the day we met at his tree farm when I went with Bella to buy a tree."

"That is so romantic. I'm glad to hear you are finally going to do it."

"Do you think six months will be enough time to get every thing arranged?"

"Sure, I'll help you. Let's get started while you're here. We can begin with a list of everything to do, and another of everything you'll need. I have to go with you to pick out your dress, so don't do that without me."

"I wouldn't dream of shopping for a dress without you. In fact, I'm relieved I'll have your help. Since you have already done this, I figure there are a lot of contacts I can make through you."

"We can go online and get ideas for invitations. The important thing is to stay organized," Sophie told her, leaving the sofa to get a notepad.

Retrieving a tablet and pen from the kitchen, she settled back in her corner of the sofa, outlining things that needed to be done. They discussed and planned for the next couple of hours expecting the twins to awaken, but when they didn't, Sophie and Brie opted to go to bed.

David glanced up from his work to see Brie standing in the doorway and knew it was his cue to give up the room. He shut down the computer, and pulled out the sofa bed before saying good night.

Tomorrow would be day two with the newest additions to the McKinley family and they were looking forward to it. The subtle awareness of the newborns' presence in their home was a reminder of new beginnings as parents.

Chapter 7

In the following days, Sophie settled into a routine becoming more confident in taking care of her babies. The breastfeeding issue was quickly resolved with the help of Brie, and Sophie was so grateful, she refused to be annoyed with her sister. When the newborns weren't sleeping, they were quiet and happy allowing Sophie time to rest on the sofa, taking short naps, as instructed by her husband and sister. She was appreciative of Brie's assistance and her sister's inclination to let her tend to the newborns, only stepping in when needed.

However, after almost two weeks of lying around the house, Sophie was eager to step out into the world again making each trip she and Brie took short excursions. David watched the twins in the late afternoon after she had fed and put them back down for a nap. Their first stop was to a jewelry store to place an order for personalized anklets.

Sophie was still periodically plagued with jealousy and tried hard to abate the feeling. There was no logical reason, or explanation as she struggled with this unpleasant emotion. It wasn't Brie's problem she was feeling this way and certainly didn't want her sister to know, having no intention of saying anything that had the potential to cause a rift between them.

In the past several years since their college days, it was at infrequent times they got together because their professions didn't accommodate such. Sabrina's traveling for the magazine kept her away, and Sophie's teaching schedule didn't allow many days off. This was before Brie moved to Asheville. However, Sabrina now makes it a point to return often which was the reason for holding onto her condominium on the beach.

When Sophie told her she was pregnant, Brie made many weekend trips to help her sister prepare for the new arrivals. And on one of those visits, Sabrina and David had secretly orchestrated a surprise baby shower. Sophie was completely clueless her sister had flown into town as Brie went directly to her condo. David had given Sabrina a key to their house to arrange the party while his job was to keep Sophie away for a few hours.

Bright and early on a Saturday morning, after setting a full course breakfast in front of his wife, David suggested they go shopping for furniture for the nursery. While they were away, Sabrina arrived to decorate and wait for the prearranged catered deliveries of food, cake, flowers and guests. There were thirty-five of Sophie's closest friends greeting her when she walked through the front door of her home several hours later. She was so overwhelmed, she sat down and cried.

David hung around filming everything with their camcorder, and later that evening, the three of them watched the video twice over leftover cake and coffee. Sophie admitted it was one of the most memorable days of her life. Now months later, Sophie's babies slept while she helped plan her sister's wedding.

"I can already tell they will be good babies, no fussiness," Sophie told her sister.

"Of course, and you'll enjoy watching them grow up."

"Yes, I will."

Sabrina loved being a part of her sister's family; however, the time was approaching for Brie to leave. Neither sister addressed the subject not wanting to break the bond they had reestablished. Both accepted that Brie had to get back to her own responsibilities and Sophie needed to adapt to motherhood on her own.

Three weeks had passed and it was time for the twins' pediatric visit, and since Sabrina was able to help Sophie, David worked a full day. Brie was glad to have the opportunity to meet her nieces' pediatrician, Dr. Tracy Smitherton, who was recommended by one of Sophie's friends. She didn't appear to be much older than they were. In light conversation while she examined the babies, Sabrina discovered the doctor had no children as her immediate interest was establishing her practice before beginning a family.

Sophie watched intently as Dr. Smitherton handled her newborns like a mother hen overseeing her chicks. Sophie and David already had this conversation with the pediatrician when they met with her prior to the babies' birth, so the conversation held no interest to her. She was focused on the twins' health and as expected they were perfect.

"It's hard to believe Faith and Grace are almost a month old. How did that happen?" Sophie asked of her sister, leaving the doctor's office with a good report.

"Your girls will grow up faster than you may want."

"I hope not too fast. I want to enjoy every moment with them."

"Motherhood is definitely going to suit you."

"Oh, it already is."

When they arrived home, Sophie breastfed the twins and put them in their cribs while Brie made lunch. She brought up the subject of leaving while they sat at the kitchen table eating sandwiches and soup.

"I suppose its time I book a flight. It's been over a month, and you and the babies are doing great. You really don't need my help anymore."

"I knew this day would come. It has been special having you here and experiencing this together. It's meant so much to me," Sophie replied, already feeling the loss.

"I wouldn't have missed this for anything, nothing would have kept me away."

"When are you leaving?"

"Probably on Friday since there is no need to delay."

"Alright, I know it's inevitable. So we have two days left together."

"I'll continue to visit often, and besides, you will be coming to Asheville in a few months for my wedding and to spend the holidays with me."

Brie noticed a visible change in Sophie's demeanor when she mentioned leaving. Sadness reflected in her sister's eyes, and her shoulders slumped forward like a blanket of melancholy was placed over her. Sabrina hated causing these feelings especially under the circumstances of Sophie's new-found motherhood, but it was time to leave them alone to enjoy their family without her presence.

"That will give me something to look forward to."

Both accepted this parting was going to be uncomfortable. The quality time of living together reconnecting as twins, along with bonding with the newborns, was something neither was ready to end.

Sabrina was up early on Friday tiptoeing into the babies' room to say goodbye to her nieces. They slept peacefully while their Auntie Brie stood by their cribs whispering endearments.

"Faith, my darling one, you stay strong and healthy," she spoke softly, while gently touching her head.

Faith stirred in understanding but made no sound. Walking over to Grace's crib, she touched her arm careful not to wake her.

"Grace, take care of Faith. I know you are the independent one, just like me," Brie told her in confidence.

Grace squirmed, gave a soft sigh and settled again. Brie smiled knowing Grace understood. Sabrina stepped back from the crib and spoke to the girls, "I love you and will see you both soon."

Sabrina was going to miss her nieces. They had captured her heart, but she refused to be saddened by the separation.

Sophie and David were in the kitchen when Brie put her suitcases by the front door. She walked in and helped herself to

47

a cup of coffee, joining Sophie at the table while David prepared breakfast. Sabrina had never experienced such turmoil in leaving her sister, as she did now, and considered if it was because of her connection to Faith and Grace that made departing so difficult.

David made a complete meal of scrambled eggs, grits, hash browns and pancakes bringing the plates individually to the table placing the first one in front of Sabrina.

"This is enough food for two people," Brie told him, staring at the plate.

"Hopefully, it will hold you until you get home."

"I'm sure it will."

"Did you say goodbye to the girls?" Sophie asked, knowingly, having heard through the monitor.

"Yes, I did. I will miss them and you, sis."

"I've gotten used to you being here, but I probably need to get accustomed to being on my own."

"You're a great mother, better than you think. They will keep you so busy you won't even know that I'm not around."

"Think so?"

"Yes, I do."

The mood at the table was solemn. After a second cup of coffee, Brie couldn't delay the inevitable any longer.

"Remember, we have a wedding to plan and we'll be together for Christmas," Sabrina stated, attempting to cheer her sister.

"I haven't forgotten. I'm looking forward to it."

"Your new life has begun, Sophie."

"I know. I'm just missing you, already."

David was taking her to the airport, and while he put the suitcases in the back of his vehicle, Sophie and Sabrina stood in the doorway hugging tightly.

"I'll call you when I get home," Brie told her, pulling away from the embrace.

"Okay, talk to you then. Have a good flight."

"You have two beautiful babies that need you, so take

good care of my nieces," Brie said on a lighter note.

"I will, just for you."

Brie slipped into the front seat and as David backed out of the driveway, Sabrina waved goodbye noticing the tears sliding down her sister's cheeks. It was difficult to hold her own in check because it wouldn't help Sophie if she saw her crying. On the drive to the airport, David confided in Sabrina.

"Do you think Sophie will be okay? It's not that she can't handle the twins, but I don't want her becoming anxious."

"Having two babies to take care of will certainly be challenging, but Sophie can do it. She'll need your support which I know you'll give her, and if you need me, call anytime."

"Thanks. You've already done so much. I'm not sure we could have gotten through this without you. You've been a big help, and I want you to know we appreciate it."

"We've only got each other, and besides, we're family. We stick together," Sabrina told him.

The conversation was limited to talk of Sophie and the babies, but once Brie had alleviated David's concerns, they fell silent absorbed in their own thoughts. When David arrived at the airport, he drove directly to the customer drop-off area leaving Sabrina at the outside baggage check-in line. She was used to navigating through airports having done so for over a decade.

More than ever before, Sabrina wanted to marry Ben having no doubt he would be a good husband and father. It wasn't that she was envious of her sister but rather knew she had misplaced her priorities, and consequently, has lost precious time having her own family.

Chapter 8

It was late afternoon when Sabrina arrived home finding the quietness of the house a bit unnerving. Taking the luggage upstairs, she quickly unpacked separating the clothes and placing the toiletries in the bathroom. After setting the empty pieces near the stairs to store in the staircase closet, Brie walked the second floor glancing into each room before going downstairs. Reassured everything was as it should be, Brie called her sister.

"I'm home and unpacked," Brie spoke first.

"Did you check the house?"

"Yes, I did."

"That's a big house, and I wouldn't want you to overlook any disturbances."

Sophie was the twin who took on the parental role often expressing her maternal instincts. That was one of the reasons Sabrina believed her sister would be a perfect mother.

"Everything is secure. How are Faith and Grace?"

"They are adorable and sleeping at the moment."

"Are you okay?"

"Yes, I am. I think David is worried about my taking care of the babies by myself."

"Two babies can be a handful, so don't let it overwhelm you. When you start feeling that way, take a deep breath, relax, and call me. It's going to be double duty, but you'll be fine.

Can we talk more tomorrow? I'm fixing a quick dinner and going to bed early."

"Sure, I'll talk to you then. Sleep tight."

Sabrina placed the cell phone on the kitchen counter and went to the pantry to find a can of vegetable soup and saltine crackers. While the soup heated in the microwave, she phoned Ben.

"Hello, love. You made it home safely," Ben spoke first.

"No delays. I got in a little while ago. I'm heating up some soup for dinner."

"I can take you out for a better meal than that."

"Sounds nice, but I wouldn't be the best company at the moment. Can you get away for breakfast in the morning?"

"Absolutely, do you want to meet at *The Country Kitchen* around eight?"

"Of course, that's my favorite diner."

"Is everything alright with Sophie and the babies?"

"They are awesome, and I miss them."

"I'm sure you do, but once you get settled into your own routine again, you'll feel better. Nothing a big stack of pancakes can't fix, I bet."

"This is true," she replied.

"See you at eight. Don't forget who loves you."

"Same to you," Brie said, laughing.

Sabrina wasn't in the mood to linger on the phone talking with Ben. She missed him but because they spoke every day while she was away, Brie was current with the events in his life. He kept her informed of the crossbreeding techniques they were experimenting with for a new generation of Christmas trees. Perhaps soon the Douglas Fir would no longer be their main tree. Ben enjoyed talking about his business especially intrigued with this latest project with the seedlings. If the bud developed and grew as predicted, they would patent the tree type.

After eating her simple meal, Brie checked the appointment book in the foyer to see what was planned for the upcoming month. There were a few local sittings but nothing scheduled with the magazine. She thought about calling Joe, her assistant, in the morning to touch base with him. Even though Sabrina no longer worked full-time for the magazine, Joe remained assigned to her and was thoughtful to scout for assignments she would have an interest in.

Sophie was thrilled to be a mother even when she felt apprehensive with the enormity of caring for two human beings who relied solely on her. She settled into a daily routine managing to maintain the household chores. Not completely comfortable with taking the twins in public places alone, she waited until the weekends when David could help which made it especially fun for them as a family. She looked forward to relaxing with her husband in the evenings, the part of the day they spent discussing their activities.

She enjoyed hearing David talk about the students in his classroom and the current school board politics from the various staff meetings and parent-teacher conferences he attended. It wasn't so long ago, when she was equally involved. However, shortly after taking her initial maternity leave, Sophie decided not to return to her profession, and surprisingly, she didn't miss teaching.

Accepting this quiet time together, each is reflective of how their lives have changed.

"I thought my life was complete the moment I laid eyes on you back in college at the museum that Saturday afternoon. And these few years before starting our family have been more fulfilling than a person could wish for. We are going to have fun as parents and hopefully having more kids," David told her.

"I feel exactly the same way and want more children, even if they are twins again. How about we have boys next time?"

"That would be ideal having four children, two girls and two boys. I'm not a religious person, but I can't help think we have truly been blessed. We gave our girls the right names, Faith and Grace."

"I agree with their names," Sophie stated.

For the next few moments, they sat in silence. There was absolutely nothing that could be added to their life that would make it anymore perfect with the exception of another set of twins. Sophie snuggled closer laying her head on her husband's chest listening to his heart beating. It wasn't possible to be any happier.

Chapter 9

Sabrina arrived early at the restaurant anxious to see Ben. She was having a cup of coffee when he walked up to the booth, and leaning forward, gave her a kiss before settling onto the opposite bench.

"Gosh, it sure is good to lay eyes on you again. I've missed you, love," he said with a smile.

"I've missed you, too."

He motioned to the waitress who brought over a coffee pot and cup filling it to the brim and refilled Brie's. They placed their order.

"How was everything at your sister's when you left?"

"David is a little skeptical of Sophie's ability to deal with two babies simultaneously, but once they get accustomed to the twins' schedule, he won't feel so apprehensive."

"Are you glad to be home?"

"Yes. It was time for me to leave, but I sure do miss my nieces."

"I see the longing in your eyes. This must be the motivation to set a date, and I'm all for starting our own brew as soon as we're married. We don't have to wait a few years like your sister to start our family," Ben told her.

"No, I definitely don't want to postpone having children. Holding Faith and Grace made me realize how I've missed being a family with you."

"I'm glad we will finally be married."

"Did you look up the date?"

"Yes, it was December twelfth."

"Are you still okay with it as our anniversary date?" she asked.

"Absolutely, it's the right one for us."

"There can be no excuses for forgetting our anniversary," she said, teasing him.

"Never."

Brie wondered what it would be like to actually live with Ben. She wasn't accustomed to sharing her personal space with anyone but was ready for marriage and new beginnings.

"Are you already having second thoughts?" he asked.

Noticing the serious expression on her face, he wondered what she was thinking.

"Of course not, it's my fault we aren't married right now. I should have planned our wedding first and everything else would have fallen into place. That is my big regret," she clarified.

"Don't concentrate on the past. Let's start with today and move forward, and by Christmas we'll be Mr. and Mrs."

"You're right, let's focus on the future."

"What do we need to do first?" Ben asked.

"We need a place to be married and for the reception party."

"Okay, do you have anything in mind?"

"Not really, I was hoping you might have some suggestions."

"That would depend if you want a church wedding, but the place is more the woman's choice."

"Since it will be cold in December, it obviously needs to be indoors. We could get married at your church. Since I have been attending with you, it would be appropriate. What do you think?"

"That's okay with me. Truthfully, I just want to marry you, so the sooner we do this the happier I'll be."

Shortly after Sabrina settled into her aunt's home, and they became inseparable, Ben invited her to attend church with him. At a different place in her life, she might have been reluctant to do so not appearing in one very often in her youth. However, since Sabrina's personal experience with *Passionate Promises*, the encapsulated revelation changed her just as it had for her Aunt Millie. She didn't necessarily feel compelled to attend a congregation, but wouldn't reject an invitation.

"We should make an appointment with the pastor to see if he's available on December twelfth. In the meantime, we need a place for the reception. Any ideas there?" she asked.

"Not at the moment, but I'll check with my mom."

"I'll ask Bella. She's on several committees and might have a few ideas."

"I'm sure between the two of them we'll find a place for our big bash."

The food arrived and they changed the subject to discussing events at the farm. Soon she would be a part of his business, not that she anticipated having any physical involvement. Finishing their breakfast, Ben announced he had an appointment and needed to leave. Brie also had her day planned meeting with a family for a portrait in the park at noon, an arrangement she had just made upon returning home.

Standing at Sabrina's car, he pulled her into an embrace, and she reached up wrapping her arms around his neck pressing her body into his. Meant to be a quick hug, it turned into an engaging kiss with neither caring their actions were on public display. Sabrina reluctantly withdrew looking up at Ben with a smile.

"Boy, did I need that," he said with a big grin on his face.

"Me too."

"Let's do it again," he remarked, planting his lips on hers before she could say a word.

It took her breath away.

"Twice is even better. Talk to you later, love," he said, smiling at her before turning and walking toward his truck.

"You'd better."

Brie slid behind the steering wheel watching him disappear around the corner of the restaurant. She was so in love with him and had been since two weeks into their relationship when he claimed they were soul mates. *What a fool I've been to wait to marry this man,* she thought. Refusing to dwell on the past, Brie knew in a short time that would be rectified. She went home to get her cameras for the photo session. It was time to get back to work.

Chapter 10

David and Sophie easily adapted to a routine with their babies. The weekend was a delight for them as new parents and on Monday morning David left Sophie alone for the first time without her sister or his help. He hoped she would be all right having witnessed the work that went into attending to them.

The twins were normally awake around six, and while David was getting ready, Sophie changed the girls into matching outfits careful to keep the little gold anklets on their legs. Feeding was a bit challenging, especially when they were hungry at the same time, but she refused to use a bottle. Sophie was proud of her conviction to breastfeed and wanted to do so for a few more months. Once the girls were fed, she brought Faith and Grace into the living room, placing them in their matching bouncers.

About the same time, David emerged from the kitchen carrying two cups of coffee, and sat with the twins enjoying this start to the day. David talked to his girls telling stories about some of his students. Faith and Grace listened to their daddy's voice and watched him with their big blue eyes giving him their undivided attention. He kissed them on the forehead and said, *Daddy loves you.* A ritual he began over the weekend. Once he left for school, Sophie toasted a bagel, and with a second cup of coffee, had breakfast with her babies. This would become their morning routine, and she loved it. Thinking of Brie, she called her sister.

"Hey, sis, are you up and about this morning?"

"Of course, how are my nieces?"

"The twins are doing great. I didn't know being a mother could be so rewarding. It evokes these feelings from deep inside that you never knew were there. Sounds mushy, doesn't it?"

"Not at all, that's the way it should be."

"How is Ben besides ecstatic you are finally marrying him?"

"Ecstatic is an understatement. He mentioned eloping."

"Well, can you blame him? He's been on hold for two years. When might you come back for another visit? I realize you just left, and we'll be there in December, but that's still months away. The girls will change, and I don't want you to miss out on their development."

"You and David should be alone with your babies."

"David and I will have many years with the girls. Brie, you should see him. Before he went to work this morning, he sat in the living room talking to them. Watching David with the twins makes me fall in love with him all over again," Sophie said with a sigh.

"You both are loving parenthood. I'll plan a trip in a couple of months which will split the time before you come up for the wedding. But for now, give the girls a kiss for me, and I'll talk to you in a day or two. I'm sorry to cut this short, but I have a photo session soon and need to get ready."

"Sounds like you're back into the swing of things."

"I put an announcement on my phone recorder that I would be out of town, and yet, potential clients left messages waiting for my return."

"That should have made you feel good."

"Oh, it does. I'm very pleased to have the business."

"Who wouldn't want to have their portrait done by the renowned, worldwide photojournalist whose photos are hanging in private museums," Sophie said, teasing her sister.

"Well, sis, when you put it that way," Brie replied, laughing.

Brie accepted her popularity, modestly, with respect toward the individuals within the industry that helped to promote her career.

Ending their conversation, Sophie sat for awhile watching her daughters and began daydreaming of seeing them at two years of age running around the house, and then at five wanting to help bake cookies. She envisioned them in their teens and wondered if they would be like she and Sabrina, exchanging identities for the sheer fun of confusing people. The thought put a smile on her face.

Chapter 11

Sabrina met with William and Ashley Carpenter and their three children exactly at noon in *Asbury Park* near downtown. In fact, the park wasn't far from the cemetery where Aunt Millie was buried. Brie planned to drive over to the gravesite after finishing the photo shoot.

The children were very attractive wearing matching outfits of solid navy cotton-twilled slacks and plain white shirts. The oldest, Robert, was fourteen, Emily twelve and Lindsey had just turned five. Unmistakably, they favored their mother with her jet-black hair, aqua-blue eyes and porcelain white skin. They were a striking family.

Brie took a variety of poses using various scenic areas of the park. Approximately an hour later, she was ready to conclude the session confident she would have some great portrait shots for them to select from. Lindsey walked up and stood quietly in front of Sabrina as she knelt on the grass placing the camera in its case. Brie looked up at her and smiled.

"Hello, Lindsey. Did you enjoy having your picture taken?"

Lindsey shook her head up and down concentrating on Brie, but didn't speak.

"Can I help you with something?"

"I like you," Lindsey said.

"I like you too, Lindsey."

"Will you take care of my mommy? She is sick, and we don't know how much longer she will live," Lindsey asked with far more maturity than a five year old should have.

"Oh, honey, I'm so sorry to hear that," Brie said, understanding the reason for the family portrait.

"You can make her better."

"Sweetheart, what do you think I can do?"

"You can make her well. I know you can, please," she insisted, tears filling her eyes.

"How do you suppose I do that?"

"You can. I know you can; please, please make my mommy better," she begged.

Sabrina fell forward on her knees pulling the young girl into her arms holding her tight, and felt Lindsey's small body trembling as she wept. Sabrina gently pulled Lindsey from the embrace holding her upper arms, compelling her to look into Brie's eyes.

"Lindsey, you must understand that I can not make a promise to you. Do you know what I'm saying?" Sabrina asked, watching her reaction carefully.

Sniffling, Lindsey shook her head and wrapped her arms around Sabrina's neck. Brie whispered a prayer in her ear. Just as Sabrina was letting go, Lindsey's mother walked over to them.

"Lindsey, honey, its time to go. I hope she wasn't bothering you."

"No, not at all."

"I'll stop by your studio in a week to look at the proofs. I'm sure we'll be very pleased. Come on, Lindsey, let's have some lunch," she said, taking her daughter's hand and walking away.

Lindsey turned around smiling at Sabrina. *Such a burden for someone so young,* Brie thought waving goodbye, as she watched them walk across the well-manicured lawn toward the opposite side of the park. Lindsey continually twisted her body, looking over her shoulder toward Sabrina, not wanting to lose connection with her. Brie also focused on Lindsey until she was out of sight.

Saddened by the ordeal, Sabrina drove straight to the cemetery for a visit with Aunt Millie before returning home. She sat on the ground next to her aunt's headstone thinking about the little girl who needed a miracle for her mother, and spoke aloud the story of her request. It was moments like this that tore at Brie's heart for she so wanted to remove the heartache.

"Oh, Aunt Millie, did you know the depth of *Passionate Promises* when you bequeathed it to me?" she asked, aloud.

Whenever Sabrina visits the cemetery, she always left feeling restored with peacefulness in her soul. This is a place where she can quietly meditate and rejuvenate, coming often for that reason. There was something about being close to her beloved Aunt Millie that seemed to always manifest *Passionate Promises* more profoundly.

After returning home, Brie prepared lunch and went into the den where she could look out through the French doors to the acreage of trees that trimmed the perimeter of her lawn. Brie often had to remind herself that forest belonged to her. It was all part of the inheritance. Temporarily putting thoughts of Lindsey aside, she phoned her sister.

"How was the photo shoot?" Sophie asked first.

"It went well. It's amazing how easy it is to fall back into work. How are you and the girls doing?"

"We're okay. They still sleep a lot which makes it easy for me. Of course, I know this won't last much longer before I'll be spending my days on the floor playing with them instead of doing the daily chores."

"Playing with the girls sounds like a lot more fun than cleaning. I called to let you know we set the date for December twelfth and are planning to be married at Ben's church."

"Finally, it's official."

"Ben has been very patient while I was getting my life in

order."

"That's for sure. He's quite a guy to wait this long."

"Yes, he is. I'll ask Bella if she can suggest a location for the reception party."

"Good idea. She would love to help. You two have become close, and she might be offended if not included in the planning. Brie, I hear the girls waking from their nap and have to go. I'll talk to you later."

"Not a problem, go take care of my nieces."

Sophie's conversations where often disrupted with the caring for her infants; however, they both accepted it as part of her new life. Sabrina tossed the cell phone on the table thinking about her wedding. There was much to do, but she refused to become stressed. After all, surely between Ben, Bella, Sophie, and herself, they could put a wedding together in four months. How hard could it possibly be?

Chapter 12

Sabrina stopped by Bella's house the next morning, and from past experience knew there was no need to call first. Their lives connected easily after Bella's best friend, Mildred, died. In those first few months when Sabrina returned to Asheville, they spent time together filling in for the loss they each felt. Bella enjoyed talking about her friend and Sabrina, likewise, wanted to hear about her aunt.

Bella was a tall, attractive woman with a slim stature who preferred to wear her short auburn hair combed in a simple style. Seldom did she wear make-up, though truthfully, it wasn't needed with her smooth, olive-toned skin and hazel eyes. She didn't like to fuss over her appearance.

Opening the door, Bella was surprise to see Sabrina on her doorstep.

"Hello, Sabrina, I didn't know you were home. Come on in."

"I've been back a couple of days."

"I'm glad you came by."

Brie followed her into the kitchen and sat down at the table while Bella poured two cups of coffee with cream and sugar. Sabrina has had many conversations sitting at this table and now was excited to share her wedding plans.

"How are Sophie and the babies?"

Sabrina had called Bella from Florida informing her that Sophie had twin girls.

"Just awesome. In fact, I brought my personal brag-book," Brie said, pulling out a small photo album from her purse and placing it on the table.

Bella opened it and slowly flipped the pages. Pictures of the twins from the moment they were born still pink and wrinkled cuddled in their mother's arms to snaps of them lying in their matching cribs at home. Sabrina photographed the entire event from hospital to home putting the pictures on a compact disk for Sophie and David. From the disk, she printed her favorites to make a small album for herself. Unbeknown to Sophie, Brie was in the process of enlarging some of the pictures to matte and frame as a surprise for the babies' room, and also making a special book for Sophie. She hoped to have everything done in a couple of weeks for the girls' three-month birthday.

"What darling little angels."

"Can you tell which one is Faith and Grace?"

"Well, let me see. I think this one is Grace. She looks a little feisty to me," Bella said, pointing at the picture.

"Good guess, you're right. Sophie thinks she will be the mischievous one."

"They certainly are cute babies."

She handed the book back to Sabrina.

"How does it feel to be an aunt, now? Carries significant responsibilities, you know."

"I love it but wished we lived closer, so there could be frequent opportunities to see them. It will be hard living this far away especially when they get older. I'll probably be making several trips to Florida."

It was Sophie's continuous encouragement that eventually brought Brie back to Florida from Washington State when she took her first full-time assignment with the magazine right out of college. Now, it was Sabrina experiencing the very emotions she often detected from her sister when she was gone at length on assignment.

"You look a thousand miles away, girlie."

"I was for a moment. I was thinking of my sister and how, once again, I have moved away from her. It always meant so much to Sophie that we are near one another, and now I understand how she felt."

"I'm sure your sister accepts your need to reside where you feel is best for you. She loves you and doesn't want to lose that connection. Mildred was like a sister to me."

"It's strange how things change. But on a different note, I came by to tell you I'm getting married."

"When did this happen? I assume it's to Ben," she said with a chuckle.

"Of course, it's Ben. We have set the date for December twelfth. By chance, does that day mean anything to you?"

"Well, let me think about this. December, yes, I bet it was the day we went to buy a Christmas tree and I introduced you."

"Correct, we're using the day we met. It will forever be our anniversary."

"That's nice. I'm very happy for you and Ben. I always thought you made a good couple. You compliment each other."

"Thank you, Bella. I could use your help, but I don't want to be presumptuous."

"I would be delighted to assist."

"For starters, do you know of a nice place for the reception party? The wedding will be at Ben's church; however, we are at a dilemma where to have the reception."

"I can think of a few places, but personally, the country club would be my first choice. I'll call and see if it's available, and we can take a drive over to check it out."

"I only have a few months to make all these arrangements."

"I'll do it right now."

Bella got up from the table walking over to a kitchen drawer and pulled out a telephone book. She quickly looked up the phone number and dialed. In less than five minutes, she had discovered December twelfth was open and made plans to meet with the club's event planning coordinator the next day at ten.

After hanging up the phone and replacing the telephone book, she went back to sit at the table.

"Wow, you work fast."

"Just took a phone call."

"So are you available for ten in the morning? I'll swing by to pick you up and we can have breakfast at *The Country Kitchen*."

"I'll be ready by eight."

Brie took her coffee cup to the sink and rinsed it. Gathering her purse and placing her brag-book in it, she turned to Bella.

"We'll have a lot of fun putting this wedding together," Brie told her.

"You bet we will. I needed a new project."

"Good, because I have one for you."

Sabrina gave her friend a hug before leaving. Bella stood in the doorway watching Brie back out of the driveway onto the street. Throwing her hand in the air for a final wave, she closed the door. *Its past time those two lovebirds got married,* she thought, returning to the kitchen. It made her chuckle reminiscing about the time they met at his tree farm.

Chapter 13

The *Asheville Country Club* on Mulberry Road was the right place for the reception. The building was set back off the main street with a well-hidden driveway to the clubhouse that was overlaid with trees and exotic plant overgrowth. After a short winding drive, Bella drove to the front of a red-bricked building with its towering white, symmetrical columns giving it a southern plantation appeal. This was absolutely what Brie had in mind, staring out the car window.

Walking up the matching five brick steps toward the etched, glass-encased white door, Sabrina felt she was stepping back in time to Scarlett O'Hara's mansion. They were greeted by Jodi Carmichael, the event coordinator, as she and Bella stepped inside.

Jodi immediately began a tour of the entire country club giving a brief history lesson of each room they passed through as they had separate themes. Retracing their steps back to the main lobby, she then led them into the large banquet room off to the right from the main entrance. The walls were painted a dark green contrasting the oak wood floor with the draperies on each elongated window a Victorian paisley print of mauve, greens and blues, rendering a dramatically rich décor. On the opposite wall to the entrance, were two separate sets of double French doors leading out onto individual private decks that overlooked the garden, and beyond to the golf course.

Sabrina immediately knew this was the place for her wedding party. Standing in the center of the room, she imagined cloth-covered round tables and padded wing-backed chairs with miniature floral bouquet centerpieces. With the tables positioned in a circle, she envisioned dancing a wedding waltz with all eyes on her and Ben as they glide across the floor. Breaking from the trance, Brie inquired of the rental fees and catering services.

Bella and Sabrina were each handed a menu and price sheet for the food. Left alone for a moment allowing them an opportunity to view the choices, Sabrina made a mental note to check with Ben about the number of people he would like to invite. He had lived in the community longer and assumed he would have a list including his family's friends, but in the meantime, what to do about the food.

"Any suggestions, Bella," Sabrina asked as they perused the menu options.

"I'm sure Ben will have something to say about what he eats, but there are a few food items you may want to consider. I've eaten here on different occasions and have never been disappointed. I suggest making a selection of three entrées and when you send out your invitations have your guests RSVP their choice. That way you can get a general count of how many of each you'll need prepared."

"I like the three entrée plan."

"You can keep the salad and vegetables the same for everyone. Talk it over with Ben. He may have some ideas of his own."

They concluded the appointment with Sabrina leaving a retainer of two hundred dollars to reserve the date, not wanting to lose it in lieu of discussing this with Ben. She had twenty-four hours should she change her mind to get the deposit back.

Bella dropped Sabrina off at her house, not staying for the offered coffee. During the remainder of the day, Brie began a of her own to compare with the one Sophie had already begun. She called Sophie with this latest development.

"How is everything with Faith and Grace?" Brie asked, getting the first word in.

"Sleep when they are supposed to and eat when they get hungry, doing what babies do best."

"If you have a minute, can we go over the wedding list?"

"Sure, hold on and I'll get it."

Sophie retrieved the notepad with the list of to-do and to-get items.

"What did you want to know?"

"Well, I have a place for the reception. It will be at the *Asheville Country Club*. Bella and I went this morning. I haven't gotten the final okay from Ben, but I don't believe he will have any objections. It looks like something from *Gone with the Wind,* very southern."

"No kidding, I love that movie. How wonderful. Do you have a commitment from the church?"

"Not yet, but I'll talk to Ben tonight about it."

"Those are the two most important things, everything else will be easy. Next, select your invitations and make a guest list," Sophie suggested, remembering what it was like when she planned her own wedding.

"Can you help with the invitations? You know my style."

"I'll get right on it. I know exactly what will appeal to you. The internet makes shopping easy. I will forward some choices for you and Ben to select from. Then, it's just a matter of ordering the one you prefer. It will save a lot of time doing it this way."

"Good."

"Anything else you want me to do? You should start looking for a dress and the bridesmaid dresses. That is another big item to take care of."

"I want my dress to be formfitting without frills or ruffles, and perhaps a touch of lace around the neckline with long, slender sleeves and no train. You always look great wearing mauve and perhaps something in soft red for the bridesmaids, but you decide on the dresses."

"You trust me to make the decision."

"Of course, you pick what appeals to you."

"So I'm researching the invitations and dresses," Sophie stated, confirming her job.

"Only, if you have the time."

"I will make the time. This will be fun."

"I'll work on the menu and flowers."

"Sounds like a plan. Between the two of us, we'll have your wedding put together quickly."

"That would be a relief."

"Not to worry. Remember, I've already done this."

"Just one thing though, I don't want planning my wedding to interfere with your duties as a new mother. Should that happen, let me know because I can also count on Bella for help."

"I plan to work while they are sleeping. It shouldn't be a problem, and besides, I will enjoy every minute of researching items for you."

"I know, but I'm serious. I would be miserable if you became overwhelmed."

"I want to do this."

"Okay," Brie conceded.

"I'll get started, but it may take a week or so before I have something to forward to you."

"There's no immediate rush. Thanks, sis."

"I'll call you in a couple of days, unless you call me first," Sophie told her.

"Sounds good and give my nieces a kiss for me."

Sabrina was apprehensive about Sophie spending time on the wedding plans which would take her away from her babies. Even when they are sleeping, Sophie should be resting. But if Brie didn't include her in some of the preparations, her sister would be offended. She hoped the internet shopping was as easy as Sophie said and wouldn't become a distraction.

Chapter 14

Ben stopped by Sabrina's house after work to discuss the latest wedding plans. They sat at the kitchen table, and Brie outlined what she had accomplished so far.

"Okay, you go first. Tell me about your day. You mentioned on the phone that you have a place for the reception party."

"Yes, Bella and I went to the *Asheville Country Club*, and it is a superb place for the party. I adore the formal plantation style of the building, and the banquet room is very large which easily accommodates tables for our guests and still allow for a nice dance area in the center. I couldn't find one fault with the arrangement. Bella vouched the food is exceptional."

"If you like it, then it's fine with me. I know for a fact they fully decorate the country club for the holidays. I deliver Christmas trees every year, and the place is furnished with all the typical holiday trimmings. They usually setup a tree in every room as well as a tall one in the main lobby. I agree it would be a very festive place for a holiday wedding party. That was a good suggestion on Bella's part."

"That certainly reassures me because I put a deposit down today. Now, we need to make sure the church will be available."

"I'll stop by their office tomorrow and verify if Pastor McDaniel can perform the wedding."

"We need to know soon because I'm already assuming we do and telling Sophie and Bella we have the church. I've talked with Sophie, and she is working on the invitations and dresses. You'll need to think about who you want to be your best man."

"How many bridesmaids will you have? I'll need to gather an equal number of friends."

"I'm thinking of keeping it small; three bridesmaids and Sophie as my maid-of-honor, four total."

"That's easy enough. I'll get to work on getting the guys together. Anything else you need me to do at the moment?"

"There is one more thing. Do you have any recommendations for the food selection? If we choose three main courses, should we go with a prime-rib steak, pan-seared chicken breast in an herbal sauce and salmon sautéed in white wine? That would give our guests a choice between a meat, fish, or a chicken meal with steamed vegetables, garlic-creamed potatoes, house salad, fresh dinner rolls and coffee, tea or cola for the beverages. What do you think?"

"It all sounds great to me, let's do it."

"Okay, I'll call Jodi tomorrow and let her know our selections. Eventually, I will need to give her the attendance, but we have time on that. When Sophie sends me the invitations, we can pick one and get them ordered. Also, whenever you give me a list of family members and friends, I can add those names to the list Sophie and I are putting together. I wasn't planning on a big wedding, but I don't want to leave anyone out, either."

"I'll talk to my mom about who she wants to invite and instruct her to keep the list short."

"Let her invite whomever she wishes. We can make the final decision when we are ready to send out the invitations."

"Good idea."

Sabrina couldn't believe she was actually discussing her wedding. *This is going to happen,* she thought. They still had details to work out. Ben would move into the house with her, but then what to do with his house that was at the back of the family's property. It wouldn't be conducive to selling and letting just anyone have access through their private acreage.

They went into the den to sit more comfortably and talk. Relaxed in her rocker across from Ben, Brie realized this would soon become an everyday occurrence. When it was time for Ben to leave, she walked him to the front door, but before opening it, Sabrina wrapped her arms around his waist. She felt his arm muscles flex when he pulled her close. They stayed locked in the embrace as she rested her head on his chest enjoying the masculine scent of spicy cologne emanating from his body. It was intoxicating.

"Thank you, Sabrina," Ben whispered.

"I love you, Ben."

He kissed her passionately leaving her standing in a daze as he always did when they parted. Every time he kissed her, it was like the first time, fresh and new with a longing for more. Very soon, she could kiss him as much as she wanted and when she wanted. That thought put a smile on her face as she closed the door.

Chapter 15

Days blended for both Sabrina and Sophie. One would call the other to exchange wedding ideas and Sabrina would check up on the twins. They were two months old now and Brie could hardly believe she had already been away from them for a month. When she let her mind drift to Faith and Grace, which it often did, she would get a longing in her heart. She missed them and called her sister often checking on her nieces. This morning was no exception.

"Sophie, how are the girls?"

"They are beginning to have more wake time. Grace seems to want to stay up more than Faith. Maybe that is a good thing, so I can take care of one at a time."

"It sounds like you've settled into a routine with them."

"I think so."

"How is David doing? I bet he is a doting father."

"I can't pry him away from them. If they are sleeping when he comes home from work, he'll still go in their room and start talking to them. Next thing I hear is all kinds of sounds through the monitor. That goes on for quite a while."

"You love it."

"Of course, I do. I'm not complaining in the least. By-the-way, I sent you an email with links to a few websites for the invitations. Take a look and if you don't care for them, I'll start another search."

"Thanks. I'll do that later today."

"Sorry I have to cut this short, but I hear the girls. Was there a particular reason you called?"

"No, just checking on you."

"We're all doing well. I'll talk to you another time," Sophie told her.

Sabrina hung up the phone deciding to take a drive to Bella's and bring her up-to-date on things in general. It was a short distance down the road as her property was adjacent to Brie's to the west.

"How did you know I needed someone to share my coconut cream pie?" Bella asked, opening the door.

"I can't resist your goodies."

"I'll put a fresh pot of coffee on. So what brings you by today?"

"I wanted to let you know of the latest development in the wedding plans. Just to let you know, Ben liked your suggestion of the country club. We decided on the steak, chicken and salmon for the meal choices."

Bella placed pie and coffee on the dinette table while they talked.

"You've been busy. Anything else I can help you with? I'm at your disposal, just name it. Mildred would be so delighted to see her niece getting married."

"Yes, this is true. I think she knows, though."

"I bet she does."

"If you have the time, I could use your help selecting flowers for my bouquets and the arrangements for the church and banquet room."

"It would be my pleasure. What colors are you thinking of for your bridesmaid's dresses?"

"Probably soft red and mauve, but I'm not sure. Sophie is in charge of that, and I'm letting her select the dresses."

"You'll need to decide on what type of flowers you want and are they in season."

"I don't have a favorite other than daisies. Do you have any suggestions?"

"Poinsettias are the typical holiday plant. I'll have to give it some thought. The easiest way is to go to the florist and check their books to find out what appeals to you."

"That makes sense."

"Mildred and I always liked the arrangements at *Petal Pushers*. I've known Jill, the owner, for years. She'll do you right. We can go there tomorrow, if you like."

"Sure, the more I can get done now, the calmer I'll be as it draws closer."

They sat talking like old friends over a second cup of coffee and pie. Sabrina enjoyed sharing part of her life with Bella as she used to do with her Aunt Millie. Perhaps because Bella was a widow and had lost her best friend, Brie felt compelled to spend time with her. However, what began as a kind gesture quickly became a mutual meshing of hearts.

Sabrina took her dishes to the sink. Grabbing her purse and walking toward the front door, Brie turned giving her friend a hug.

"Thanks for helping, Bella."

"It's truly my pleasure."

Brie stepped outside and walked down the sidewalk to her car. Believing her wedding plans were moving along smoothly, she needed to switch gears and think about work. There were negatives waiting in the darkroom to be developed. The next few months would be a shuffling from work to wedding, but with the help of her sister and Bella, it shouldn't be difficult getting everything accomplished.

Chapter 16

Sophie was becoming concerned about Faith. Though she didn't know anything about raising babies, it seemed Faith was sleeping far too much. While Grace would awaken to discovering her surroundings, Faith chose to sleep. Since they were twins, Sophie naturally expected her babies to do the same things simultaneously, but that wasn't the case.

"David, I'm noticing Faith is sleeping a lot, and when she is awake, makes no effort to stay alert. Grace is looking around and being playful. Why isn't Faith doing that too?" Sophie asked, pressing her point.

"Honey, I don't have an answer for you. Even though they're twins, we have to remember they are two separate individuals with their own unique personalities and will have different habits. Faith may be more interested in sleeping."

"You could be right. Do you suppose that's all there is to it?"

"Yes, Faith will catch up when she is ready, but if it will alleviate your concerns, discuss it with Dr. Smitherton when you take the girls in for their next checkup. She's the baby expert."

"That's a good idea. I'll talk to her about it at their next appointment in two weeks. I knew Grace would be my more adventurous girl, and she is proving me correct. She doesn't miss anything. When I talk to her, she stares at my face, and it's so cute, but Faith doesn't respond the same way."

"I don't expect you to remember when you and Sabrina were babies, but possibly it was that way with the two of you. Maybe one of you was more alert than the other. If that be the case, I already know who the overzealous twin was," he said, teasingly.

"Oh, is that so. You believe you know us that well."

"Of course, I married the one bold enough to sit beside me in the coffee shop at college. Of these two beautiful women willing to meet with a stranger, I knew then who the more assertive twin was."

"You are a very perceptive man, Mr. McKinley. I'll take your advice about Faith; however, I will mention it to Dr. Smitherton. I'm so glad we talk about things. I feel better already. You are such a good daddy, David."

"I'm doing my best."

Sophie knew he was right. The twins are two individuals, and she should remember not to compare Faith to Grace's performance. It would not be fair to Faith. Putting that concern out of her mind, she and David enjoyed their evening with the girls already asleep for the night.

The next morning after breastfeeding, bathing and playing with the babies on her lap, Sophie put them in Grace's crib, and while sitting in the rocking chair, phoned her sister.

"Hi, Brie, what are you doing today?"

"I have a busy day scheduled in the darkroom; lots of photos to develop."

"Your life has always been hectic ever since college. David and I were talking last night about the twins. Do you remember mom mentioning anything about us being different when we were babies? Like either of us displaying separate habits or learning abilities."

"Not that I can think of, except in our teens. You were the outgoing one and I the hermit. Remember, you always liked to be around crowds, and I didn't care for the family reunions."

"I mean when we were babies."

"Now, I'm curious. Why do you ask?"

"I've noticed Faith sleeps when she should be awake. Even when she has slept for hours, and wakes to be fed and changed, she goes right back to sleeping. Grace is studying everything around her, and if Grace is doing that, I would think Faith should be also. David suggested I discuss it with Dr. Smitherton when I take the twins in for their next appointment. What are your thoughts, Brie? " Sophie asked, feeling her concerns manifesting again.

"I agree with David, and you should discuss it with their pediatrician."

"Faith is going to be my serious, thoughtful daughter."

"Kind of reminds me of us," Brie told her.

"When you mention it, yes it does. They are following in our footsteps. That takes a load off my mind. How is the wedding planning coming along?" Sophie asked, ready to change the subject.

"Everything is on course. Bella came through with a florist. She knows a woman who owns a floral shop and is working on the bouquets."

"Between the three of us, we'll get it done. We can put your wedding together."

"I couldn't do this without your help."

"Of course not," Sophie replied with a chuckle.

They ended their conversation and Sophie tiptoed to the crib to see Faith sleeping on her back, and Grace staring at the mobile hanging above her bed. She scooped Faith up and gently placed her in her own crib. Leaving the room with the monitors turned on, she went about her daily chores. Sophie fleetingly thought of calling the doctor's office for an earlier appointment but decided against it. *Now, I'm being foolish,* she thought.

In a few more months, Sophie knew all this peacefulness will vanish as they begin to crawl and eventually walk. It will be fun to watch as they discover things and learn about animals, colors and how to count. It occurred to Sophie that she would become a teacher again, but this time with her own children.

Chapter 17

Sophie was sitting in an examination room waiting for Dr. Smitherton. The girls were content in their double-seated stroller dressed in matching yellow and white print sundresses, and soft white sandals. Yellow barrettes barely held their blonde hair in place on top of their head.

She sat daydreaming about the past few years spent in a classroom, and knew as much as she enjoyed being a school teacher, being a mom was exceedingly more rewarding than she ever imagined. She loved her life. Sophie became alert when the pediatrician walked in. With a smile on her face, the doctor bent down to take a closer look at the twins.

"You have grown since I last saw you," she told them.

Grace replied with babbling while Faith stared at her.

"Who wants to be first?"

Grace responded again.

"Okay, Grace, you're it."

"How do you know which one is Grace?" Sophie asked.

"I cheated and looked at the anklets."

While Dr. Smitherton went to the sink to wash her hands, Sophie lifted Grace from the stroller and laid her on the examination table. She examined Grace carefully from feeling the soft spot on the top of her head to touching her pea-sized toes. Grace watched the lady doctor, and when she gently squeezed her tummy, Grace let out a giggle. Taken by surprise,

Sophie let out a squeal of her own.

"Oh my gosh, did you hear that?" Sophie exclaimed in amazement.

"I must have tickled her when I pressed on her belly. Let's try that again and see what she does."

She did it again and Grace made the same sound pulling her legs up in the air, playfully.

"Oh, you are so adorable," the doctor told her.

As though Grace understood what was said, she let out another vocal sound, and for good measure blew a stream of bubbles. Sophie stood on the opposite side of the examination table in complete awe of what her daughter was doing. She couldn't wait to tell David.

"Alright, little one, we have to let your sister have equal time or it wouldn't be fair, so I need you to have a seat back in your stroller while I have a talk with Faith."

She talked to the girls as though they understood. Sophie sat Grace back in the stroller and reached for Faith, placing her on the exam table. Doing the exact same thing, Faith didn't give the expected response. She showed no interest in what the doctor was doing to her, and apparently, wasn't ticklish when her tummy was touched. Even when Dr. Smitherton did it a second time, there was no reaction from Faith. Sophie thought this would be an appropriate moment to bring up her concern.

"Dr. Smitherton, do you notice anything different about Faith? I don't mean to compare the girls against one another in their developmental stages, but Faith doesn't seem to have the same interest as Grace does."

"Explain what you have observed."

The doctor was still focused on Faith as she continued her examination.

"For example, like now. Grace responded, but Faith didn't. What I have noticed is that, unlike Grace, Faith wants to sleep all the time. Even when she awakens from a nap, she eats and basically goes right back to sleep. She has very little wake time, and it doesn't seem natural to me. Maybe I'm overreacting like David said, but he did tell me to discuss it with you."

"While Grace may appear to be more enthusiastic at this age, it doesn't mean that Faith won't catch up, or surpass Grace in her activity level in time to come. Let me finish my exam, and we'll talk more," she said, reaching for her stethoscope from around her neck.

Sophie stood quietly as the doctor examined Faith. Dr. Smitherton listened carefully to her heart and lungs pulling the stethoscope away for a few seconds, and positioning it over Faith's heart again. Gently rolling Faith onto her side, she placed it on her back listening for what seemed to Sophie longer than necessary. It didn't take this long with Grace, so why was she repeating herself with Faith? Sophie noticed the frown on the doctor's face.

Finally, Dr. Smitherton finished the examination. Sophie was becoming apprehensive waiting for the doctor to speak, and her serious expression was disconcerting.

"I suggest we run a test on Faith for peace of mind. Now don't get upset on me. We don't have anything serious here, but I would feel better if we did an echocardiogram of her heart. Just humor me on this," she said on a lighter note, seeing Sophie turn completely pale.

"Is there something wrong with Faith's heart? What is it?" Sophie asked, stunned.

"I'm not sure, but I may have detected a murmur."

Sophie's own heart was beating way too fast. What was Dr. Smitherton trying to tell her? Was something wrong with her baby's heart? She wished David was with her because it was all she could do to stay calm, listening to the pediatrician.

"What is a murmur? I don't understand."

"A murmur is an abnormal additional rhythmic sound along with the heartbeat; however, let's not get too far into that conversation just yet. It may very well be one we don't even need to have."

Though Dr. Smitherton felt confident in her medical findings, she wasn't going against standard protocol and discussing concerns without performing tests. She wrote out two scripts, one for an ultrasound and the other for an echo-cardiogram, handing them to Sophie.

"Once you have these tests done, bring Faith in and we'll go over the results. In the meantime, don't worry."

"If this is a heart murmur, what caused it?"

There could not possibly be anything wrong with either of her babies.

"Get these tests done, and we'll talk about it when you return. Make an appointment before you leave. If you do this in the next day or two, I'll have the reports within a week."

"Okay," Sophie said, putting Faith back into the stroller.

She took the scripts before maneuvering out of the examination room and down the narrow corridor to the receptionist desk to make another appointment in a week. Sophie's mind was numb as she pulled her thoughts together. What did this mean?

When she arrived home, Sophie placed the girls in Grace's crib and sat in the rocking chair waiting for David. She didn't even call her sister, so shocked by the news. *This isn't happening,* she told herself repeatedly as tears slid down her cheeks. That's how David found her when he returned home from work.

Chapter 18

The moment David walked into the house, he sensed something was wrong. Leaving his briefcase in the foyer, he walked down the hallway to the girls' room to find Sophie sitting in the rocking chair, crying.

"Honey, what's wrong?" David asked, quickly checking on his girls.

Seeing they were fine, he stooped down in front of Sophie looking intently into her face. She flung herself at him wrapping her arms around his neck, letting the tears flow. Holding her close, he asked again.

"What is it Sophie? Why are you crying?"

"Something may be wrong with Faith's heart," she blurted out, pulling away from the embrace.

"What do you mean?"

"I did what you said and talked to Dr. Smitherton today when I took the girls in for their regular check-up. She thought she heard a heart murmur when she listened to Faith's heart. She gave me scripts for some tests, and I have an appointment in a week to go back. When I asked her questions about the murmur, she didn't want to talk about it until she had the results," Sophie explained, choking on the words.

David felt as if someone had just punched him in the stomach. He stood up and took Sophie's hand leading her back into the living room. He needed a few minutes to regain his composure before he could deal with this hit.

"Come on, let's not talk in here."

They sat down on the sofa, neither saying a word until Sophie spoke.

"What are we going to do if this is true?"

"First, let's not jump to conclusions without having all the facts. It could be nothing. What kind of tests is she recommending?"

"An ultrasound and echocardiogram."

"Then we should get the tests done and see what they reveal."

"But aren't you worried. Doesn't this bother you that something might be wrong with Faith?"

Needless to say, it had been a very stressful day, and David's apparent calmness to her news wasn't sitting well with Sophie. From her viewpoint, whether it is true or not, she expected more emotion from him.

"Yes, I am concerned, and I don't want to consider our daughter having anything wrong. It doesn't sound good when a doctor talks about the heart. I'm trying to not let my mind race to unpleasant thoughts. Sophie, believe me, I am upset," David explained, feeling her unease with him.

"I'm sorry, David. I know you would be too. I guess I was expecting an outburst, but that isn't your way of dealing with matters. I'm scared. What if this is true? What if Faith has something wrong with her heart?"

David pulled Sophie into his arms and held her close refusing to allow his imagination to conjure up anything distressful regarding his baby. They sat cuddled together for a long time without saying a word. Sophie realized she didn't need conversation but rather her husband's strong arms holding her. Slowly, her body relaxed, and she knew everything would be as it should be. This was simply a mistake. Nothing was going to happen to her family.

Later in the evening once he believed Sophie had calmed down, David went to the guest bedroom to do schoolwork. He expected Sophie to call her sister with the details. In fact, he was surprised she had not already phoned Brie, but secretly appreciated his wife waiting until she told him first. Settled on the sofa, Sophie dialed her sister.

"Brie, I need to talk to you."

"You sound so serious, what is it?"

"I took the girls for their regular visit with Dr. Smitherton, and she detected a murmur in Faith's heart. We have to go back in a week after having two tests done," she said solemnly, tears welling up in her eyes.

"Oh, Sophie, you must be worried. Why does she think Faith has a heart murmur?"

"She wasn't positive. I asked her what that meant and she said it was an abnormal extra sound. When I pressed for more information, she withdrew stating we needed to wait for the results. I won't be able to handle anything being wrong with either of my babies."

"Your girls are healthy. Faith will be alright."

"I know you're trying to cheer me, but really, Brie, you don't know that for sure."

"I do believe it, but there is one who does know for sure."

"What are you saying?"

"I'm saying that God knows."

"Please, Brie, I don't want to talk about God. I called to tell you about Faith. I thought you would say comforting words to make me less fearful," Sophie said, feeling a bit spiteful that her sister wasn't showing alarm.

Never had she been at odds with her sister and didn't want to start now especially over the twins. She thought everyone around her should exhibit the alarm she did, and it bothered her that her own husband and sister didn't react the same way. More so with Brie because she was her twin, they shared everything more intimately.

"We won't talk about it," Brie said, not taking offense to her sister's attitude.

"I'm sorry, Brie. I'm really on edge. I don't mean to take it out on you, but I'm not into God."

"I won't press you about it right now."

"I'll call you when we get the test results," Sophie said, agitated.

"I know how upsetting this is for you, and I haven't been very consoling, but try not to worry. Faith is okay."

"I appreciate what you're saying, but you're speaking out of turn. You don't know what's going to happen."

"We'll leave it at that. What tests have to be done?"

"An echocardiogram and ultrasound; I'm making the appointment in the morning since Dr. Smitherton stressed to have them done right away. I'll ask David to take that day off and go with me."

"Those are non-invasive tests."

"I can't imagine anything being wrong. Do you think this is why she sleeps all the time?" Sophie asked.

"Did you ask the doctor about her sleeping habits?"

"Yes, but she didn't address it, so I don't know if there is a connection."

"You'll have all your answers in a few days, but in the meantime, don't stay upset. You must be calm for the girls."

"I'll try, but it will be hard."

"Take your mind off it, and think about other things. I know that is easy to say and harder to do, but you have to, Sophie."

"You're right. I'll call you in a couple of days after we do the tests," Sophie told her, ready to end the conversation.

It wasn't one of their better talks leaving Sophie disappointed and annoyed that Sabrina didn't respond as she expected. Until experiencing that brief brush with jealousy, she never had reason to get into any confrontations with her sister. They didn't always agree, but it never caused any rifts between them.

Returning to the girls' room to check on them before retiring to bed, Sophie was discouraged by the lack of concern from both her husband and sister, finding it unacceptable. How could they not feel the same way she did?

Chapter 19

David made arrangements for a sub to take over his classroom, and together they went to the *Thornton Pediatric Diagnostic Center* recommended by Dr. Smitherton for the tests. As expected, they were not scheduled back-to-back, so most of their time was spent waiting. By the end of the day, Sophie's nerves were frayed, but at least it was over, and Faith did well throughout the ordeal. When they arrived home, she got the girls ready for bed. Sophie walked into the kitchen, exhausted, just as David was putting dinner on the table.

"Honey, I'm sorry to say this, but you look beat."

David walked over putting his arms around his wife, holding her close.

"So do you, what a day. I am so glad it's over. I was dreading Faith going through that, and I'm not looking forward to the visit with Dr. Smitherton," she told him, pulling away.

"Neither am I, but let's not get ahead of ourselves."

"You're right. When my mind wants to wonder, I'll have to refocus on positive thoughts."

"I know a week is a long time to wait for the answer, but the best thing is to not talk about it. I'm not denying anything, just not jumping into the unknown," he told her.

"I agree, it would only stress us more to dwell on it."

Dinner was fairly quiet with each self-absorbed in thought. They only spoke about uneventful topics. After they ate and cleaned the kitchen together, David took off to do schoolwork while Sophie phoned her sister, having promised Brie she would call.

"We got through the cardiology test today," Sophie began.

"I wish I could have been there with you. Faith was on my mind all day. How did everything go?"

"Besides being there for four hours, mostly waiting, it went smoothly. Faith was good and didn't seem to be the least bit affected by the techs putting probes all over her. It was upsetting, though, to watch them connecting devices to her body and hooking her up to a machine. I know she wasn't in any pain or discomfort, but I didn't like them handling my baby. We have to wait a few days to get the results. It is so nerve-wracking. I'm trying not to think about it like David suggested."

"Everything will be okay," Brie said, knowing her sister wouldn't appreciate her statement.

"Can we talk more tomorrow? I called to let you know how things went today, but I'm stressed and tired at the moment. "

"I understand. It has been a grueling day for you. Sleep well."

"I hope I can sleep."

Even though the conversation was brief, Sophie expected more outward concern from her sister. Perhaps it was wrong of her, but she wanted Brie to express distress which would give her comfort. Instead, Sabrina keeps telling her everything will be alright. It was not encouraging.

After checking on the twins, Sophie walked into the guest bedroom approaching her husband who reached out pulling her onto his lap. Wrapping her arms around his neck, she kissed him before leaving David to continue with his schoolwork. Not a word was spoken between them, it wasn't necessary.

Alone in the master bedroom, Sophie sat on the edge of the bed, and though she agreed not to think about the outcome, it weighed heavy in her thoughts. After a lingering shower, she slipped into bed pulling the covers over her head. She was so emotionally depleted she couldn't even shed a tear. Thinking she wouldn't be able to sleep, it came quickly sending her into a deep unconsciousness where dreams await.

Chapter 20

The drive to the pediatrician's office was very solemn. David understood the nervousness in Sophie and knew there wasn't anything he could say that would alleviate it. When they arrived, the receptionist ushered them straight into an examination room. While sitting in the hardback chairs, David reached over taking his wife's hand and gently rubbed his thumb pad over her knuckles.

"Sophie, stay focused."

"I just want this over."

The door swung open and Dr. Smitherton walked in holding a folder in her hand. She addressed David and Sophie with a smile before bending down to say hello to Grace and Faith. Leaning against the exam table, she opened the folder pulling out two sheets of paper. Sophie squeezed David's hand tightly.

"I know you are anxious for the results, so I'll get straight to the point. As suspected, Faith has a hole in her heart which is the cause of the murmur I detected a week ago. The medical term is a Ventricular Septal Defect or VSD for short. Sophie, remember when I explained that a heart murmur is an extra sound along with the regular heartbeat. It is an additional flowing sound simultaneous to the heart's rhythm. In Faith's case, this is due to the hole," she paused to allow this news to register.

"How did this happen? How could she have a hole in her heart?" David asked, shocked.

"We don't know, but most likely Faith was born with it. It's not as uncommon as you may think. Sometimes there isn't a specific explanation, but most often it occurs while the baby is developing in the womb. What we need to address, at the moment, is what to do about it. I recommend setting up an appointment with a pediatric cardiologist. More than likely, he will run some additional tests to determine the size and severity of the hole. This is out of my expertise."

Sophie's own heart sank when she heard the word cardiologist. It's never good news when there is a need for a heart specialist. It was all she could do to not grab her babies and run out of the room until she was safe at home.

"I strongly recommend not delaying getting Faith in to the cardiologist. I'm referring you to Dr. Phillip Whalton, and his office is in the *Thornton Pediatric Diagnostic Center* where theses tests were done. I prefer using their radiology department because of the state-of-the-art equipment. I'll give his office a call and let them know to expect hearing from you."

Dr. Smitherton was writing on a prescription pad as she spoke, tore off a sheet and handed it to David. He took the piece of paper without looking at it and shoved it into his shirt pocket.

"There isn't anything else I can do for Faith, and I don't need to see them for another month."

David took that as their cue the visit was over and looked at Sophie who was silent. There were questions she wanted to ask, but wasn't able to gather her thoughts. Looking at her babies lying peacefully in their stroller, Sophie could barely manage to hold herself together. It seemed her world had just stopped spinning.

"Do either of you have any questions?" Dr. Smitherton asked.

"If you're saying Faith was born with a hole in her heart, why wasn't it detected before now?" David asked.

"I'm saying most likely she was born with it, but I don't know that for sure. The cardiologist would be the best source for the answers to your questions. It is possible it occurred as she grew and her heart enlarged, but realistically, it was probably always there but so microscopic in size, it wasn't detected by the stethoscope."

"Is she in any danger of her heart stopping? Should we be worried?" he continued.

"No, her heart will not stop beating. If I thought Faith was in any immediate danger, I would have her admitted to the children's hospital."

Sophie almost fell off her seat when she heard the word *hospital* taking her gaze from her babies to looking up at Dr. Smitherton.

"What is this cardiologist going to do?" Sophie asked, coming back to reality.

"I'm sure he'll have other specialized tests, but I can't say what he will consider. If you prefer, I can have my staff make that appointment for you while you're here, and we can get things started for Faith."

"Sure, I don't see anyway around it," David commented as he looked at Sophie for approval.

"Faith will be in good hands with Dr. Whalton. He is young but very good at his specialty. I wouldn't put Faith under his care if I didn't believe he was one of the best pediatric cardiologists in this area."

"Let's go ahead. You are sure Faith is in no danger?" David asked again, wanting to verify that his daughter will be alright while they await her next appointment.

"Yes, she is stable," Dr. Smitherton reiterated, hoping to calm their concerns.

Sophie couldn't accept that Faith actually had a physical imperfection. In a state of disbelief, she stood up and reached into the stroller tucking the blankets around her babies. David navigated the stroller out of the examination room following the doctor back through the corridor to the receptionist desk.

As she gave instructions to the young woman, David reached over and pulled Sophie close.

Sophie didn't respond, standing very stiff, attempting to hear the instructions to the receptionist. She couldn't quite discern the words as Dr. Smitherton turned and smiled, placing a hand on David's shoulder.

"Don't worry. Faith will be in good hands."

On that final statement, she walked away.

The receptionist handed David the appointment cards for the cardiologist and the return check-up with Dr. Smitherton. They left the office in a trance.

After securing the twins in their individual car carriers, David glanced at his wife before pulling out of the parking garage. Seeing she was distraught, he thought perhaps having lunch at one of her favorite restaurants would be comforting.

"Let's get a bite to eat. Where would you like to go for lunch?"

"How can you think of food at a time like this? I don't want food. I want to hear that nothing is wrong with Faith," Sophie replied, raising her voice.

"Honey, you heard the doctor. It's a very small hole that I'm sure the heart doctor can easily fix. I know you must be hungry so let's stop somewhere."

"I can't eat anything right now. I just want to take my babies home."

"We can go home," he said, maneuvering through the mid-day traffic.

The longer he went without saying a word, the more upset Sophie became until finally she couldn't hold her thoughts any longer.

"Why is this happening?"

"All kind of things happen to people all the time. I guess it was our turn."

"That's a stupid answer. It isn't a matter of whose turn it is."

"Well, how else do we explain it?"

"I don't know, but that is not an acceptable explanation," she stated, sharply.

"I'm just saying, we don't know why this is happening to Faith. Hopefully, we'll learn more after we see the cardiologist."

Sophie didn't want to pick a fight with David, but he was quickly becoming a target for the fear she was feeling. She was scared, and perhaps unreasonably angry at the situation, but it agitated her that he was so calm, not showing signs of distress. They didn't discuss it on the drive home.

She took the girls straight to their room, changed their outfits, fed them and put them down for a nap. David went into the kitchen. They had yet to say another word to each other, however, when Sophie walked in, David broke the silence by offering lunch.

"I just put a casserole in the oven for tonight. Give me a minute and I'll heat up the leftover lasagna for lunch and throw a salad together."

"I can do that," she replied, pulling the dish out of the refrigerator.

Dividing off two portions and placing them on individual plates, she heated each in the microwave and started on the salad. It wasn't normal for there to be discord between them, but Sophie was frustrated with David for his lack of compassion. With the meal on the table, they sat down to eat. Sophie confronted David about his behavior.

"David, I don't understand why you aren't upset and talking about this?"

"I don't believe it's anything serious. The doctor will fix the hole, and everything will be back to the way it was."

"I can't take this lightly like you seem to be able to do."

"The doctor told us Faith is okay, and I believe her. This is a small problem we have to take care of, that's all."

"You see this as a *small* problem? I can't believe you just said that."

"That's all it is, nothing that can't be fixed."

"What if it's more serious than Dr. Smitherton told us?"

"She would have said so."

"We don't know that. Maybe she didn't want to alarm us or perhaps she knows more from reading the reports than she's willing to disclose, leaving it to the cardiologist to break the bad news."

"Those are the kind of thoughts that aren't good for either of us to have. Where is your faith in Faith?"

"Oh, that's real cute. Don't test me, David. I'm truly not in the mood to be questioned about my faith, my acceptance of the doctor's diagnosis, or anything else at the moment. You're irritating me, and I'm trying real hard to not get into an argument with you."

"Why argue with me? There isn't anything we should be on opposite sides about and especially when it comes to our girls."

"That's the point. We aren't seeing this situation the same way. You apparently have little concern while I am a nervous wreck."

"I trust what Dr. Smitherton told us."

"Please don't side with the doctor. That is not an acceptable statement to me at the moment."

On that note, Sophie got up from the table taking her dish to the sink. With nothing else to say, she walked passed David sitting at the table. She wanted him to feel the same way she did, but instead he was being practical. She checked on her babies and stood by Faith's crib watching her sleep. It was impossible to imagine there was anything wrong. How could her baby have any imperfection? The reality was like a slap in the face, one Sophie felt she was taking over and over, each time she replayed the diagnosis in her mind.

Not in the best of moods, she promised her sister she would call and knew Brie would be waiting to hear from her. She walked back into the living room retrieving her cell phone on the table and punched her sister's number.

Chapter 21

The phone rang several times before Sabrina answered and Sophie was about to leave a voicemail message.

"What took you so long to answer?" Sophie asked, curtly.

"Well, hello to you too, sis?"

Brie thought the news must not be good for her sister to sound so discouraged. She would wait for Sophie to begin.

"I told you I would call as soon as we had the results. We came home about an hour ago, and I put the girls down for a nap and had lunch. David and I almost got into a fight."

Sabrina noticed Sophie was avoiding the issue of Faith, but wasn't going to push for information, knowing she would talk about it when ready.

"You should take this opportunity to relax too."

"I can't right now. David is so calm and accepting of whatever the doctor says."

"How is David?"

"Better than I am, that's my point."

"Don't let that cool facade fool you. I'm sure David is dealing with his own emotions and is not going to show them, causing you further anxiety."

There was a noticeable pause in their conversation as Sophie gave credence to her sister's comment. Perhaps, there was some truth to her statement.

"Well, I admit I didn't look at it that way. He keeps telling me everything will be alright. If one more person tells me that, I'm going to scream. I swear I will."

"Forbid, I would say such a thing to you!"

It got the reaction she expected and made Sophie laugh.

"You had better not!"

Sophie felt better talking with her twin. She began to explain everything Dr. Smitherton told them. Brie listened without interruption as Sophie went into great detail.

"So the hole in Faith's heart has been confirmed and Dr. Smitherton wants a cardiologist to take a further look to see what he recommends," Brie reiterated her sister's words after a long pause.

"Yes. There may be further tests he will want to do."

"Perhaps nothing has to be done, and the hole will close as she grows," Brie said, offering her thoughts.

"I didn't think of that. Maybe nothing needs to be done."

With her imagination running rampant conjuring up terrible images, Sophie had not given any consideration to a solution of allowing Faith's heart to repair itself over time. Thank goodness Brie was grounding her. Sophie desperately needed to hear those reassuring words which gave her some-thing to hang onto. For the first time since being told of the heart murmur, she felt somewhat better.

"Thanks for the encouraging words. I was expecting to hear them from David and when he didn't give me the response I wanted, I faulted him for it. I need to talk with him."

"I'm always here for you."

"I know you are. I should make amends. I'll call in a couple of days and thanks, sis."

"Give your husband a hug for me," Brie said with humor.

"Will do."

Maybe Sabrina was correct and everything would return to normal. She knew she needed to focus on that thought feeling somewhat relieved as she walked down the hallway to the twins' room to find her babies were still asleep. She went in search of her husband locating him in his usual place; however, not wanting to interrupt him, she turned in the doorway to leave. He called her back.

"What is it Sophie? Are the girls okay?"

"Yes, they are sleeping. I didn't mean to disturb you."

"Honey, you can disturb me anytime you want to."

David always said the sweetest things, and it was one of many reasons why she loved him because he had a way of making her feel special. He didn't deserve her poor behavior even if she was under duress, and for him to say something sweet now, only made her feel worse.

Sabrina was right that David would be upset but dealing with this in his own way. She walked into the room to the small sofa where he was sitting and sat down on his lap. Instinctively, David put his arms around her pulling her close.

"I'm sorry. I had a bad attitude this afternoon and took it out on you. I was being selfish," she said with tears in her eyes.

"Oh, honey, its okay. This is difficult for both of us, but I believe it isn't anything serious and there will be an easy remedy."

"You think so? Because that is the same thing Brie said. She isn't worried, either. I mean not in the sense that something grave is wrong."

"See, there are two opinions expressing a positive out-come. I know this is upsetting you, but try not to dwell on it."

"You're right. I'll have to guard my thoughts."

Sophie felt relieved to have her husband's confirmation also. She kissed him and left him to grading papers. In the small room, she walked over to the computer desk and booted up the internet to research wedding dresses. It would be a good distraction keeping her mind clear of things she'd rather not think about.

Chapter 22

As they sat in Dr. Whalton's office, Sophie took a visual inventory of the room noticing the walls were painted a peach color and trimmed with a turquoise print wallpaper border near the ceiling. Nicely framed artwork of beach scenes was strategically arranged on the walls. The sofa they sat on was cream-colored leather placed opposite a desk and matching bookcase of solid teakwood. The décor was inviting and friendly, understandably so.

The pediatric cardiologist was a young, energetic man with a soft spoken voice. His sandy-blonde hair, worn longer than most physicians, trimmed the top of his collar; however, because it was styled away from his face, it was not an unattractive cut. He had warm brown eyes and a very friendly smile.

Rather than sitting behind his desk, Dr. Whalton pulled a chair up close to the sofa and sat across from David and Sophie. The twins were in their dual-stroller to the left of their father. He had received a copy of the tests ordered by Dr. Smitherton and was carefully studying each sheet while they waited patiently. Sophie jumped when his voice broke the silence in the room.

"Well, let's see who we have here," he said as he turned to get a glimpse of Grace and Faith.

With an easy smile, he took his index finger and pretended

to tickle each girl. Grace enjoyed the attention, but Faith watched him unimpressed by his antics.

"It does appear from these reports that your daughter may have a problem with her heart, but to know exactly what is happening, there are additional tests needed. I recommend we add to the echocardiogram and ultrasound a chest x-ray, electrocardiogram which will tell us the electrical activity of Faith's heart, along with a pulse oximetry test to measure oxygen levels in her blood. I'm sure you must be very anxious so having these done today while you are here, I can give you some preliminary information about Faith's condition without any further delay," he said in a matter-of-fact tone, glancing at the twins.

David and Sophie looked at each other and with a quick nod, David agreed. They both wanted to know as soon as possible, and waiting wasn't an acceptable option. These were non-invasive tests, annoying but not harmful.

"Faith's heart has been listened to many times since her birth, and no one has mentioned this until now. If she has a heart murmur, why wasn't it detected before; especially, if you think she was born with it?" David asked.

It was a reasonable question, he thought.

"Infants have a faster heart rate than we do as adults, and this underlying sound is so subtle it can initially go undetected. A murmur is an additional sound produced by blood moving through the heart's valves making a swishing noise. It is possible for it to go unnoticed for awhile until the heart grows and develops more. Then it becomes easier to detect the anomaly."

"How did this happen?" David questioned further.

"The simplest way to explain it is this area of her heart wasn't supplied a sufficient amount of blood, thus inhibiting the cell formation required to make the tissue in that particular spot as the organ matured. This can easily occur in the developmental stages as a fetus; perhaps, by the position of her body in the womb. We don't always know, but this is probably the cause."

Sophie listened carefully to every word spoken by the doctor. The more she heard, the faster she was losing her resolve everything was going to be alright. She had to ask the question weighing on her mind.

"Can she outgrow this?"

"That is an understandable question, but one I can't answer just yet. After these additional tests, I'll give you a better prognosis for Faith."

That word prognosis didn't sit well with Sophie. She didn't like any of this and was finding it extremely hard to be calm.

"I want to know what is going on with Faith's heart and what we can do to help her," David stated.

"We have an excellent radiology department which I see by these reports ordered by Dr. Smitherton were done here."

"Yes, this is where she sent us."

He grabbed the stethoscope hanging around his neck and leaning forward listened to Faith's heart, but she wasn't amused by his presence. Walking back to his desk, he picked up the phone and asked for one of his staff. Shortly, the door opened and a tall, slender woman came in with bright red hair pulled back in a ponytail.

"Amy, this is David and Sophie McKinley, and their twins, Grace and Faith. I need some tests on Faith, STAT, and would like for you to make the arrangements and accompany them to the third floor."

The nurse turned and smiled as she was handed the scripts.

"Certainly, I'll take good care of them. If you'll follow me, please," she said.

David took charge of the stroller.

"I'll see you later this afternoon once I have all the results. We should know something more affirmative by then."

"Thanks, Dr. Whalton," David said, before maneuvering the stroller out of his office.

They followed Amy through the adjacent corridors to an

elevator. As she pushed the button to the third floor where the diagnostic imaging equipment was located, she told them the building had seven levels, a surgical wing and eight cardiac specialists on staff. Unbeknown to the nurse, this was their second trip to the third floor.

Stepping off the elevator, they were directed to a circular receptionist desk. Amy handed the scripts to the young woman sitting behind a monitor wearing a headpiece with a microphone wrapped around her face, explaining the tests where to be done immediately. As the receptionist looked up, she recognized the young couple and smiled before rapidly punching keys on her keypad. Within minutes, Faith was on the schedule with minimal lapse of time between each test. Slightly off-center to the receptionist's desk was a small carpeted waiting area where they were instructed to wait until called by a technician. Sitting in the same padded chair in less than two weeks seemed very abnormal to Sophie.

"Let me know if you have any questions. These tests are not painful for your baby. If you have ever had or known of someone who has had an EKG or ECG then you know how this works. The part that is probably annoying is having all the probes stuck on her body, but it doesn't hurt."

Neither David nor Sophie corrected the nurse that they had been through this procedure recently with Faith.

"How does the pulse oximetry work?" Sophie asked, wanting to understand every minute detail of what they would be doing to her baby.

"That's an easy one, I'll do it myself. It is a small sensory probe that we attach like a clip to a body extremity such as a toe or finger. It is connected to a monitor that reads the oxygen in the blood and tells if an adequate level is supplied throughout the body."

"How long do you think our wait will be? It's almost lunchtime, and I'd like to get my wife something to eat since it appears we could be here awhile," David asked the nurse.

"There's a cafeteria on the first floor. You can go down to

eat, and I'll call your cell phone when they are ready for Faith, or bring a tray up here, if you prefer."

David looked at his wife for her preference.

"I'll stay here. Just bring something back."

"Do you want a hot meal or a light deli plate?"

"If they have a hot meal, I'll take that and iced tea."

"I'll be right back. Amy, would like anything?"

"No, but thanks for the offer."

David took off for the elevator while Sophie kept close guard on her babies. Amy walked over to talk with the receptionist for a few minutes. Because she was very apprehensive about the tests, Sophie was glad the nurse didn't hang around for small talk.

Chapter 23

Faith wasn't bothered by all the people swarming around probing and sticking things on her body. David and Sophie were solemn hanging on emotionally by invisible threads, and even Grace was quiet. The answer could be unexpected, and David was becoming concerned it may be one they weren't anticipating. Sophie was finding it hard to maintain a strong-hold, to be hopeful; she was so frightened for Faith. She wasn't sure her own heart could withstand anything other than good news.

Sophie stayed with Faith while David waited with Grace just outside the doorway of one of the radiology rooms. Standing next to the gurney that Faith was placed on, she watched intently how the technicians handled her baby. There were two of them working diligently adhering adhesive probes on her chest, arms, neck, temples and a few on her upper back. Though Sophie understood Faith wouldn't be in any discomfort, she didn't like her baby being messed with.

It took several hours to complete the tests; however, individually they were approximately thirty minutes. It was the preparation time that seemed to take the longest. Now they were back in the same waiting area expecting Amy to return them to Dr. Whalton's office on the second floor. Instead, she deposited them in the reception area and informed them he was waiting for the results, and it may take awhile. They sat forty-five minutes before the nurse came and took them into his empty office to the same position as earlier that day. David grabbed Sophie's hand and held it firmly.

"There can't be anything wrong with Faith," he reassured her.

She wasn't given the opportunity to respond. The door opened and Dr. Whalton walked in holding papers in his right hand. Pulling up a chair in front of them as he had done earlier, he paused reading the reports once again.

"I have all the results. The hole in Faith's heart appears to be about the size of the head on a straight pin. In comparison to our own heart, that may seem insignificantly small, but to an infant's heart it can be a measurable size. Oxygen levels are good. However, to determine with accuracy that her heart is indeed providing an adequate blood supply, it would be wise to do a more invasive procedure called an angio-cardiography which will tells us exactly how her heart is functioning. This test measures pressure within the heart chambers and the blood vessels. With a hole in the heart, it can affect the valves in pumping the flow of blood in and out. If there is a problem in this area, we need to address it now rather than later," he said, pausing to let them absorb this information.

This didn't sound good.

"How do you do that?" David asked.

"We would need to sedate Faith and run a dye and watch as it travels through the heart. This placement in a vein is called a coronary angiography or arteriography. Following on a monitor will show us how her blood is flowing throughout the heart, the rate it flows and if there are any places that slow down this flow. If the blood isn't being pumped at a normal rate, there could be a deficiency reaching all the other organs. We can also detect if blood is seeping out of the chamber via this hole."

"What are you saying? Because she has a tiny hole in her heart, there may not be enough blood to all parts of her body. This sounds serious," David questioned.

"It can be, however, I don't want to jump to conclusions without this additional test. If it comes back that blood flow is adequate, we aren't looking at any immediate danger of other organs becoming damaged for lack of blood thus oxygen. Then we direct our attention specifically on the hole and not any subsequent issues it could be creating."

"If I understand you correctly, you are addressing her heart as a whole in its function at the moment, rather than what to do with the hole that is in it?" David asked.

"Correct. We need to make sure the heart is performing properly supplying the needs for the remainder of the body's functions. Once we know this organ is doing its job, we can isolate the incident of the hole and look at what to do about it," Dr. Whalton reiterated.

As the doctor and David talked back and forth, Sophie thought she was going to die right there in his office. She glanced over at her twins lying together in the stroller. With eyes upon Faith, who was sleeping through the discussion centered on her, Sophie wanted to burst into tears. This could not be happening. David was still holding his wife's hand sensing the tension and knew instinctively what this news must be doing to her. He asked the questions that were on both their minds.

"I would like to schedule this procedure for next week."

"How long will it take?"

"It doesn't take long, maybe forty-five minutes or so. However, it's the preparation that's longer in the duration. We will need an anesthesiologist for the sedation, and an intra-venous specialist for the injection of the dye solution."

"You mean they will use anesthesia like in surgeries?" David asked, alarmed.

"Yes, but it will be appropriate for an infant."

"What does an intravenous specialist do?"

"Because Faith's veins are so small, we have intravenous specialists available who are specifically trained in locating minuscule veins, to place the needle correctly the first time avoiding continual attempts which becomes stressful for the patient."

"What about this dye you mentioned? What is it?"

"It is a radioactive substance we monitor as it travels in the veins and passes through the heart. It gives us a mirrored image of how the blood is moving by creating a shadow effect. By doing this test, we make sure we aren't missing anything concerning the blood flow through the arteries and valves."

David didn't like what he was hearing. His heart sank as the words registered. There didn't seem to be any way of getting around having their daughter subjected to this invasive procedure with its needles, radioactive dye and anesthesia.

"I realize this is a lot to take in, but I suggest not delaying doing the procedure. The sooner we have the results the better we will know what to do next," he stated, writing out a script.

"What if we decide to not do this procedure? What would be the next step?"

Sophie let out a silent thank you. At least her husband was directing the questions at the doctor that she would be asking if she had not lost her ability to speak, feeling completely numb.

"We would have to think about closing the hole assuming it will enlarge as her heart grows."

"So you think if we don't do anything at all, the hole in her heart will get larger?"

"Yes, that possibility does exist."

"Could the hole simply close up as she grows?"

Thank you, David, she thought.

"It's not likely that it would. As Faith grows, her heart grows also and the hole continues to stretch or open further. It would be a simple solution if that were the case."

"What would you do to close the hole?"

"It would require surgery."

"You mean like open heart surgery."

"Yes, in a manner of speaking."

"What does that mean?" David asked, persistently.

"There is a relatively new technology using laser. I don't

know, at the moment, if that is an option with Faith, but there are cases when we can correct some heart issues with a laser beam rather than a scalpel."

David couldn't believe what he was hearing as each question he asked led him deeper into the unknown. The mere thought of open heart surgery on his baby girl was unthinkable. He glanced at his wife to see Sophie had gone completely pale realizing it was time to get his family out of this office and back home where they belonged.

"We want to think about this."

That was all David could say. He was ready to leave.

"I would advise you not to take too long. Any delays could become potentially harmful, especially without a positive assessment of the condition of her heart at this time."

"We'll get back to you in a couple of days. We need to think about this. It's a lot to digest."

Dr. Whalton handed the script to David and stood removing the chair in their path. David stood also and politely shook the doctor's hand. He turned to help his wife and they left his office with Sophie in such a state of shock, words escaped her. All she could think about was this could not possibly be happening to them. Her greatest fear had just become a reality, and it wasn't going to be alright as David and Brie had told her.

Chapter 24

Sophie had yet to utter a single word since leaving the doctor's office, and her facial expression had not changed, nor the paleness of her skin. David was worried she had truly gone into shock. It wasn't like Sophie to act this way.

"Sophie, honey, it's going to be alright," he said, trying to comfort her when he didn't feel it himself.

He reached over and grabbed her hand, giving it a firm squeeze, while keeping a tight grip on the steering wheel with his left. His attention was divided between traffic and his wife.

"No, it's not going to be alright. You're wrong. I don't want you telling me everything is going to be alright," she yelled at him.

"We can't think the worse. We have to stay positive," he told her, not affected by her tone.

"No, we don't. There is absolutely nothing, I repeat, nothing remotely positive about this."

"Honey, Faith is okay. It's not productive for either of us to get upset. Yes, we took a hit today, but the hole in her heart can be fixed."

"Fixed! You talk as though she is a piece of equipment to be put in a shop to be repaired, and then she'll run good-as-new. She is not an object to be fixed!" Sophie shouted.

Was David really looking at Faith as something to be repaired? Sophie found his reserved attitude unnerving and his words unacceptable. She didn't want to hear anything about fixing Faith. It was appalling he would even say such a thing.

"Sophie, you're putting words in my mouth. You know I don't see Faith that way. I'm just saying we need to keep a clear perspective. We were blindsided by what the doctor told us, but it is important to consider what he said and carefully think this through."

"I have no intentions of letting them put a single mark on my baby. There will be no cutting on her. I heard what he said, and I'm not interested in his method."

David was fast losing his stance on the conversation, sinking into proverbial quicksand by every word he spoke. He postponed any further discussion until she had a chance to calm down and see the situation more rationally. He couldn't fault her for how she felt because he felt the same way. This just wasn't the right time to discuss it with both of them on edge.

"Let's put this conversation on hold until we get home," David suggested.

That was fine with her. The remainder of the drive was in silence. After getting the twins changed, fed and tucked in their cribs early for the evening, Sophie disappeared to their bedroom. Entering the adjacent bathroom and closing the door, she took a warm shower lingering longer than usual. She could no longer hold back the tears mingling with the droplets of water. *This can't be real. Why is this happening to me? Why my baby,* she silently pleaded. Crying uncontrollably, Sophie became fixated in the shower not ever wanting to step out and face the fate in store for Faith.

Perhaps the water would wash away all the day's bad news, and when she dressed and returned to the living room, everything would be right in her world again. However, when she finally made an appearance, nothing had changed. She passed through to the kitchen to find David cooking dinner. Sophie felt badly for the way she had spoken to him earlier taking her anger out on him. Realistically, her attack wasn't fair. That was twice now she had been irritated with her husband which was completely out of character for her.

"What are you fixing?" Sophie asked, breaking the silence.

"A couple of steaks on the grill with steamed vegetables and salad."

"That sounds good. I'll make some iced tea."

Neither seemed ready to talk about Faith. David made the decision to let Sophie take the lead to begin the discussion. They ate dinner with conversation centered on school and plans for the weekend. Afterwards, David made a fresh pot of coffee and they went into the living room. Sophie had yet to call her sister which was another very unusual occurrence because she always talked to Brie about everything. Sitting on opposite ends of the sofa, David waited patiently for Sophie to initiate a conversation, but when she didn't speak, he decided to nudge her.

"Honey, we need to talk about this."

"I can't do it, David."

"Do what?"

"I can't let them cut on Faith."

"I don't want that, either. But we need to take things in the order of Dr. Whalton's concerns and think about this procedure first. I don't see how we have any choice but to do this one additional test."

"Sedating Faith and running radioactive dye in her veins is disgusting to me. That stuff is harmful, how can it not be?"

"I agree, but there isn't any way to avoid it."

"Oh, there is, we don't do it."

"But if we choose not to, how are we going to know what is happening with her heart and whether this hole is causing other problems?"

"I don't have an answer, but this isn't right."

"We have to know what is going on with Faith. Ignoring the matter isn't going to make it go away."

"You think I am pretending it doesn't exist. I understand the severity of this problem and don't like the options we've been given."

"I wasn't implying that. So what are your thoughts? How do you think we should handle this?"

"I'm not sure, I have to think."

"Well, the doctor doesn't want us taking much time. He is expecting this to be done soon and will be waiting for the results."

"I don't care what he wants. I only care about what is best for Faith."

"If we don't do the test, we'll never know for sure. We can't take the chance of not doing anything and something goes wrong later. Is that what you want to do, nothing?"

"There has to be other options. It's just a tiny hole."

"Yes, but that hole is causing problems," he reiterated.

"We don't know that for a fact. Even the doctor said he wasn't sure until he did the test."

"Exactly, we're back to the angio-cardiography."

"I realize we have to make a decision, but can we talk about it later. Right now, we are just talking in circles. I want to call Brie. She's waiting to hear from me," Sophie told him.

"Call your sister. Brie is very insightful; perhaps she will have some comforting words."

"David, I don't mean to be ill-tempered with you."

"It's okay, honey. This is hard for both of us, and I understand."

"I know you do."

As he stood, he leaned down and kissed her.

"Call Brie, I'm going to grade papers."

Sophie needed to talk to her sister. If anyone understood how she was feeling, it would be her twin even more so than her husband. She knew Brie would have encouraging words, and perhaps, even some thoughts on the matter they hadn't considered, or at least she hoped so.

Chapter 25

Sophie checked on the twins before retrieving her cell phone and returning to the sofa. When Brie answered, Sophie got right to the point telling her about the doctor visit.

"Faith does have a hole in her heart. The pediatric cardiologist had a few more tests done today, basically for confirmation, but wants to do a more invasive procedure to see how this hole is affecting her heart's function. He recommends an angio-cardiography which requires putting Faith to sleep and running a radioactive dye through a vein. How harmful does that sound?"

"It sounds daunting. Once they have this test result, then what?"

"He's talking about surgery to close the hole. But first, he wants to see how the heart is performing to make sure there is an adequate amount of blood flowing to all the organs which is the reason for this test. If the heart is functioning properly, he'll then discuss closing the hole."

"Does he think it may close on its own as she grows?"

"David asked that question, but Dr. Whalton didn't think so. If anything, probably the opposite and it could get larger."

"Did the doctor say how this happened?"

"Her pediatrician and the cardiologist both believe she was born with it, but aren't absolutely sure. I don't think they really know."

"And this is the only solution."

"At the moment, yes, that's what he presented to us today."

"This must be very hard for you and David. And Grace is alright? I mean being a twin, they haven't detected anything wrong with her heart as well."

"No, apparently it is only Faith that has the problem."

"Sophie, I'm so sorry to hear this, but Faith will live up to her name."

"What does that mean?"

"Faith has her name for a very special reason."

"Please, Brie, if you are implying something religious; drop it. I'm not in the mood."

"I don't mean to add to your stress. So what happens next?"

"David wants to do the procedure. I hate that she has to be subjected to any of this. It isn't right."

"I agree. What would happen if you and David decided to leave it alone and wait to see how she does in the next few months?"

"Dr. Whalton seems adamant we do this procedure and not delay. I haven't actually asked David, but I would be surprised if he agreed to hold off."

"I'm sure you both want to know for sure."

"Why is this happening? I feel like I'm in a bad dream."

"You and David should pray about this."

"No, Brie, I don't want to hear about praying, or having faith. God gave Faith a defective heart," Sophie stated, sharply.

"You don't mean that, Sophie. I know you are very upset at the moment, but I don't believe for a minute that you really blame God."

"Yes, I do. This is His fault."

"Why would you say such a thing?"

"I don't want to talk about it."

"Okay, okay, but I'm praying for you and Faith."

"Whatever," Sophie said sarcastically, too upset and angry

to listen to what Brie was saying.

Sophie didn't want to talk about God even though she was the one to inadvertently bring up the subject with her comment, and hearing her sister defend Him was unsettling. With the mood she was in, their conversation was headed toward an argument so before that happened, Sophie cut it short.

Sabrina remained supportive with encouraging words knowing how hard this was for her sister, having no intention of expressing her own thoughts anymore than Sophie would allow. Brie expected a trip to Florida was imminent for both Faith and her sister.

Chapter 26

Sophie called Brie three days later informing her that David believed they should have the procedure done before proceeding with any other decisions. He didn't think they had the liberty to wait, and Sophie's adamant disagreement didn't sway him. Neither wanted to put their baby through the ordeal, but David was more realistic about it. It was scheduled for Friday morning and could take up to two hours including the prep time and recovery.

Two days later, they were driving Faith to the *Thornton Pediatric Diagnostic Center* for the third time. Sophie was having difficulty controlling the fear that engulfed her. She understood doctors did this all the time, but didn't know if she could actually let them do it to her baby. Tears filled her eyes as she glanced over her shoulder to look at Faith. David parked the car but before opening the door, he reached over and took Sophie's trembling hand and held it firmly.

"Sophie, let's say a prayer before we go in," he said, squeezing her hand.

"No, I can't do that."

"Why not, it certainly won't do any harm. Let's give Faith some extra protection," he continued, gently encouraging her.

"David, I won't do it."

"I don't understand why not."

"Because this is God's fault we are here right now."

"Oh, Sophie, you don't mean that."

"I do, and don't pretend to know my thoughts," she stated, harshly.

"I want to say a prayer, so give me a minute."

David was surprised by Sophie's reaction having never known her to be upset with God, and couldn't believe she was actually holding him responsible for Faith's condition. However, now wasn't the time to delve into that subject as he continued to hold her hand, not sure if she would bolt out of the vehicle. He closed his eyes and prayed aloud for their daughter. Sophie yanked on her hand attempting to disengage from David, but he held firm. She resented him doing so but wasn't going to argue. Sophie was extremely upset with the circumstances, and to compound the matter with anger toward her husband, was more than she could deal with. His support was needed right now, so she kept silent.

They reported directly to the third floor and were instructed to wait in the now familiar patient area. Within thirty minutes, a young man of average height wearing green scrubs walked up and introduced himself as Dr. Perry Stonewater, the anesthesiologist, who would be putting Faith to sleep. He grabbed a chair pulling it close, and sat down explaining what he would be doing and the anesthesia medication of choice. Both David and Sophie listened carefully throughout his explanation. Sophie's initial reaction was he was far too young to entrust her baby in his care.

"Are there any side effects to the anesthesia?" David asked.

"There can always be residual side effects from any medication. However, I will be administering a very minute amount. It's predetermined by body weight and the age of the child. In this case with Faith, it will take less than half a milliliter which, trust me, is like a few drops. It is administered intravenously once a butterfly is inserted in her vein," he informed them.

"Is Dr. Whalton doing the procedure?"

"Yes, and he is very good. Once we are done, Faith will be

taken to a recovery room and you can be with her there. It's precautionary after anyone has had anesthesia to monitor their blood pressure and heart rate for approximately thirty minutes post procedure. After that, you can take her home. If you don't have any further questions, we'll get started."

"Where will they place the needle to run the dye?" David continued.

"We try to use the back of their hand even though the skin is very thin. If that doesn't work, the intravenous specialist will try for the foot. In Faith's case, since we are doing an angio-cardiography, the specialist will attempt to place it in her left hand or inner elbow. Dr. Whalton will want the dye to travel the least distance before reaching the heart."

Sophie was split between disconnecting from the conversation to control her emotions, and not wanting to miss any part of what the doctor was saying. Still finding it hard to believe he was an anesthesiologist.

"So who wants to bring Faith with me?"

"I will," Sophie finally spoke.

"Are you sure, honey. I can take her."

"I want to," she said, reaching for Faith in the stroller.

With Faith in her arms, Sophie followed Dr. Stonewater down a long, cold corridor to a sterile operating room with its large, oval light hanging above a oblong table. Instruments and supplies were neatly arranged on a rollaway tray, and two nurses were preparing something Sophie couldn't identify in the far corner of the room.

"Put Faith on the table on her back," Dr. Stonewater instructed.

Sophie kissed her baby on the cheek before, reluctantly, laying Faith on a long sheet-covered stainless steel surgical table. She remained by her daughter's side intently watching Dr. Stonewater withdraw the anesthesia, Propofal, with a syringe that would put Faith to sleep. They were waiting on the specialist to put the port in her hand to begin.

A plump woman pushed a waist-high cart into the room

stopping short of bumping the table. She immediately began grabbing various syringes, foiled alcohol packets, two-by-two gauzes and sterile-packed butterfly needles. Before slipping on a pair of surgical gloves, the nurse slid her cart to the side gaining access to the patient, and it was at this point, Dr. Stonewater told Sophie she would have to leave the room. Sophie backed away from the table to the outer perimeter, but didn't take her eyes off the nurse. She glanced at Faith lying peacefully and then locked eyes with Dr. Stonewater. Tears filled Sophie's eyes as he came to her putting his arm around her shoulder and guided her from the room.

"Please, trust me. I'm not going to let anything happen to your baby. We do this all the time and haven't lost a patient yet," he said, trying to console her.

Once the words were spoken, he realized it was the wrong thing to say. She went white as a sheet. He personally walked her back to the waiting room, not trusting she could make it on her own. David took one look at his wife and then focused his attention on Dr. Stonewater.

"I apologize; my sense of humor has backfired on me. I was trying to alleviate her fears and only seemed to have made them worse," he said, concerned for causing a mother un-necessary duress.

David stood up putting his arm around Sophie helping her to a seat. He could see she was barely holding herself together. This was so hard for her, and he knew words were not going to be of comfort, but he tried anyway.

"Sophie, go ahead and cry. It will probably make you feel better."

"It's too late to do anything about it. I want it over so I can take my babies home."

"Just keep thinking in less than two hours, we'll be out of here," he said, not knowing what else to say.

Two hours went by in silence. Grace was such a good baby lying in the stroller content with her soft toys, unaware of what her sister was going through. After two and a half hours and no report on Faith, they were getting worried.

"Why aren't they calling us to be with her? She should be in recovery and we're supposed to be there," Sophie spoke up.

"I'm sure someone will be coming to get us soon."

"Go ask the receptionist if she can find out what's going on."

David walked over to the desk and inquired about Faith. The young woman placed a call to the recovery room and was told Faith was there.

"She's in recovery, but not awake yet. That's why you haven't been called," she explained.

"How long has she been in recovery?"

Directing that question to the nurse, they learned Faith had been there almost forty-five minutes. This news put David in alarm.

"Why hasn't she awakened?"

The receptionist continued to carry on a three-way conversation, directing his questions to the recovery room nurse.

"Apparently, her blood pressure dropped during the procedure, and it hasn't stabilized yet. They aren't sure if that's why she isn't awake."

"How was she through the procedure?"

"I'm being told there were no complications."

"When can we see her?"

"Not until she is awake. If no one has come for you in the next thirty minutes, I'll call them again."

He nodded without saying another word and went to sit down next to Sophie.

Sophie saw the worried expression on her husband's face.

"What did you find out?"

"She's been in recovery for the past forty-five minutes, but isn't awake. They won't let us go back to see her."

"Why isn't she waking up? I want to be with her."

"The nurse also said her blood pressure was being closely monitored. Apparently, it dropped during the procedure, and they are waiting for it to return to normal," David told her.

He deliberately ignored her statement.

"I knew this was wrong. I had a bad feeling from the beginning, but you insisted we do it."

"Are you saying this is my fault?"

"It's not mine!"

"I don't believe you just accused me of putting our baby girl in harms way."

"I was never for this and you knew it," she claimed harshly, venting her anger.

David backed off. Sitting on the edge of his chair with his elbows digging into the tops of his legs, he buried his face in his hands. They were actually arguing while Faith was in another room unconscious. Getting a grip, he addressed the issue once more with his wife.

"Sophie, I know you don't mean what you just said, so I'm not going to take offense. Regardless, this is neither the time nor the place to discuss our personal feelings when our daughter is having issues. Let's just keep our cool, okay," he told her.

"David, don't patronize me. I don't need you to tell me to keep my cool. I'll feel however I want to, and right now, I'm very angry as if you haven't noticed."

He had never seen his wife so upset. It had to be fear motivating her to say things he knew she would regret later, and couldn't fault her for having them, he did too. The clock on the wall indicated another thirty minutes had passed. He expected to hear from the receptionist, but instead Dr. Stonewater walked up.

"I have some good news, and not so good news," he began.

Seeing the worried look on both their faces, he didn't hesitate to continue.

"The procedure went smoothly without any complications. However, Faith hasn't awakened yet. All her vital signs are now strong and normal."

"Then why isn't she waking up?" David asked.

"We don't know, but we expect she will at any moment."

"What is the result of the test? Is her heart pumping the blood sufficiently?" David pursued.

"I don't have that information. I just put the patient to sleep. Dr. Whalton will answer that question."

"Did you give her too much anesthesia?" Sophie asked, pointedly.

"That is a fair question that I will answer. No, I did not. The amount of anesthesia was minimal," he answered without taking offense, looking her straight in the eye.

"What do we do now?" David asked, fearful.

"We can only wait. It's all in Faith's timing now," Dr. Stonewater replied.

"I want to see my baby," Sophie demanded.

"We don't allow family members in recovery until the patient wakes up."

"You said she was fine. I want to see my baby, now" she reiterated, staring him down.

"Alright, I'll take you back."

David took charge of the stroller with a sleeping Grace as they followed Dr. Stonewater to the recovery room. Faith was in a crib tucked away in the far corner of a room having several beds with fabric wraparound curtains, dividing each for privacy.

As they stepped behind the drape, a nurse turned to greet Dr. Stonewater who made the introductions, informing the nurse to allow the parents to stay with Faith. Turning to leave, David thanked him with a handshake. Sophie remained focused on Faith. She was so tiny lying on her tummy with a blanket over her.

"Why isn't she waking up?" Sophie asked David.

"I don't know, honey."

"Will they let us take her home if she doesn't wake up soon?"

"They will want to keep her under observation, so my guess is she stays put."

"I want to know the results of the procedure. Can you track down Dr. Whalton?" Sophie asked the nurse standing nearby.

Their nurse, Brenda, immediately placed a page for Dr. Whalton who stopped in recovery an hour later with the report and getting to the point.

"The hole isn't causing any obstruction in blood flow; however, it's larger than first estimated. With the dye running throughout the organ, it gave a much clearer picture than the ultrasound as to the size, shape and placement. If the hole is not repaired, the blood leaking from it will hamper the development of the right side of the heart, eventually damaging that area, and could even affect the lungs which, at that point, can have the potential for respiratory failure or cardiac arrest," he told them without preamble.

Sophie looked at Dr. Whalton as though he had slapped her hard across the face. Even David stood stunned by the doctor's words. How could a tiny hole cause so much trouble? This was not what they were expecting to hear.

"What are you suggesting?" David asked.

"Surgery."

"Are you talking with a scalpel or laser?"

"I haven't decided yet, but I'm leaning toward exposing the heart and suturing the hole."

"Why wouldn't you consider the laser instead? Isn't it less invasive?"

"Yes, however, it's a procedure that is only effective depending on accessibility. In Faith's case, unfortunately, the hole is not in a place that is conducive to being cauterized. It remains an option, but not a strong viable one at this time."

They were talking about her baby as though Sophie wasn't even present. She should resent it, but instead, stayed focused on the conversation not wanting to miss anything the doctor said. She was grateful, once again, David was asking the right questions.

"Is Faith in any danger? How soon does this need to be

done?" David asked, not believing he was having this conversation.

"Faith isn't in any immediate danger, but on the other hand, I wouldn't delay too long. We can give her a couple more months until she is around six months old, but definitely no later. As we get closer, we'll sit down and go over all the details," Dr. Whalton informed them, drawing the conversation to a close.

"Can you explain why Faith isn't waking up?" Sophie asked abruptly, inferring he was to blame.

"I honestly don't know. Faith did great through the procedure, and all her vital signs are good. I'm sure she will shortly," he said, reassuring them.

That was not a satisfactory answer, but the only one she was going to get. Dr. Whalton left them standing by the crib. For Sophie, there was no need to get into a conversation about her baby having heart surgery because it wasn't going to happen. She wanted Faith to wake up, so she could take her daughters home and be done with this whole ordeal.

Neither David nor Sophie said a word. The impact of the doctor's words was a devastating blow. As Dr. Whalton was talking, David watched the expression on Sophie's face, knowing his wife was crushed by this latest development, just as he was.

"I'm going to the cafeteria and get us something to eat. We haven't had any lunch, and I know you must be hungry," he told her attempting to deflect the bad news.

David needed to remove himself from the scene for a few minutes to gather his composure, believing an excursion to the cafeteria might help.

"I'm not sure I can eat anything. Just bring me a sandwich and iced tea."

He didn't ask permission to bring food into the recovery room and dared anyone to confront him when he returned carrying a tray. No one objected. They sat in their corner and ate silently watching for some movement from Faith. She had yet to show any indication of waking up, not even a stir.

As the hours passed, David and Sophie were becoming more alarmed and no one could tell them why their baby was still asleep. Sophie left the room and went outside the building to call her sister. It was time to give Brie the heart-wrenching news.

Chapter 27

Sabrina answered the phone on the fifth ring. Unfortunately, the expected call from her sister came when she was finishing a photo session. It wouldn't be professional to leave her clients waiting which meant she would have to postpone talking with Sophie.

"We're still at the diagnostic center and Faith hasn't awakened yet," she blurted out as soon as she heard Sabrina's voice.

"I'm wrapping up a shoot. Let me call you right back."

"That's okay, we can talk later. Sorry to bother you," Sophie said with a clipped tone in her voice.

"Sophie, stop that. You aren't bothering me. Give me five minutes to finish with my client, and I'll call you right back. Okay."

"Sure," she said, disappointed.

Sophie hung around outside the front entrance to the building waiting for Brie's call, and as promised, six minutes later her cell phone rang.

"Okay, now tell me what's going on."

"Faith isn't waking up. Dr. Whalton said the procedure went smoothly, and her vital signs are normal, but she's still asleep and they don't know why. We can't take her home until she is awake."

"The doctors have no explanation why she won't wake up."

"Isn't that what I just said," Sophie snapped in reply.

"So what happens next?" Brie asked, ignoring her sister's sarcasm.

"I don't know, but it gets worse. Dr. Whalton recommends heart surgery when she is six months old. He said the hole is larger than the first tests revealed, and believes if we don't do the surgery, complications will occur creating the potential for heart failure."

"Oh, Sophie. No, this can't be."

"Oh, Sophie. Yes, this is happening," she retaliated with same.

Sophie was so distraught that every word she spoke reflected her fear. She didn't care who she assaulted with her remarks, including her sister.

"Let's take this one step at a time. First, we have to get Faith to wake up. What can I do to help?"

"If you can make Faith open her eyes, that would be a start," Sophie said with hostility.

"Sophie, I know you're frightened, but stop with the attitude. We'll get through this together. I assume unless she wakes up, they will keep her overnight."

"We've been told we can't take her home until she is completely alert, so that possibility exists."

"Do you want me to fly down?"

"No, there's nothing you can do. I'm sure she will wake up soon. I left David in the recovery room with the girls, so I could take a break and call you. I should go back and see if there is any change."

"How is David handling this?"

"He's upset but doing better than I am, for sure. I'm sorry to take this out on you. I don't understand how this can be happening, and I'm so scared."

"I know you are, so go check on Faith and call me back. She may already be awake."

"I'll call you as soon as I know what's next."

"I'll be waiting."

"Brie, I can't do this without you. I know I have David, but you're my other half, and I need you."

"I'm always here for you."

"I'll call you later," Sophie said, disconnecting the call.

Even with her misplaced anger, Sophie felt comforted talking to Brie in a way that perhaps only twins can relate. She walked back inside to the recovery room slipping behind the drapes, noticing David holding Grace while Faith continued to sleep. There had been no change and the stress was showing on David's face.

"Has she stirred at all?"

"No. It's like she's knocked out cold, if you'll forgive the expression."

"What are we going to do?"

"If she doesn't wake up soon, they will probably put her in another room. They won't keep her in recovery indefinitely."

"What did Brie have to say?" he continued.

"She offered to fly down, but I told her to hold off at the moment. There isn't anything she can do."

"That was nice of her to offer."

"Why is this happening?"

"That's the million dollar question," he said, shifting Grace on his lap.

An hour later, Brenda informed them that Dr. Whalton wanted Faith moved to a private room just as David had suspected. Because this was a surgical center, the facility was equipped similar to a general hospital. Even though David and Sophie were expecting this, it still was hard to accept. Brenda unlocked the wheels setting the crib in motion toward the doorway with David pushing the stroller, and Sophie carrying Grace. Faith was placed in a room across the hall.

"Dr. Whalton will be in to see you shortly," Brenda announced, snapping the locks on the crib in place with her foot before leaving them alone.

Sophie placed Grace in the stroller and stood by Faith tucking the blanket close to her body, and gently rubbing her back. Perhaps, jostling Faith might awaken her but not even a sigh came from her baby.

Chapter 28

It had been nearly six hours since Faith was wheeled into recovery. Dr. Whalton was not able to explain her not waking up, but assured them it had nothing to do with anything pertaining to her heart. Apparently, this just happens which was not consoling in the least. *Just happens* was not an explanation acceptable to Sophie.

"I wish I could give you a better answer, but at the moment, we are not certain why Faith isn't waking up," Dr. Whalton informed them.

"If this doesn't have anything to do with her heart, then it has to be the anesthesia. Could it be an allergic reaction to the drug?" Sophie questioned him.

"I can't say that it's not possible, but highly unlikely."

"Why is that? It's a drug that puts people to sleep. Surely, you have experienced this before. Faith can't be the first baby that has gone through something like this."

"As a matter-of-fact, she is for me. I haven't had a child not come out of the anesthesia."

"Don't you have a drug that can wake our daughter up?" David asked, interjecting his own thought.

"Not for infants. She will have to wake up on her own."

Dr. Whalton left the room leaving them with unanswered questions. Sophie felt like screaming, and even David was feeling despair. Sophie told David she was staying with Faith, and he could take Grace home after she was breastfed. David offered to let Sophie go home and get some sleep, but she refused. There was no way Sophie could leave Faith alone. She had to be here when her baby woke up. And besides, Faith would be hungry as Sophie explained and he understood. It was logical.

But as the evening drew in and shadows filled the room, David wasn't compelled to leave part of his family behind, so they settled Grace beside Faith, and she slept peacefully alongside her sister. Sophie phoned Brie and explained they had been moved to a room for the night. Brie offered again to fly down, but Sophie stalled since it was a matter of waiting.

Periodically, Brenda stopped in to check on Faith also wheeling in another matching recliner as it was evident they both were staying. She informed them of a shift change, and their night nurse's name was Heather.

David went to the cafeteria bringing back two plates of salad and fruit. Eating in silence, neither was willing to address the issue of heart surgery. After putting the empty plate on the tray, she curled up in the recliner staring at the crib watching her babies sleep. David pulled his chair next to hers. He knew Sophie was hurting and didn't know what to say to console her. Words evaded him, so they sat together silently waiting.

Sleeping in recliners and waking often to check on the girls, neither got much rest. Heather made an appearance a few times during the night, but there wasn't anything she could do. Everyone was waiting on Faith.

Early in the morning, David went down to the cafeteria bringing back two cups of coffee. When he returned, Sophie was breastfeeding Grace.

"It's been over eighteen hours, and Faith hasn't stirred and longer than that since she has been fed. Remember, because of the anesthesia she wasn't allowed anything past six o'clock yesterday morning. What are we going to do?" Sophie asked her husband.

"I don't know. We'll have to talk to Dr. Whalton, but this just isn't right. Something is terribly wrong," David told her.

He finally expressed his own thoughts.

"No kidding, you wanted this done and see what happened."

"Sophie, that's a low blow. We've already been there."

"You're right, sorry."

She couldn't seem to say anything without ill-tempered words coming out of her mouth. It wasn't David or Brie she wanted to attack, but the doctors. They did this to her baby. She wanted to talk to the anesthesiologist again.

Brenda was back on duty stepping into the room to check on Faith. Sophie expressed her concerns about Faith not eating, and Brenda explained she would start intravenous nutrition but was waiting for the orders from Dr. Whalton. Shortly after the nurse left, he walked in and listened to Faith's heart. He tried to awaken her, but she didn't respond.

"I'm putting Faith on a TPN drip for fluids and nutrition to keep her hydrated," he explained.

"She's been like this for almost a day. What have you done to my baby?" Sophie asked, raising her voice in anger.

"For her to remain status quo for this long, I'm thinking she has regressed into a comatose state," Dr Whalton informed them with his matter-of-fact approach, purposefully ignoring Sophie's allegations.

"Comatose! Are you saying Faith is in a coma?" Sophie screamed at him.

"Yes, at this point, I believe so. She should have awakened within a few hours at most. The fact that she has not and shows no visible signs of coming around can only mean that her body has withdrawn into a deeper sleep."

"And how do we get her out of this *deeper sleep,* as you call it?"

"We don't completely understand what happens when a person goes into a coma, but it is theorized that the body does so as a safety mechanism."

"Why would Faith's body need to do that unless something was done to her like the procedure, or the anesthesia, or the radioactive dye? You did this to her, and now you tell me she's in a coma. I want my baby awake, now!"

Sophie was livid.

"I want her awake just as much as you do, more so, Mrs. McKinley, but there isn't anything I can do, or I would have done it. We need to keep her hydrated and fed while we wait for Faith to decide when she will wake up. I'll check back later today," he said, before leaving the room.

Sophie wanted to continue screaming at the top of her lungs and beat the doctor to a pulp. How dare he do this to her baby and walk away without a remedy. She looked at David standing next to the crib.

"David, our baby is in a coma," she said, sobbing.

He pulled Sophie close and she wrapped her arms around his waist holding tight, dealing with this latest crisis. In a stronghold embrace, Sophie's emotions fluctuated between anger and fear.

"I don't understand what's happening. Why won't she wake up? I want my baby awake," she pleaded.

"So do I, honey."

Sophie recalled her ill-behavior towards her husband, making her feel worse, and attempted to make amends.

"David, I'm sorry for things I said that I didn't mean."

"We're both in shock, and I've kept my distance because you've been upset with me. I feel so helpless for Faith and for you. I would give anything to make this go away."

"How are we going to get through this?" she asked.

"Somehow, we will."

Sophie had been so self-absorbed that she never gave thought to David, barely speaking to him since the procedure, and when she did, it was with harsh words and blame. His tender words against her unkind statements intensified the moment. She felt ashamed for the way she had behaved and began to cry again.

Chapter 29

Within an hour, Brenda came into the room pushing a tall, metal tree with a bag of opaque-looking liquid hanging from each end. Behind her was the intravenous specialist Sophie recognized when they did the angio-cardiography. With no choice in the matter as Faith needed fluids, they solemnly watched as the specialist placed a butterfly in the back of their baby's right hand which had no effect on Faith as the needle slid into her tiny vein. Faith was already sporting a small bruise on the back of her left hand.

The nurse ran the tubing from the bags through a dispensing machine that monitored and controlled the quantity and pressure the fluids entered into her body. Brenda talked the entire time she prepared the lines explaining how everything worked. Once she had Faith connected and the two drips running simultaneously, she informed them of the content in each bag. One was a potassium solution to maintain her electrolyte balance and the other liquid nutrition.

Through everything that was happening, Grace remained a happy baby and both David and Sophie did not forget they had another child that required their attention. He picked up Grace from the crib, and sitting in the recliner, situated her on his lap. Sophie took advantage of this time to call her sister.

"David, I'm going out for a minute to call Brie. If she still wants to fly down, do you have any objections to her being with us?"

"Why ask me that? Of course, not. Brie is family, and you should know that I'd never object to her presence," he replied, surprised by the question.

"I thought you would say that. I know she will want to be here when I tell her Faith is in a coma."

"Go call her. I'm sure she is waiting."

Sophie walked outside the building pressing the call button on her phone.

"I couldn't sleep last night, but I didn't want to call and bother you. Tell me what's going on," Brie spoke first.

"Faith is in a coma and the doctors don't know how this happened and can't do anything about it. Dr. Whalton said it's up to Faith."

"I'll get a flight and will be there this evening. Give me the address and room number."

"I knew you would want to be here."

She stepped out further from the entranceway to catch the street number on the building, and recited it to Brie.

"Sophie, please don't get hostile with me for saying this, but everything will be alright. Our little Faith will wake up, I promise you."

"My baby is in a coma," she said, bursting into tears.

"Hold it together, Sophie. I'm on my way. You have to be strong for Grace as well."

"Okay, let me know your flight time."

"I'll call you back, shortly. Hang tight, we'll get through this."

"Yes, we will," she said, not sure how they would.

Sophie felt solace for talking with Brie; however, the brief conversation amplified the severity of the situation with her sister's positive attitude contrasting the dilemma with Faith. Sophie knew there wasn't anything Sabrina could do but render moral support which was why she wanted her to be there.

It had now been over twenty-four hours and counting. David thought they needed to go home and freshen up, but neither made the suggestion. At least they had fresh outfits for

Grace and plenty of diapers. Sophie continued to breastfeed Grace but noticed her milk supply wasn't as plentiful as usual, accepting the stress was affecting her production. It meant she would have to resort to canned formula, and she didn't want to do that. She had to relax.

Brie was expected around seven o'clock taking the first flight she could get. The *Thornton Pediatric Diagnostic Center* was across town from the airport and took almost forty-five minutes through evening traffic. Sophie flew out of the chair into her sister's arms when she saw Brie walking into the room. David came over and gave his sister-in-law a hug and kiss on the cheek.

"Thank you for coming, Brie," he said.

"Has there been any change?"

"No, not yet. I was waiting for you to arrive before getting dinner. What would you like from the cafeteria, Brie?" David asked.

"Whatever you're having."

"Honey, you want anything special?"

"A fruit plate."

Brie walked over to the crib and addressed Grace first as she laid next to her sister.

"Hello, my sweet Grace. I see you are protecting your sister," Brie said with a smile, taking hold of her tiny hand.

She looked at her Auntie Brie and let out a howling squeal that Sophie had never heard from her before. Grace was becoming more vocal with her baby sounds, but never something as loud and direct as what came out of her mouth just then.

"I've missed you, too, sweetheart," Brie told her, touching her cheek with her index finger.

Sabrina knew she was under scrutiny by her sister and had to be cautious with the twins. Brie didn't need to lay a hand on Faith for her to be aware of her aunt's presence. Stepping away from the crib, she turned to Sophie.

"Why don't you and David take Grace home tonight and get some sleep. I'll stay here with Faith."

"That's a nice thought, but I need to be here when she wakes up."

"You look beat, sis. What you do need is rest for Grace's sake."

"I know."

David walked in with the cafeteria food interrupting their conversation. He handed out the plates with iced tea and brought a bowl of fruit for Sophie. Brie and Sophie sat in the chairs while David stood, holding his plate.

"David, I just suggested to Sophie that you both should go home and get some sleep. I'm sure you want to freshen up."

"Is that a polite way of saying we stink?"

"Of course not, but I can stay with Faith tonight."

"Sophie, can you leave Faith and come home?" David asked.

"I know she will be fine with Brie, but I'm not sure I can."

"You decide what you think is best, however, I'm taking Grace home. She's been a real champ but needs to sleep in her own bed and might enjoy a bath."

It was late and Sophie knew it was better for everyone if they went home so she agreed, leaving Brie alone with her baby. They would be back early in the morning. Sabrina gave Sophie a hug and bent down to the stroller giving Grace a kiss on the forehead.

"I'll see you in the morning, sweetie," she whispered to her niece.

Closing the door behind them, Brie walked over to the crib.

"Okay, little one, it's just you and me."

Sabrina lightly placed her hand on Faith's back gently rubbing in a slow circular motion and witnessed her tiny fingers move. This was the reaction she expected and the reason she didn't touch Faith earlier. It wasn't something for Sophie to witness, at least not yet.

Chapter 30

Neither David nor Sophie had the desire to engage in conversation, nor did either want to talk about Faith's pending heart surgery, though the subject was at the forefront of their thoughts. When they arrived home, Sophie took Grace straight to her room to bathe, breastfeed and settled her in for the night while David disappeared into their bedroom. He was already showered and in bed when Sophie walked in heading straight for the bathroom to do the same.

Slipping between the sheets, she snuggled next to David who was still awake waiting for her. He wrapped his arm around her waist and pulled her close, and they fell fast asleep in each other's arms without a spoken word between them.

Sabrina gently picked up her niece and rested Faith against her chest with one hand while carefully maneuvering the metal tree to the nearby recliner. She settled into the chair, reclined the position, and gently rubbed Faith's back as she slept on her breast. Softly and methodically, Brie spoke to her niece throughout the night. Often, Faith stirred as Brie continued whispering to her. That was how Sophie found them the next morning when she walked into the room, preceding David pushing Grace in the stroller.

"What are you doing?" Sophie asked, alarmed when she saw Faith out of her crib.

"She's okay."

"Shouldn't she be in her bed? How long have you been

holding her like that?"

"All night."

"What! You held her all night. Did you sleep?"

"No, it's been very enjoyable, sitting peacefully, holding her."

"Well, let's put her back in the crib. I think she'll be more comfortable there."

Sophie didn't know why she suddenly felt so irritated with her sister when she saw Brie holding Faith, but it bothered her, just as it had at other times, when she felt she was intruding on something sacred. It was that jealousy again. She hated these emotions that surfaced every time she witnessed her babies with her sister. *I need to get over this,* she told herself.

Sabrina did as she was told and placed her niece back in the center of the mattress on her tummy, the way she liked to sleep. Faith began rotating her head back and forth while opening and closing her hands.

"Oh my gosh, she's moving! Is she awake?" Sophie asked, excitedly.

"I don't know, we'll have to see what Faith does," Brie answered, deflecting any attention to herself.

Faith continued her movements, yet her eyes stayed shut. Sophie reached into the crib and turned Faith on her back watching her with anticipation. Faith started kicking up her legs and flinging her arms in the air, but she had not opened her eyes.

"What is she doing? She seems to be awake, so why isn't she opening her eyes?" Sophie asked with uncertainty.

David maneuvered the stroller closer to the opposite side of the crib and stood watching Faith.

"Look David, I think she's waking up."

All three stared at Faith as she continued her bodily movements. Finally, Sabrina stepped away and went to the stroller to visit with Grace.

"Good morning, Grace," Brie said, picking her up.

Sabrina walked the length of the small room whispering to

Grace who let our vocal sounds of recognition. It made Sophie take notice.

"David, I swear there is something weird happening between our babies and Brie. Every time she is around them, they becomes so active, responding to her."

"They are doing what babies do when someone gives them attention. That's all it is."

"No, I don't think so. I've been watching when Brie holds them, and they react to her. I'm not sure how to explain what I mean, but there is something that happens when she is with them. I've seen it on more than one occasion. Take notice and you'll see what I'm talking about."

Sophie and David returned their attention on Faith to see her eyes were wide open.

"David, she's awake! Brie, come here, she's awake!" Sophie hollered.

Sabrina returned and stood beside Sophie peering into the crib making direct eye contact with her niece.

"Good morning, Faith. It's good to see you so happy this morning," Sabrina told her, expecting no less.

Faith looked directly at her Auntie Brie releasing a babbling sound. Sophie's eyes leaped to meet David's giving him a furtive look. It wasn't the right time to address the subject, but Sophie was definitely going to have a talk with her sister. She wanted answers. This was not her imagination. Her girls *knew* their Auntie Brie.

"Thank goodness. Let's get her unhooked and out of here," David said.

"Let's do it," Sophie agreed, relieved.

David walked out of the room to fetch a nurse who immediately placed a page for Dr. Whalton. He appeared thirty minutes later.

"I hear our patient is awake this morning, that's good news. I'll give her a quick check, and she'll be all yours to take home. We should get her on the surgical schedule even though it's a few months away," he told them as he examined Faith.

"We aren't ready to make the appointment. We haven't had a chance to discuss it," David replied.

"Don't take too long. It's not something you want to delay."

David nodded, and Dr. Whalton left the room with orders for the nurse to remove the drip and discharge Faith. Within the hour, David and Sophie were checking out glad to be getting back to normalcy. There still remained the surgery, but at the moment they were thankful to have Faith back with them.

The drive home was quiet as no one wanted to initiate a conversation. Sophie didn't believe there was a coincidence to Faith's sudden awakening. It was strange, she admitted, but the evening of Brie's arrival and alone with Faith for the night, she find's her daughter awakened from a coma the next morning. Her sister had everything to do with Faith waking up. There was no doubt in her mind.

Chapter 31

Sophie and David carried the twins into the house and placed them in their bouncers in the living room. Brie and Sophie sat on the sofa watching the girls, especially Faith who was her usual quiet self while Grace made babbling sounds and blew bubbles.

"It doesn't seem Faith has any side effects from everything she has been through," Sophie said, observing her daughter closely.

"No, it appears not. Since there is no need to delay, I'll book a flight for tomorrow afternoon."

"Can you stay a few days?"

"I wish I could, but I have clients scheduled. Have you thought about what you'll do regarding Faith's heart surgery?"

"No, we haven't talked about it. But after this experience, there is no way I will let them use anesthesia on Faith again. I believe that's what put her in the coma. Something went wrong, or she had a reaction to it, but they are not getting a second chance."

"What are your thoughts, David?" Brie asked.

"I'm not sure what to do. Dr. Whalton believes the hole will enlarge as she grows. But after this scare, I can't imagine letting them put her under a second time, and yet, that is what we are facing."

His reply was solemn as he thought about his answer.

"Is the doctor positive the hole won't close without the surgery?"

"Yes, he was adamant it wouldn't. Looks like we'll have to trust him no matter how much we hate it," David told her.

"Not my baby. They are not cutting on Faith," Sophie declared, abruptly.

"Honey, I don't think we have a choice. If we do nothing, we would be putting Faith's life in jeopardy."

"And if we do what they want to do, they could put her back in a coma plus her little body would be cut up. Is that what you want?"

"Of course not, but what other choice do we have?"

"Just thinking of them using a knife on her soft baby skin makes me want to puke, and I certainly won't risk another coma episode. Maybe we could monitor her heart ourselves and see what happens."

"You heard what Dr. Whalton said. The sooner we do the surgery, the safer it is for Faith. We would be the ones taking the risks if we don't do anything."

"It's a microscopic-sized hole. I don't see this as an emergency situation."

"Yes, but the hole will enlarge and that's the problem. It isn't going to go away."

David stressed the point.

"So you're willing to gamble with the possibility of her going into another coma."

"You make it sound as though I want this. I can't see a way out of it. If we don't do anything, which is apparently your position, we are potentially putting Faith's life in danger. Are you willing to take that chance?"

"I would never deliberately put Faith in harms way and neither would you. It is very hard to believe that she has a problem much less having to deal with resolving it. I'm not exactly accepting what Dr. Whalton said and truthfully probably never will," Sophie told him.

It was the best answer she could give her husband without

causing a major argument because the conversation was becoming intense, each appearing to take opposite positions in the matter. The fact that they were at odds was adding strain on Sophie. Sabrina listened to their discussion without contributing. After a brief pause, David spoke up.

"What is your opinion, Brie?"

"Yeah, sis, what do you think we should do?" Sophie asked in an agitated tone.

Sophie wasn't sure she wanted her sister's opinion unless Brie's input would support her concerns. She was aggravated with her husband, and she didn't want her sister to be the referee.

Sabrina felt trapped, not wanting to be in the middle of their conversation, knowing her sister would not appreciate or accept her comments. She hesitated gathering her thoughts and then answered carefully.

"I'm not sure I can give either of you an adequate answer. I understand the decision you both face, but I don't have a say in what you do, so my opinion is moot."

"Brie, we're asking what would you do in this situation," Sophie remarked in exasperation.

"Well, since you want to pin me to make a comment, I would first pray about it."

"Oh no, here we go again," Sophie said, rolling her eyes upward.

"That's a good thought and I think we should pray, but it's not going to solve our problem," David interjected, ignoring his wife's ill-behavior.

Brie never knew Sophie had an attitude of mistrust toward God until recently when she confessed to blaming Him for their plight with Faith. She was determined to break through the emotional barrier her sister held and help Sophie overcome the hostility she harbored, expecting to get to the root of the problem.

"Why are you so opposed to praying? It's not like we are expecting God to do anything, but it might make us feel better to know we prayed about it," David told her.

"David, that's a stupid remark, but I do agree with you on one thing, it won't do any good."

"Okay, I'm losing ground here. Explain to me your aversion to praying. I guess I didn't realize you had it in for God," David remarked.

"He isn't going to help us, David. In fact, He gave us an imperfect baby on purpose."

"Sophie, stop. You don't know what you're saying," Brie interrupted, not wanting to hear another word.

"Don't you dare tell me what to do," Sophie said, angrily.

Sophie was scared. Her well structured world was falling apart, and seeing Brie sitting so calm without a worry in the world was revolting. She had never been this way with her sister, but the nasty jealousy was rearing its ugly head again, attacking, and she was helpless to control it.

David was appalled by his wife's behavior never having seen Sophie act this way before. Her open hostility toward him and her twin was shocking, and he wasn't sure what to say but before he responded, Brie spoke up.

"Sophie, I'm not going to tell you what to think, say, or do. And your words, I know, are not meant to attack, but it is obvious we see this situation from a completely different perspective. You are wrong to blame God."

"I'm tired of you pressing me about God. And you have interfered, but for a reason I could never hold against you. Whatever you did, it brought Faith back to us, and I'm grateful to you for that."

"What do you mean?"

Sabrina was expecting this topic to come up, eventually. She knew her sister was detecting the subtle awareness her babies had toward their aunt and anticipated she would bring it up for discussion.

"You know perfectly well what I'm talking about. Faith didn't just *wake* up, and we both know it."

"You think I had something to do with that."

149

"Yes, and don't even try to deny it because I won't believe you. I have seen how my babies react to you. I may not understand what the connection is and why, but it is *real* and you are going to tell me."

"How did we get off the subject?" Sabrina asked.

"We can postpone this conversation for the moment, but we're going to have it before you leave my house."

"Fair enough, but let's get back to Faith."

Suddenly, the conversation had switched topics and David sat spellbound listening to them, unbelieving what he was hearing. Sophie was so determined and straightforward with her sister and to think it was over their girls. *What is going on here*, he questioned. Before he could speak up, Sophie picked up Faith and walked back to the girls' room to breastfeed and put her down for an afternoon nap, and would be back for Grace.

Brie took Grace to hold until Sophie was ready for her. David watched intently how his sister-in-law handled his daughter. It never would have occurred to him before to study them together, but after this recent development, he was fascinated to see for himself what Sophie was accusing her sister of doing.

"David, you're staring."

"Sorry, but I seem to be drawn into believing you have this mystical power over my daughters."

"Of course, I do," she said, unable to resist teasing him.

"You'll have to spill the spell," David countered, without missing a beat in their conversation.

"Well, first it isn't a spell but a spirit."

"Okay, I'll bite. What do you mean a spirit?"

"Oh, David, you look so serious."

"I am serious. If we are talking about spirit stuff, isn't that serious?"

"Not always."

"I can't believe we're talking about spirits."

"Don't worry, David. It's okay to talk about things pertaining to the spirit. In fact, we could all learn a lot if we did talk about the subject more often."

His expression was priceless as David sat in silence trying to comprehend what Brie was saying. Before he could reply, Sophie reappeared to retrieve Grace, and the conversation was dropped. He didn't pick up the subject again, but rather excused himself and left the room. Brie pulled her cell phone from her purse and booked a flight home.

Chapter 32

Once the girls were asleep for the night and David had retired to the bedroom as usual, Sophie and Sabrina sat enjoying a cup of coffee as they often did when she visited. Sophie had calmed down and felt better now that they were settled at home.

"Brie, I can't handle this situation by myself. David and I are already at odds, and I don't want to alienate myself from you as well."

"I know the uncertainty you feel, but you may not find everything I say acceptable. How can I help you if you shoot me down?"

"I guess that is what I'm doing, but I can't seem to overcome these terrible feelings. I get so emotional at times, and I do take it out on David and you. I'm really scared for Faith."

"You and David should be together with things that concern your children."

"I know that. This is the first time we have been at odds with each other. I don't want us to fight over Faith. And, Brie, I'm sorry for the things I said earlier. I didn't mean them. I see you with my babies, and I can't help but get jealous. Another thing that bothers me is you have kept something from me. I thought we had no secrets from each other, but obviously, we do. You do. Can you understand how deeply that hurts me?"

"Oh, Sophie, you shouldn't feel this way."

"But you don't deny it."

"I won't deny that I have changed in the past couple of years, but you already know that. However, you are right. My life's purpose has been redirected through Aunt Millie's legacy. For now, you will have to trust me and not be upset by what you see."

"Why can't you tell me?"

"I promise you will know soon, and I'm not trying to purposefully be evasive."

"We shouldn't have secrets between us."

"I'm sorry, Sophie. Please, just trust me."

"You want me to have trust. Wow, that's very intuitive," Sophie declared, irritated that Brie would not confide in her.

Sabrina accepted her sister's unpleasant attitude in stride. It was best to change the subject.

"What do you think you'll do about Faith's surgery?"

"We'll talk about it and David will want me to agree," Sophie replied, gaining some composure.

"You have a few months before making that decision."

"It isn't going to change anything but only add stress."

"A lot can happen."

"What needs to occur is for the hole in Faith's heart to disappear. Truthfully, I was hoping you might be able to do something since you apparently have a connection to my girls, and I did witness you bringing Faith out of the coma. What other abilities can you perform in lieu of your discussing them with me?" Sophie asked, intending to put her sister on the spot.

"What exactly do you think I can do?"

"That's what I want you to tell me."

"Sophie, you talk as though I have some innate ability to change the circumstances, but I don't."

"I need help. I'm begging, Brie."

"You are putting your faith in the wrong person. It's not me who can give you what you are seeking."

Sophie looked away ignoring the implication. She knew

153

where this conversation was leading and didn't want to go there. If Brie wasn't willing to help her, so be it. She would have to find another way on her own. Seeing the disturbed expression, Brie still felt the need to continue even when it would be upsetting to her sister.

"You want a different resolution for Faith, however, the very subject you refuse to discuss with me is the one conversation we must have."

Sophie felt the deflating impact of Brie's words. She had hoped Brie could take away this problem and make everything right. After all, she did it once already, why wouldn't she be willing to do it again.

"You're telling me I have to deal with God. I can't do that."

"He is the only one, and the only way, to Faith's heart being healed. You must turn to Him."

"Well, that is so unfair of Him to put me in this kind of a dilemma. Figures!" she said, disgusted with the conversation, slumping down into the sofa with her arms crossed in annoyance.

"What happened to turn you off to God? I don't remember you having such hostility toward Him growing up."

Sophie felt betrayed both by her sister and a long time ago by God. Right now, the disappointment with Brie was unsettling. Her expectations of soothing words, and perhaps, a remedy weren't forthcoming from her twin. Instead, Sabrina was persistent in her seeking God. This discussion was a huge calamity.

Not wanting to contribute further to Sophie's unhappiness, Brie decided to drop the subject. It wasn't going to help matters for her sister to remain on edge. However, before she could do so, Sophie flared at Brie.

"I get it. This is where God comes to the rescue. Well, I have news for you, sis. He isn't wanted here."

"Sophie, you are hurting right now, but you can't mean that."

"No, no, no! I don't want to hear another word about God. How many times do I have to say that to you and David? Both of you need to stop ganging up on me. Let's just drop it. I don't want to talk about it anymore tonight. I don't want to hear it!" she screamed.

David heard his wife yelling and came into the living room to investigate the cause. He looked at Sophie and then glanced at Brie. Though she didn't appear to be as distraught as his wife, her expression was seriously somber. He had never witnessed a hostile scene between the sisters before.

"What's going on? I could hear your voice across the house," he asked, looking at Sophie.

"It's nothing, I'm just upset. Go back to grading papers, we're fine."

"Are you sure because you don't look fine to me?"

"Yes, we are having a difference of opinion, that's all."

David studied them both for a minute before leaving the room. It was obvious he couldn't do anything to help.

"I'm sorry, Sophie. I've caused you to be upset more than the situation deserves. You know I would never intentionally do that. I think it best for us to accept a truce. I'm here for you always, but right now you have a lot to think about."

Sophie knew her behavior was deplorable. The words that shot out of her mouth were sharp, directed to inflict pain, and it was wrong to verbally attack Brie simply because she wasn't saying what she expected. She couldn't have her sister leaving with bad vibes between them, that was unacceptable.

"I'm not mad at you, Brie, but I'm taking things out on you. You have this carefree 'everything is going to be alright' attitude that rubs me the wrong way. Then to make it worse, you always want to bring God into the conversation when you know how I feel about that. It's not your fault, but it isn't helping me, either."

"Well, that certainly puts me in my place. Do remember, though, that I'm always and forever at your beck and call," Brie told her with a wink.

That did the trick. Sophie saw the sincerity in her sister's eyes and couldn't remain in a bad mood. It was impossible with her twin so aptly teasing her. She knew she was riding a rollercoaster of emotions with outbursts on the slightest provocation, but at least she could still resume peace with her sister.

"Sophie, I..." Brie began, but was interrupted.

"You're going to tell me everything will be alright."

Sabrina merely nodded. As though they shared the same thought simultaneously, each stretched across the sofa leaning into a warm embrace. It was time to call an unspoken truce.

"I'm sorry. I seem to be saying that a lot, lately," Sophie told her.

"You are under duress. I can't relate as a mother, but I do have empathy for what you are dealing with and compassion in my heart for you."

Sabrina's endearing words only made Sophie feel worse for her previous harshness. She sat quietly, without responding, as there was no need to say anything further between them. After making their amends, she left the room to check on the girls while Sabrina stayed. When Sophie returned, neither was in the mood for further conversation and agreed to retire to bed early.

First thing in the morning, Brie quietly slipped into the girls' bedroom to say goodbye, as she had done once before, finding Grace awake lying quietly on her back. Grace became very excited making vocal sounds when she saw her Auntie Brie lean over the crib. Brie gently ruffled her golden blonde curls while noticing the monitor, knowing to be careful of being overheard.

"Grace, what are you doing up so early? You should be asleep," Brie told her.

Grace focused on her aunt listening to her voice as though waiting for instructions.

"Sweetie, don't worry about your sister because Faith is doing well. I know you understand, sweetheart. I have to return home, but I'll see you again soon. I love you, Grace."

She took her tiny hand and held it for a minute, rubbing her thumb pad over the back of Grace's fingers, before leaning forward over the crib's railing to kiss her on the forehead. Letting go, Sabrina walked over to Faith's bed, finding her asleep.

"Faith, darling, I love you. Stay well, sweetie, and I'll be back soon," Brie said as she gently placed her hand on her back.

Faith released an almost inaudible sigh as Sabrina leaned in placing a kiss on her head, however, the attention from her aunt didn't awaken her.

Brie walked into the quiet kitchen to find David and Sophie sitting at the table with the baby monitor base on the counter. She went directly to the coffeemaker pouring a cup of coffee and joined them. Feeling embarrassed they had eavesdropped on Sabrina, David stood up to make breakfast.

"So you've said goodbye to the girls," Sophie remarked, admitting to overhearing her talking to the twins.

"Yes, and I certainly am going to miss them."

"You'll see the girls again soon."

Sophie and Brie were reserved toward one another having had time to ponder their previous conversation, and though they were no longer upset, there were unresolved issues between them. David watched closely surprised by their unusual quietness. He had never known the sisters to be at odds, and not knowing what to say, he was silent concentrating on preparing breakfast.

David didn't understand Sophie's behavior with her sister. It was completely out of character and questioned how deep the emotional bondage was that gripped her. Apparently, his wife was more distraught than he realized and hoped to encourage her to talk about it later.

Chapter 33

David walked down the hallway to check on his girls and found them together in Faith's crib watching a mobile slowly circling above their heads. Faith focused intently on the object while Grace was having fun lifting her legs in the air and grabbing her pea-sized toes. After noticing they were content, he went in search of his wife finding her on the computer researching wedding items.

"I checked on the girls," he said, not expecting an answer.

She looked at him without saying a word.

"Can you take a break? We should talk."

"I'm really not in the mood to talk right now. Is it really important?"

"Yes, there is a lot happening and we need to discuss it."

She saw the worried expression on his face and could put him off, but she couldn't postpone the inevitable issue concerning Faith's heart. She knew he wanted to talk about it, so agreed, putting the computer in hibernation mode. David went into the kitchen to brew a fresh pot of coffee meeting Sophie in the living room. Sitting with their mugs, David spoke first.

"What happened between you and Sabrina? When she left, there was uneasiness between you that I've never seen before. Will you tell me about it?"

"I was upset with Brie for keeping a secret from me."

"What kind of a secret?"

"She wouldn't tell me. She said I'll understand later when the time is right, whatever that means."

"Does this secret have anything to do with Faith? The reason I ask is because of your statement while we were at the center when she came out of the coma. You implied Brie is responsible for Faith's awakening."

"Yes, I definitely believe that. It's not a coincidence the night we leave Brie alone with Faith, she's awake the next morning."

"What exactly do you think she did?"

"I don't know. I've seen how the twins react to her from the moment they were born. They seem to *understand* when she talks to them. This is a strange thing to say about my sister, but I've witnessed it. Whatever her abilities, it's real."

"Honey, do you know how weird this sounds?"

"Yes, but I also know something has happened, she's changed. When she refused to discuss it, I got upset but we're not mad. Besides, I'm on edge about everything right now."

"Well, whatever Brie may be keeping from you, she has a good reason. It's not like either of you to keep things from the other."

"That's why even though it hurts, I can't be angry with her. She said I would understand soon and then it would make sense, so I'm waiting for her explanation."

"You have to trust her. I know you're upset with everything Faith just went through and now Dr. Whalton wants to do surgery. We have a little time, but we should know what we are going to do," David said, changing the subject.

"After this incident, I think what the doctor is suggesting with his surgery and anesthesia is potentially more harmful to Faith than anything we would consider. What if she goes into a coma again and doesn't recover? Or other issues occur during the surgery or after? There are too many risks," she told him.

"What do you suggest? Something has to be done. Dr. Whalton believes complications will develop if the hole is left unattended. You heard him, it could become fatal. I'm scared not to do anything, and yet, I'm equally afraid to do the surgery. We really aren't given a choice," he said.

"No, we aren't, but I can't put my baby through that."

The impact of their different viewpoints brought a momentary end to the conversation, each in self-reflection. David took the coffee mug from her hand and went into the kitchen for a fresh cup. Sitting back down on the sofa, he continued.

"Obviously, we aren't going to agree. So what do we do now? Is your idea to take the risk even if something more serious could develop?"

David had never experienced such discord between them, and it bothered him they weren't in agreement about Faith. He wanted them to be together in this major decision, but his words weren't reaching his wife. What could he say to get her to understand there was no other answer?

"You want me to agree with you, and if I do, I feel we are putting Faith in danger with the anesthesia much less the surgery. We have no idea what could happen to her. What if we lost her on the operating table? Have you thought about that?"

"No, I haven't."

"Well, maybe you should. They are going to cut her open and expose her heart. What if it stopped beating while the doctor is suturing the hole? You know, as well as I do, anything can happen in surgery."

"I won't deny it is possible, but you're dwelling on the negative and not looking far enough ahead when she gets through this. It will be behind us, and we can go on with our lives. Sophie, we may not like it, but we have to do it for Faith's sake. She needs her heart working properly. How else are we going to achieve that?"

"I want to think it will close as she grows."

"The doctor told us plainly that won't happen."

David couldn't get through the fear that was enveloping Sophie and wasn't sure they would ever come to an agreement.

"Sophie, I know you're in emotional pain, but you aren't alone. I'm hurting too. I don't want them cutting on Faith, but there isn't another answer."

"Let's hold off making the surgical appointment. I need time to think," Sophie told him, solemnly.

"That's not a good idea and besides what's there to think about. We don't have another solution, this is it. We need to get her on the schedule before they are completely booked, and it pushes back Faith's surgery date. It's going to happen, Sophie, and you need to accept it," he told her more forcefully than he meant to.

Sophie looked at her husband not believing they were actually having such a conversation. Never in her imagination did she think they would ever take a stance against each other concerning anything in their life together. She understood David would be just as upset, but she wasn't expecting him to push so strongly for the surgery, not even considering another alternative, whatever that may turn out to be.

Furthermore, it was troubling that he wasn't sympathetic to her, focusing more on the surgery and the doctor's words. This was driving an invisible wedge between them. Sophie didn't want to be in opposition with her husband, and especially over their baby, but she couldn't control the black mood enveloping her, and she snapped.

"You're wrong, David. I don't need to accept anything. There will be no surgery, not now, not ever!"

Sophie couldn't take another minute of their conversation and got up from the sofa, leaving him in a state of complete shock. Not once in the years they have been together, had she ever raised her voice against him. Things were rapidly spiraling out of control. Stunned, he remained sitting in the living room.

Between the contention with her sister, and now David's lack of compassion, for the first time, Sophie felt isolated and alone. The two people she depended on for emotional security were letting her down. Didn't they understand how she felt as a mother protecting her infant? *This is so wrong*, she told herself. Slowly, Sophie felt herself sliding further into an abyss, and fleetingly, wondered if she would ever escape it.

Chapter 34

The following days in the McKinley household were quiet as the invisible tension had not dissipated. There existed an unspoken truce discussing everything but the surgery, a subject that was taboo. David knew an affirmative agreement needed to be made, and not talking about it, wasn't going to make it go away. He felt compelled to take the initiative, and called Dr. Whalton's office putting Faith on the surgical schedule, not wanting to miss the opportunity for the time allotment the doctor had mentioned. Sophie wouldn't take kindly to his making the decision without her consent, but he believed in time, she would understand his reason for doing so.

He needed to tell Sophie what he had done. She wasn't going to be happy with him. In hindsight, he regretted having made the appointment. It wasn't right to do this behind her back; however, calling and canceling only to reschedule later wouldn't make matters better. With the escalating strain between them, David feared this would completely take her over the top, but he decided to mention it after dinner.

Sophie was at odds with herself. She wanted her baby's heart healed but didn't know a direction to take to resolve this urgent medical crisis. By default, she was now alienated from her husband, and to some extent with her sister, believing herself to be without support. Brie would only want to talk about God, and David wanted her agreement to go forward with the surgery.

David worked in the kitchen preparing dinner placing two prime-ribbed steaks on the built-in stovetop grill along with foiled potatoes and steaming fresh green beans. While he was attending to dinner, Sophie bathed the twins hoping they would settle early for the night. She had them dressed, fed and in their cribs when David walked into the room.

He picked up Faith and went to the rocking chair. Holding her close against his chest with her head lying on his shoulder, she was content in her daddy's arms and soon fell asleep. He held her for awhile enjoying the feel of her soft body, inhaling her sweet baby scent. *She is so fragile. It's not right she have this problem,* he thought, finally relinquishing his daughter to her bed, gently laying her in the center of the mattress.

Grace showed no signs of sleepiness when he lifted her from her crib and high over his head, twirling her in circles. After a few minutes of playtime, he returned to the rocker and did the same routine as Faith, hoping she would be ready to sleep. Though she was still awake, he placed Grace in her bed and turned on the mobile. They lingered a few seconds adoring their babies before turning on the monitors and stepping out of the room.

Dinner was relatively quiet as each meditated on their private thoughts. It was strange to be living in the same house, estranged. What David was about to tell his wife wasn't going to help the situation. Once the kitchen was in order, they went into the living room with their usual cup of coffee. He wasn't going to delay any longer.

"Sophie, I did something I regret."

"What did you do?"

"I made an appointment for Faith's surgery."

There, he said it.

The impact of his words hit her like a punch in the stomach. She looked at him with unbelieving eyes. When the reality of his words settled, Sophie was stunned feeling betrayed by the man she loved.

"You did what?"

"I got ahead of myself. I wanted an appointment for the timeframe Dr. Whalton mentioned, so I called and scheduled it."

"I don't believe you. You wouldn't do that without us being in agreement."

"I should have waited, but I didn't. I was afraid we'd miss our opportunity. I'm sorry."

"When did you do this?"

"A couple days ago."

"Just because I opposed the surgery, you went behind my back without our discussing it further. We are supposed to make decisions together. Do I mean so little that you wouldn't consider my opinion? How could you do that, David?"

"I made a mistake. I wasn't thinking."

"You made a big mistake."

"I said I'm sorry."

"Sorry is just a word."

Sophie could not find the words to express the devastation that instantly washed over her. She didn't want to talk about it anymore. Crushed, she got up from the sofa taking her coffee mug into the kitchen. There was nothing to say and yelling wouldn't take the pain away. Walking back through the room, she grabbed the monitor from the table and without a glance toward her husband, headed straight to the master bedroom.

Not able to hold back the tears, she sprawled across the bed crying. Even when there were no more tears to shed, she stayed in that position for a long time. Reluctantly, Sophie got up and methodically dressed for bed with little attention to her nightly routine. No brushing her hair, applying facial moisturizer, and barely concerned if she brushed her teeth. Slipping under the covers, she pulled them over her head unable to bear another assault as, once again, she felt herself being drawn deeper into darkness.

Chapter 35

It had been several days since Sophie spoke to her sister. Normally, the time in between phone conversations didn't exceed two days, but she simply wasn't interested in lingering over idol phone chats. However, now she felt an urgency to call her twin.

"Brie, I need to talk to you."

"Okay, but we always talk."

"Don't be funny. This is serious."

"Then you talk, and I'll listen."

"David made an appointment for Faith's surgery."

"Did you agree?"

"No, of course not. He did this without my knowledge. He said he was sorry for doing it, but that doesn't change the fact he did it without my consent."

"Have you talked about it?"

"Sure, but I can't forgive him."

"That seems so completely unlike David. He must be afraid for Faith. We can do crazy things when we are enveloped in fear."

"Are you trying to make excuses for him? What he did was wrong, period."

"Of course, it was wrong, but you said he admitted to making a mistake and apologized for it."

"That's just not good enough, he betrayed me."

"Sophie, you know David loves you. I'm sure deeply regrets his actions. The appointment can be cancelled. That doesn't erase the hurt, but you both are dealing with a serious situation, and under such conditions some allowances have to be made for each other. You would expect no less from David if it had been you to make a mistake."

"The point is the decision should have been made together. I wouldn't have done it without us being in unison. He should have thought of that before he did it. David knows I'm opposed to this surgery, and I even told him I wanted to delay making the appointment. He knew how I felt and did it anyway."

"Don't hold it against him. He is scared, as you are. You both are in a crisis mode, and perhaps things will be said or done that neither of you mean, but it's not done on purpose. There's the difference."

"I know you're right, but he wasn't even thinking about me."

"You're upset. You love each other and need to stay strong together supporting one another. This will pass and you will forgive him because you love him. Right now, you are very sensitive about Faith and rightfully so as her mother."

"You aren't even married yet, so when did you get to be so smart on relationships?" Sophie asked, glad she had called her sister.

"I've learned first hand by watching two people I love dearly, and witnessing the love blossom between them over these past years."

"Good answer."

"He's the love of your life and you're his. You'll get through this."

"Thanks, sis. I appreciate your thoughts, and it has helped. I'll talk to you later."

Sophie hung up the phone feeling only slightly better for the conversation, understanding what Brie was saying, but couldn't get past the emotions. She wanted and needed her husband's support, and yet, felt it wasn't there thus pushing her further into indifference.

David was giving her space and allowing her to make the first move toward amends. It had already been several days without them speaking with the exception of things pertaining to the twins. How did everything become such a mess?

Sophie wasn't accustomed to managing problems and issues. Her life had always been a fairly easy one from childhood to teenager, to college where she fell in love, and then on to marriage and now babies. She was the twin who was grounded and homebound living life in the safety zone while Sabrina lived a fast-paced career, accustomed to dealing with matters on a frequent basis. She would be more adaptable to handling a crisis, Sophie thought. This simply wasn't fair.

Sophie believed she did everything right leaving no room for error in her precisely planned and nurtured lifestyle. That's why this recent development with Faith, and now the disagreement with David, was chipping away at her solid foundation of security, and she felt completely helpless to know what to do. Loneliness was becoming a distant friend pulling her further away.

Sabrina was concerned for her sister hearing the despair in her voice and wanted so much to reach out with words of wisdom that could change things, but they would not be welcomed. She briefly thought of calling David to talk with him about Sophie, but that would be an act of unkindness going behind her back, not the right thing to do. She had to wait and simply be there for her twin when called upon.

As Grace and Faith celebrated three months of age, Brie sent a package containing the brag-book of photographs along with the framed pictures. Sophie would be receiving it soon and Brie hoped the surprise would cheer her sister. It was the only thing she could do at the moment.

Chapter 36

David needed to make amends with his wife. She wasn't coming around and forgiving him as expected, and it wasn't healthy in their relationship for this to continue indefinitely. He thought to have flowers delivered and ordered two dozen blood-red roses, set in a designer vase, to be delivered that afternoon requesting they arrive before four o'clock when he returned home.

He hoped to sit down and discuss the differences that had come between them and get everything out in the open. There was more to his wife's unhappiness than his mistake, knowing Faith was at the forefront of her thoughts just as she was with him, but even so, he shouldn't have let so much time lapse before attempting to remedy the situation.

As expected, David arrived home to see a beautiful vase of roses situated on the coffee table in the living room. His card was lying face up next to the flowers. It read, *Remember who loves you.* Putting his briefcase by the entranceway, he walked through the quiet house down the hallway to the twins' room to find Sophie holding Faith in the rocking chair. It was a beautiful mother and child moment had it not been that his wife was crying. She briefly made eye contact with him and then closed her eyes as more tears streamed down her cheeks. Sophie held Faith upward against her shoulder with her baby's tiny head buried face inward toward her neck. She was sleeping, something Faith did more with each passing day.

David stood watching them. Even though Sophie refused to look at him, he lingered in the doorway deeply moved by the vision. It disturbed him to see his wife in such turmoil. At that moment, he didn't know whether to step into the room and plant a loving kiss on her forehead, or quietly withdraw leaving them in peace. He opted for the later.

After a change of clothes, David went into the kitchen to prepare dinner relaxing from the school day to concentrate on home issues, and his thoughts were focused on Sophie. He needed to bring her out of the funk she was in and thought of calling Sabrina to discuss his wife's possible depression. But after the fiasco with the appointment, he didn't dare do another thing without her knowledge.

One of the telltale signs that sent David in this direction of thought was the house. Sophie took great pride in maintaining a spotless and sparkling clean, interior-designed home, even after the arrival of the twins. Nothing was ever out of place, at least not for long. However, he noticed the bed remained un-made all day, clothes to be washed were piling up in the laundry room, and baby items washed, yet not folded and put away. For Sophie to leave these chores unattended was completely out of character for her, a not-so-subtle giveaway that something was drastically wrong in their household.

Sophie made an appearance in the kitchen just as David was putting the casserole dish on the table. She placed the monitor base on the counter and made herself a glass of iced tea. Lately, she broke down in tears more frequently though attempting to maintain control. It bothered her that David saw her in such a hopeless state.

"I was just about to get you. I suppose the girls are sleep-ing."

"No, they're awake but ready for bed. I need to feed them later."

Her reply was short and direct, no elaborating on the twins activities. He thought about starting a conversation over dinner, but if interrupted, they may not finish or worse leave things hanging on a more detrimental note. So David held onto patience for awhile longer until his girls were settled for the night, and then hoped to coax Sophie into a conversation.

As usual, these past couple of weeks, dinner was shared with minimal talk, and afterwards, Sophie left the kitchen to check on the twins while David cleaned the dishes. Usually they worked together; however, under the unforgiving turn-of-events, he had lost his kitchen partner. While putting things in order, he brewed a fresh pot of coffee.

It was customary after dinner, to retire to the living room whereby they enjoyed discussing their day's events over a cup of one of David's special blends. Being somewhat of a perfectionist in the culinary department, he always made his coffee selections from the finest beans, keeping a well-stocked assortment and grinding them fresh daily. He liked to mix the various flavors creating his own originals filling the house with a wonderful aroma. Thus, coffee became a delicacy they savored.

Bringing two cups into the living room, he waited for Sophie to join him. She was breastfeeding the twins and he left her alone expecting she would appear shortly. Though they weren't on the best of terms, they continued to share their evening coffee. However, when she didn't show, and her cup grew cold, he went in search of her.

The twins were asleep, and he gently leaned over each crib and kissed them. Retracing his steps, he went to the guest bedroom thinking Sophie might be on the computer, but she wasn't there. Next, he walked into the master bedroom to find her sitting in the middle of their bed clinging tightly to one of the pillows, staring straight ahead. *This is not a good sign*, he told himself. The impact of the situation hit hard, and David was frightened for what was happening in his life. He already has one crisis with Faith's heart, and now to unexpectedly have another with his wife was more than he was equipped to deal with. But he had to, this was his family. He wished Brie was with them right now because she would know how to help her

171

sister. David couldn't call her, at least not without trying on his own first. His wife needed him, this much he did know.

He sat down on the edge of the bed and reached for her left hand. She held tight to the pillow refusing to let go. The more David tried to persuade Sophie to release her grip, the tighter she clung. He wanted to touch his wife, hold her in his arms and whisper that everything was going to be alright. What should be an easy gesture between them was now foreign. When did they drift so far apart?

She continued to stare ahead not acknowledging his presence. What could he say that would penetrate the un-happiness written on her face? For the first time, David studied her appearance closely and what he saw broke his heart. Purple smudges rested under her lower lashes, and her eyes were sunken without any sparkle. Her skin was very pale and had lost its beautiful radiance. If not for sitting next to her, he would have broken down and cried.

Chapter 37

David had to try because he loved this beautifully spirited woman who became his bride. She was lost to him, but not for long. He left Sophie to fetch his briefcase and locate a short list of substitute teachers whom he trusted to take charge of his students when he was away. Calling the first on the list, his favorite, Crystal, confirming her availability to sub his classroom. Next, a second call was to the school's automated answering service leaving a message of personal leave for one day and that his classes were covered. David needed to be home.

Stepping back into the bedroom, he went directly to the bed and sat down beside Sophie who had not moved in his absence. With his arm around her shoulder, he gently tried to sway her into an embrace, but she was unrelenting. He changed positions to the middle of the bed sitting Indian-style in front of her. He reached for her hands hoping she would let go of the pillow and allow him this little pleasure, but it wasn't happening.

"Sophie, honey, let go of the pillow and hold my hands, please."

Sophie focused on him momentarily, but she had no words to speak to him, nor was she interested in hearing his.

"Go away, David."

"She speaks," he mocked, trying to tease her.

"Come on, honey, we need to talk."

"No, I don't have anything to say to you, and I don't want to hear anything you think you want to say to me. So leave me alone."

"Alright; if you don't want to talk, then please listen."

He cautiously hesitated a moment for her rejection, and when it wasn't forthcoming, he proceeded with a silent sigh of relief.

"Sophie, I am so deeply sorry for hurting you. I was afraid we would miss our window of opportunity for the surgery. I wasn't going to do anything else without our being in agreement, but it was a security to have the appointment. I made a mistake."

He paused, waiting for her reaction. At least she was focusing on him and not staring over his shoulder at the wall. That had to be a good indication she was listening, he thought.

"Talk to me and tell me what's bothering you. You look so unhappy and it's breaking my heart. Please share your thoughts with me. We love each other and it should never be this way between us. Talk to me sweetheart, please," he repeated again, reaching for her hand.

Sophie allowed him to hold her right hand when he tugged it away from the pillow. He braided their fingers and held loosely giving her the option to pull away, waiting patiently for her to speak. She didn't know how she got to this place in her life where everything seemed so hopeless. What was most important and kept her going were her babies because they needed her. Sophie knew David wanted an explanation for her behavior, but she didn't have one. She was at a loss what to say to him.

"Don't try to calculate. Just speak from your heart, not your head. Tell me what's bothering you."

"Everything is upsetting to me."

"You look so sad. Are you still angry with me?"

"I do feel sad, I feel sad for Faith. This is so unfair to her."

"I agree. She doesn't deserve this. She's an innocent baby, untouched."

"Yes, that's the word, pure and untouched. The doctors want to slap her on an operating table and cut her open. They'll be stripping Faith of her innocence and leaving a permanent scar on her body."

"Wow, that's a powerful statement. Have you always viewed it this way?"

He had never given such a graphic thought to the surgery.

"Not at first, but I've had plenty of time to think about it."

"Now I understand why you so strongly oppose it."

David was treading carefully as this wasn't the time to discuss that particular subject.

"Do you forgive me, Sophie?"

She saw the worried expression on his face and the pleading in his eyes. He so desperately wanted to be forgiven. No matter how badly she felt, it wasn't going to help matters if she remained upset with him. There were other emotions crowding out anger toward her husband.

"David, I'm not mad anymore."

"Okay, that's a start. I'm taking tomorrow off, so we can spend the day together."

"Why did you do that? You never take a day off."

"We should take the girls and do something. We can go to lunch, walk through the mall, or take a drive. Whatever you like to do, we'll do it."

"That's a nice thought, but I really don't want to go anywhere."

"It would do us good to get out of the house for a few hours. When was the last time you went shopping? Let's do that tomorrow, and we'll have lunch at one of your favorite restaurants. How does that sound?"

"Sounds like too much trouble."

"It'll be fun. We can head out when the mall opens and have all day to shop. I'm sure there must be something you have though of buying."

"No, I don't need anything."

Sophie didn't want to leave the house. She had no interest

in shopping, lunch out, or anything else outside her own world with her babies at home. David meant well and was trying to cheer her up, but she didn't want to be coddled. What she wanted was to be left alone.

Chapter 38

David's attempt to help Sophie by getting her out of the house and into public places backfired. He thought perhaps part of her problem was staying home too much, and if he took her for an outing, she would instantly perk up, but it seemed to send her further into a slump. The most zeal she expressed all day was at the baby section in the few stores she volunteered to enter. She purchased a couple of outfits for the twins but had no interest in shopping for herself. The trip was cut short.

When they arrived home, there was a large box at the front door. Sophie walked right past it, unnoticed. She was carrying Grace heading for the girls' room, and he followed with Faith. Backtracking, David brought the box inside recognizing it was from Sabrina.

"Hey, Sophie, that big box out front is for you. Brie sent you something," he told her as he walked into the twins' room.

"Okay," she replied, unconcerned.

Any other time, she would be elated to receive a surprise package especially from her sister, but now she showed little interest. With nothing else to say, David left. Sophie followed going into the kitchen to retrieve a knife returning to the living room with David on her heels. He was anxious to see what Sabrina had sent to them. Sophie sat on the floor slicing the top of the box. Folding back the flaps, she saw that Brie had carefully secured the items with bubble wrap and Styrofoam peanuts.

"She sure did package this good. Wonder what she sent?" he asked, trying to initiate some enthusiasm.

Sophie didn't respond but instead opened the envelope lying on top. It read, *Something special for someone special, Love, Brie.* Carefully folding the card and placing it back in the envelope, she set it aside and pulled out the first wrapped item. It was the brag-book done in pink checkerboard fabric with white eyelet trim, Sophie's favorite colors. Slowly turning the pages, Brie had captured the twins from birth through her most recent visit a month ago. Sophie didn't realize how much her little girls had changed in their short three months until she saw her babies in pictures.

Handing it to David, she took out an eleven by fourteen portrait of Faith. It was breathtakingly beautiful, exquisite. Setting it aside, she knew the next one was of Grace. Identically matted and framed, the portraits were unbelievably realistic capturing a heartwarming pose of the twins. Sabrina had imposed a very delicate pink backdrop with small white baby rattles in an intricate shadowed imprint on the back-matter. The girls carried the same position in matching outfits of cream-colored gowns and booties. As they rested on their tummies with their head turned to one side, a tiny fist was tucked under their chin and large, adorable blue eyes stared straight at the camera.

These were her babies, Sophie thought and began to cry.

David took the frame from her hands setting it aside so it wouldn't get broken and pulled his wife into his arms. She didn't resist. It felt good to hold her knowing he should have been consciously aware to be there for her. Shortly, she pulled away and picked up the frames again studying the portraits.

"Would you like to hang them now?" David asked.

"Yes, I want to see them on the wall."

"You got it. I'll get a hammer and nails, and meet you in the girls' room."

Sophie took one in each hand walking down the hallway.

David went for the supplies and joined her.

"Where do you want them?"

"If you can secure them so they won't fall into the crib, I'd like to place each over their bed centered underneath their name plagues."

"That will look nice. I'll use screws in the wall instead of nails. I see Brie already thought of placing picture wire on the back. That'll make my job easier."

As David worked over each crib, Sophie took the girls and held them in the rocking chair, watching him. It was the best gift, being of her daughters, and completed their bedroom décor. When he was finished, she returned the girls in Grace's crib and turned on the overhead mobile as it was too early for bedtime. As she and David silently studied the portraits, Sophie recognized Brie had taken them in the bedroom, one at a time lying on the changing table, and wondered when her sister did this not seeing her with a camera. She would ask her when she called later to thank her.

"Sabrina sure has talent with a camera. That is a great present she sent you."

"Yes, it is. Only Brie could have made it so special."

They left the girls alone walking back into the living room. Sophie stopped to clean the mess from the box while David headed for the kitchen. He thought Sophie seemed a little more alert once she opened the package and owed that to Sabrina. *Perhaps, it wasn't such a disastrous day after all*, he thought.

When the household settled for the evening, Sophie curled up in her favorite corner of the sofa and punched Brie's number. She had not talked with her sister in a few days, and surmised Sabrina was giving her space to work things out between her and David. When Brie answered, Sophie took the lead.

"Hi Brie, I got the package today. It was a wonderful surprise, and I absolutely love it," she said with an exaggerated cheerfulness she didn't feel.

Sophie didn't want her sister to sense her sullen mood, so

she made a deliberate effort at sounding happy.

"I knew you would. It's a three month birthday present."

"David hung them immediately. Can you guess where they are?"

"I bet you put them over each crib."

"Yes, and they are beautiful."

"How are my nieces?"

"They are doing well. To look at Faith, you would never know she has a problem with her heart. Without a comparison to Grace, I probably wouldn't have questioned her sleeping so much."

"It's not likely to have gone unnoticed since you take them to regular pediatric visits."

"You're probably right. It was just something that crossed my mind."

"How are you and David doing?"

"Not the best right now, but it's my fault. He took today off from work to spend with the girls and me. We went to the mall for a few hours."

"For David to sub his classes, there's more going on. He would never do that if not for what he considered an emergency. What's happening, sis?"

"Nothing really, we still don't agree and the surgery is imminent."

"Is that what bothers you the most?"

"Yes, things are tangled together, and I can't get a grip. I'm not close to David right now. I'm so alone."

"Sophie, you're not alone. You have David and me, we're here for you. I'm always available to help you."

"Can you give me a miracle?"

"Oh, Sophie, I truly wish I could. What else can I do?" Brie asked, noticing her sister's good cheer had quickly faded.

"There's nothing you can do. We're getting closer by the day to Faith's surgery date, and I'm helpless to prevent it. David has told me I am fettered by my fear. And please, Brie, if you're going to tell me everything will be alright, I may just have to hang up on you. Sorry, but that's the way I feel right now."

"No, I wasn't going to say that. You've heard it too many times from me. You already know my thoughts and beliefs in this situation."

"Yes, I know where you're coming from. We just don't agree."

"Sophie, you're my sister, and I don't like being helpless when I know you need me. Please don't shut me out. We've had times in the past when we didn't necessarily see things the same, but we always stayed firm in being there for each other. This is no different."

Sabrina detected the depression in her sister believing it to be worse than she first surmised.

"I know we don't let differences get in the way of our sisterhood," Sophie said.

"Would you like me to fly down and spend some time with you and the girls?" she asked, offering her services the best way she knew.

"That's okay. I don't want to take you away from your business. You have important things to do."

"Nothing is ever more important to me than you and your babies."

"Maybe later."

It was all Sophie could muster to say. They ended the conversation. Sophie always enjoyed her sister's visits, and under different circumstances, would be thrilled to be together, but she didn't want Sabrina to see her in such disarray. She couldn't help how she felt, but it was irritating being around her sister who was always cheerful and spouting words that everything was going to be fine, when in her heart she didn't see the situation the same way.

Chapter 39

David was clueless how to bring his wife out of her des-pondency. This was something he never had dealt with before. Talking to her had minimal effect, flowers arrived with-out a mention, and the outing was a flop. Much to his dis-approval, he called and cancelled Faith's surgical appointment informing the receptionist he would reschedule. David hoped Sophie would be pleased, and it might work in his favor to cheer her. The next day when he returned home from work, she was sitting in the living room with the twins in their new matching swings.

"Hi, honey, how was your day with the girls?" he asked, cheerfully.

"The same, nothing out of the ordinary."

He walked over and sat down next to her on the sofa, wrapping his arm around her shoulder pulling her close, eager to tell his news.

"Sophie, I called and cancelled Faith's appointment to-day."

"Why did you do that? You wanted her to have the appointment, so why change it now?" she asked, turning to look at him.

"I thought you would be happy if I canceled and took her off the schedule."

"At this point, it doesn't matter. There is no escaping this."

"We're in a horrible position. Neither of us wants to accept the circumstances, but we have to," he told her.

David was disappointed to not get the reaction he had hoped for. But Sophie was right, whether it was scheduled or not, it wasn't going to change the facts. Accepting she wasn't discussing it further, he changed the subject talking about his day at school. Noticing she showed no interest in his topics, David gave up trying to draw her into a conversation.

Instead, he picked up Faith and held her on his lap. Her big, blue eyes focused on her daddy's face with his animated attempts to get a playful reaction. David saw the gloom on his wife's face as she watched the lack of response from their daughter. Shortly, he placed Faith on Sophie's lap.

Removing Grace from the swing, David twirled her in the air as she babbled spontaneous vocal sounds, anticipating more. After several minutes of playful behavior, he placed her back in the swing. He looked at Sophie cuddling Faith, and regardless of the intensity of the situation, they were a lovely sight.

"What would you like for dinner?"

"It doesn't matter, whatever you want."

"How about something quick like pasta salad and steamed vegetables?"

"That's fine."

Sophie worried about the future believing she did everything right, but somehow things still went wrong. *Why?* she asked herself. As the twins' mother, Sophie believed it was her duty to protect her babies and she was experiencing the failure.

To her thinking, there was only one person who could do something of such magnitude. She believed this had God's fingerprint stamped all over it. Unequivocally, the blame rested on Him. What Sophie didn't understand was why would God take an innocent baby and inflict a potentially fatal condition as a means of punishment for her wrongdoings? What did she do that was so terrible He would do this? She was so angry with

Him she couldn't tolerate the very mention of His name. It was His fault everything in her life was spiraling out of control.

Sitting quietly as Faith had fallen asleep on her chest, she turned her thoughts, as she had done so many times in the past month, to finding a resolution. There has to be an answer. Her mind drifted to her sister remembering the incident with the coma. Brie wouldn't confide what she did to awaken Faith, but maybe she should talk to her about it again. Later that evening Sophie phoned her sister.

"Hi, Brie, are you busy?"

"Not at all, how are things with you?"

For starters, the last time we talked, I forgot to ask you about the wedding plans? Did you pick out your flowers?" she asked, prolonging the reason for calling.

"Yes, Bella suggested miniature red rosebuds wrapped in a long-leafed fern and baby's breath. Small arrangements will be easier for the bridesmaids to carry."

"That was a nice idea. Did you order your invitations yet?"

"Yes, to that also. Ben and I selected the first of the three you emailed, and they should be arriving in another couple of weeks which gives me plenty of time to send them out."

"How is Ben doing?"

"He stays busy with the business. Sometimes, I think he is more excited about our wedding than I am."

"I bet he is. He's been ready to marry you for a long time."

"That's true."

"Did you get the photos of the wedding dresses I sent to you a couple of days ago?"

"I did, but haven't studied them yet. I'll do that in the next day or so. Everything is coming along smoother than I actually expected. We have the church reserved, the reception at the country club, and the meals selected. Did you decide on your dress and the brides-maids?"

"Not yet, I wanted to concentrate on yours first. I'll start a search on the others soon."

"Have you decided on the three bridesmaids?"

"Yes, actually some friends from the magazine I've known for years. They'll fly in together before the wedding, so if alterations need to be made we have time to get it done. Once you select the dresses, I'll email a picture to them and get their sizes and place the order."

"You have been busy. I'm sorry I haven't thought of your wedding lately to ask you about it."

"Sophie, you have far more pressing matters to deal with than thinking about me. Besides, it's my responsibility to plan it. Remember, I told you I didn't want it interfering with the twins, and I meant it. In fact, after you select the dress you are wearing you're officially off-duty to do anything else."

"You shouldn't have anything else that needs to be done."

"Well, if I do, I have Bella who is more than willing to pitch in."

"I hear you, sis."

Sophie couldn't bring herself to mention what was on her mind. Instead, discussing her sister's wedding became a neutral topic; however, by the end of their conversation, it exacerbated her already unpleasant temper. Weddings were supposed to be a happy event, so why did discussing Brie's make her feel so sad?

Chapter 40

Sabrina contemplated making a trip to Florida to see her sister. Again, she thought of phoning David of her suspicions but decided against it, knowing Sophie may not take kindly to what she would perceive as interference.

She was meeting Ben for an early breakfast and planned to mention this trip for his opinion. Arriving at the diner first, she enjoyed coffee as her thoughts drifted to Sophie. Brie unmistakably detected the heartache her sister tried so hard to conceal. Some things simply cannot be hidden. Observing Ben walking into the restaurant toward their booth, she smiled as he slid onto the opposite bench. He quickly leaned across the table planting a kiss on her lips. Often his actions were spontaneous.

"You're looking prettier each time I see you. How do you do that?"

"It must be you."

Her answer made him chuckle.

"So are we having our usual today?" he asked.

"Of course."

The waitress brought a fresh cup of coffee placing it on the table in front of Ben, and warming Brie's cup from the decanter she held in her right hand. Knowing them to be regulars, she was certain of their order and began reciting it verbatim. Ben and Brie looked at each other and grinned as Ben nodded his approval.

"They know us too well," Brie said, still smiling.

"Only our breakfast choices, we could throw them off if we ever came for dinner."

"This is true."

He was aware of the development with Faith's heart condition; however, it wasn't a common subject for discussion between them. He was just as concerned, but believed it best to take his lead from Brie on the topic of her sister and nieces. This was one of the rare times when she wanted to mention her thoughts.

"I'm considering a trip to Florida this weekend to check on Sophie."

"Does she know you're planning to fly down?"

"No, and I'm not telling her. I want to see for myself how she's doing. She tries hard to be cheerful on the phone when we talk, but I can read through her facade."

"She may get upset with you for dropping in unannounced. Have you talked with David about this?"

"I've thought about calling him, but I think it best to just show up."

"Then you should go. When will you leave?"

"Friday afternoon, and I'll go straight to my condo that night and drive back into Orlando Saturday morning."

"That will be a surprise. I hope it's a welcoming one."

"Even if it isn't, I feel a need to do this."

"Can I take you to the airport?"

"No, it's easier to leave the car at the parking garage."

"Well, good luck and give them my best. Let them know I'm looking forward to seeing them at our wedding."

"I will."

The remainder of breakfast was spent discussing Ben's business, as usual. He enjoyed talking about his projects and his enthusiasm was contagious. They discussed briefly some wedding ideas before parting ways for the day.

Having made the decision, Sabrina was anxious to make the trip. If nothing else, maybe her arrival would help Sophie with companionship. It also gave Brie another opportunity to spend time with Faith and Grace.

Just as planned, Sabrina arrived at her sister's house at eight o'clock Saturday morning knowing they would be up. Ringing the doorbell, it was David who answered with a surprised look on his face, actually one of relief.

"Am I glad to see you," he whispered as he gave her a hug.

They broke apart, and she smiled at him without saying a word. He grabbed her hand leading her into the kitchen where Sophie was sitting at the table.

"Honey, we have a visitor this morning," he announced, dragging Brie behind him.

When she looked up to see who it was, Sophie jumped out of the chair and flew into an embrace, thrilled to see her sister. However, the realization kicked in of exactly what Sabrina might discover that she had labored to conceal.

David poured a cup of coffee handing it to Sabrina as she sat down.

"This is a great surprise, Brie. When did you get in?" David asked.

"Late yesterday afternoon and I went to the condo. I had a few things to take care of and thought to make this a surprise visit. I didn't think either of you would mind."

"Not at all," he replied.

David was pleased to see her and hoped Sophie would feel the same way.

"I'll make some breakfast. For you, Brie, I'll mix up a batch of your favorite multi-grain pancakes."

"How did you know I have a taste for them?" Brie asked, teasing him.

Brie chatted with David while watching her sister who had yet to contribute to the conversation. She couldn't help but recognize the fatigue and dark circles under Sophie's eyes, also detecting uneasiness at her presence, which only confirmed her initial concerns. Not wanting to bring attention to her sister by mentioning her appearance, Brie took a different approach of inviting her out for the day.

"Sophie, I purposefully sprung this visit hoping you don't have plans, so we could do some shopping and have lunch, or go to the art museum in Winter Park for the afternoon. What do you think?"

Sophie looked at her sister wondering if she could muster the energy. Everything was a struggle and getting out of the house was not something she did very often. It seemed like too much trouble.

"I don't know, Brie. I need to stay home with the girls."

"We can take them with us. It'll be fun and David can come along. We can make it a family affair if you prefer. I've wanted to check out the *Millennia Mall*."

Another time, Sophie would have been excited to spend a day shopping with her sister, but now she didn't have that same energetic spirit. The lack of enthusiasm was a dramatic indication that Sophie wasn't doing well which made Brie glad for the trip.

"Could we just hang around the house today, instead?"

"Sure, but it's a beautiful day. If you don't want to shop, we can do a picnic at *Lake Eola*. Let's get out for a few hours," Brie said, trying to coax Sophie without making her angry.

"Those are some good ideas, honey. I can stay home and watch the girls. Why don't you and Brie go out and have some fun. You haven't had a chance to do that since the twins were born," he said, gently encouraging her.

David and Brie knew she needed to get out of the house. They hoped it didn't backfire as it was apparent they were ganging up on Sophie, and she was smart enough to realize it. She looked at them with such expressionless eyes. They didn't know what her next words would be.

"Well, I see I'm outnumbered, so I suppose we could go out for awhile. If you're okay watching the girls, Brie and I can go to the mall," she told her husband.

"Of course, I can take care of my girls. I want you to enjoy yourself."

"Good, we should go right after breakfast," Brie said, confirming the plan and not allowing Sophie a chance to change her mind.

In the past, it was always Sophie practically begging Sabrina to slow down from her busy traveling schedule, so they could spend time together. Now, Brie was prying Sophie out of her own home to do what used to come so naturally.

They ate breakfast with David and Sabrina carrying the conversation. Afterwards, Brie heard the twins were awake and went in to see them while Sophie got ready. The girls were so adorable, and Brie noted the subtle changes that occurred since she last saw them.

"Hello, Faith. I've missed you. I see you have done some growing. Good for you, sweetheart," she told her, gently rubbing Faith's cheek with the back of her index finger.

Faith listened to her Auntie Brie's voice staring at her face. Sabrina smiled before turning toward Grace's crib.

"You are such a cutie. I see you have been doing some growing, too."

Sophie walked into the room halting the baby talk. However, she had stood in the doorway long enough to witness another episode of her twins communicating with their aunt. She refused to allow it to bother her.

"They get cuter by the day, if that's possible," Brie said.

"Yes, they do."

Sophie gave David instructions for the twins before leaving the house. He was happy to watch his daughters and hopeful that Brie could put his wife in better spirits. At least, he was counting on it because he certainly wasn't having any luck.

Chapter 41

It had been awhile since Sabrina and Sophie spent a day together doing miscellaneous things with the exception of the very short outings right after the twins were born. Since neither had been to the *Millennia Mall*, Brie thought it would be a treat to browse the unfamiliar stores. Sophie loved to shop; however, she showed no interest.

Another noticeable difference in Sophie was her lack of conversation and general nonchalant attitude. Sabrina finally suggested they sit and have an iced tea at a restaurant inside the mall. Sliding onto opposite benches at a booth, they settled in while a young waitress stepped over to take their order of drinks.

"Sophie, talk to me. It is obvious you are not doing well."

Sophie saw the concern in her sister's eyes but didn't really understand herself. Everything was fine one day and the next life had changed, just that quick it seemed. She stared at Brie, without attempting to explain, while picking at the paper napkin containing the wrapped flatware.

"How are you and David doing since he made the appointment for Faith?"

Perhaps that would draw her sister into a conversation. She had to start somewhere, and maybe talking about David would be considered neutral conversational material.

"David and I are fine. He cancelled the appointment, but I

got over being mad at him before he did."

"What have the two of you decided?"

"David still believes we should do the surgery even with the risks."

Her brief answers weren't giving Brie knowledge of what happened to put her perfectionist sister into such a degenerative frame of mind. Was this solely because of the pending surgery? Or was there more that Sophie wasn't sharing?

"I know you are frightened about Faith. Is that what has you feeling so down?"

"Every time I think about it, I get such a horrible feeling. You want to know what's bothering me. Everything is bothering me. Life is bothering me, sometimes David bothers me, and most of all Faith's heart condition bothers me. And I don't have anyone or anyplace to get the help I need to resolve this crisis, not even from you. I'm totally helpless to help Faith. You're not a mother, so I don't expect you to understand. Not having a choice or say in what happens to her makes it worse. No one can help me help my baby!" she said, raising her voice.

Brie wanted Sophie to talk, and it all came out in one big gush. Sabrina wished she could say what her sister wanted to hear, but Sophie wouldn't appreciate her words, so she sat in silence waiting for her sister to calm down. They sipped on their tea, and when it was apparent Sophie wasn't going to speak, Brie took the lead.

"That is a lot of pain to carry around everyday. How do you manage it?"

"Honestly, most days I don't. I take care of the girls and that's all I have the desire to do. As you probably noticed, my house is no longer the well-kept home I prided myself on maintaining."

"Sophie, your home always looks good."

"I'm only thinking about my babies."

"Do you really believe you have no one to help you?"

"If I knew of someone who could give me a solution, don't you think I would have gone to them by now? I thought maybe you could."

Brie twirled the straw in her glass accepting the root of Sophie's pain; however, Brie was more concerned to finding the reason for Sophie's refusal in acknowledging God. Sophie needed to come to terms that the resolution she was seeking lies within her belief. How do you convey that to someone whose heart is closed to hearing the truth? This wasn't the place to hold such a conversation. However, before the weekend was over, she would have answers. In the meantime, she needed to cheer her sister.

"We should hold this conversation until tonight, and instead, spend our time having fun shopping. I haven't bought anything for my nieces yet, and I can't leave this mall before I do," Brie said, attempting to enlighten her sister's spirit.

"Sure, if you're ready, we can go."

Sabrina left money on the table to cover the drinks and tip. She hoped to take Sophie's mind, even though temporarily, off her problem. Sophie, knowing what her sister was trying to do, wanted to go home but couldn't bring herself to say anything. Shopping didn't hold any appeal, but for Brie's sake, she kept stride in every store they entered. Sabrina bought clothes and toys for the twins going directly to the baby department. She was now intent on helping Sophie select a few things for herself.

"I don't need anything, Brie."

"That's not the point. We're going to find you a couple of lounging sets for relaxing around the house with the girls."

Obviously, Brie was on a mission, and she wasn't taking no for an answer. Sophie followed her sister idly looking at the racks of clothing, but adamantly refused when Brie held up matching top and bottom sweats for her to try on.

"What about this Sophie? How about one set in navy and the other in pink?"

"That's fine."

Sophie gave up trying to convince her sister that she didn't want any clothes. Slinging them across her arm, Brie headed toward the lingerie department for some cute cotton pajamas. Pretending to be perusing the items for herself, she selected a soft blue print bottom with the matching solid jersey top.

"Anything else you want to look at?" Brie asked.

"No, not really."

"Then let's go checkout."

Once they were in line, Sophie asked for the clothes to pay for them, but Brie pretended her arms were too full to relinquish the outfits. When it was their turn, she plopped down her bundle. Sophie reached over to pull her clothing out of the mix, but Brie refused.

"I'm getting this."

"No, you're not. Let me have the two that are mine. I'll pay for my own clothes."

"Not this time, it's my treat."

"Brie, you don't need to do that. Just give me the clothes," Sophie said, irritated.

Sabrina pushed the items towards the sales clerk informing the lady they were all her purchase, putting a stop to the conversation. Sophie wasn't going to make a scene, allowing Brie to have her way.

"Brie, can we go home now? I'm too tired to do anything else today."

"Sure, I think we covered every store in this mall anyway. I wonder what David's fixing for dinner. He always prepares such great meals."

"Since you're here, he may make one of your favorites. He likes to do that for you."

"Really, that's so thoughtful of him. He's a good man."

"Yes, he is."

Sabrina normally reserved shopping for when she visited with Sophie, so it felt good spending the day together. However, Brie understood her sister was anxious to get back home to her babies. Unfortunately, this particular expedition wasn't as successful as Brie had hoped for.

Chapter 42

The house was quiet when they walked in, thus, all was well with no crying babies or flustered daddy. Sabrina handed the two big bags to Sophie.

"This isn't all mine, you have some things in one of these bags," Sophie said, accepting the packages.

"No, everything is yours."

"What about the pajamas you bought."

"Yours."

"Brie, I can't take these things without paying for them."

"No need, everything I bought is for you and the girls. I felt generous today."

Sophie stared at Brie for a moment and conceded.

"I'm not going to argue, thank you. I'll put them in my bedroom."

The twins were sleeping, and David was in the kitchen with the monitor on the counter preparing dinner. Brie walked in as he was placing a pot roast on the top rack in the oven.

"What did you make?"

"Your favorite; pot roast with vegetables."

"David, you didn't have to go to the trouble. A sandwich would have been sufficient."

"It's no trouble. Between us, I enjoy spoiling you with my cooking," he told her.

"Sophie sure is lucky to have you."

"Did you girls have fun?" David asked.

David was curious how Sophie fared being away from the twins and considering her depressive state of mind lately.

"For the most part."

Sophie walked into the kitchen ending their conversation.

"I checked on the twins. How were they today?"

"No problems, we played all day."

"Did you remember to feed them?"

"Feed them! I was supposed to feed them. You're joking, right?"

When Brie snickered, he winked at her while Sophie barely smirked. It was his best attempt to deflect the somberness surrounding them.

"Of course, I followed your instructions, and we had a great day. How was yours?"

"We had a good day. Brie bought some cute things for the girls."

Making a glass of iced tea, she handed it to Brie and then another for herself.

"When will dinner be ready?"

"In about an hour, I've got a pot roast in the oven."

"What did I tell you? He made your favorite. Let's sit in the living room."

"David, can I help you with anything?" Brie asked.

"No need, just have to wait for it to cook."

They left David and took their respective places on the sofa. Sophie spoke first.

"You didn't have business with your condo this weekend, did you?"

"No. I was worried about you, and if I asked to come down, you might refuse. So I took it upon myself to make the trip," Brie explained, without guilt.

"If you had business, you would have told me on the phone the last time we talked."

"I knew you weren't doing well and didn't plan to tell me, so I had to take the initiative. Admit it, if things were reversed, you would have done the same."

"For sure, so when is your flight tomorrow?"

"Around noon."

"Did you pick out the dresses from the last email I sent to you?" Sophie asked, deferring the subject away from herself.

"Yes, I definitely liked your choices. I decided to go with the second wedding dress, the slim-fitting one with the long, tapered sleeves. And I took your idea for the maid-of-honor dress and the bridesmaids, and sent the pictures to my friends at the magazine. I'm waiting to hear back before placing an order. This internet shopping sure is making my life easy."

"Who are these friends? What are their names?"

"Becky, Tanya and Deborah; Becky works in accounting, Tanya and Deborah are editors. I've known them for years and they are married with families. Actually, I was surprised how excited they were to be in my wedding. You'll get to spend a few days together since they are flying in early."

It didn't seem they had chatted for over an hour when David made a quick appearance to announce dinner was on the table. Following him back into the kitchen, Brie noticed he had done all the work, including setting the table.

"David, I could have helped," Brie said.

"No need, you know the kitchen is my personal domain," he replied with a wink.

As they sat at the small table, conversation was purpose-fully kept on neutral subjects such as David's classroom students, or Brie's photography, but no mentioning what was pressing on their minds.

"David, did you feed the twins all the breast milk I pumped into the bottles?" Sophie asked.

"Every drop and I stuck to the feeding schedule just like you told me. The twins were good, neither complained. This has been the first time I've been alone with my girls for the entire day, and we did good."

"It seems so," Sophie replied, surprised.

David was proud, handling the responsibility of his babies without a glitch. As they ate, Sabrina told tales of past photo assignments embellishing the stories making them laugh. It was a great antidote to the tension. After dinner, Sophie and Sabrina cleaned the kitchen while David brewed one of his special blends, and they all retired to the living room.

"Do you think the girls will wake up soon?" Brie asked.

Sabrina wanted to hold them, especially to see how Faith was doing. She didn't get the opportunity earlier that morning.

"I have no idea."

"How is Ben these days?" David asked.

"He's a happy man. Always goes around with a big smile on his face."

However, it wasn't unusual for Ben to grin frequently. In fact, Sabrina wondered if anything ever bothered him because he was never perturbed about issues, always taking everything in stride. She had yet to see him upset.

"Ben is a great guy, a nice addition to our family."

"That's a thoughtful thing to say."

"It's true. I will enjoy having another male around. I'm completely outnumbered with a house full of females."

"You love it, David," Brie reminded him.

"I certainly do, but it could be fun having some male bonding once in awhile with a fellow insider."

"You mean within the family," Brie confirmed.

"Exactly."

Sabrina noticed Sophie slowly withdrawing to a quiet demeanor. After brief small talk, David excused himself leaving them alone. They sat for a few minutes engrossed in their own thoughts before Brie spoke up.

"I would like to spend time with the girls before I leave in the morning."

"Not a problem. I'll make sure you do."

Brie knew the conversation she wanted and needed to have with Sophie would be very upsetting, but there was no way to get around it. Perhaps the best way was to jump right in.

"Sophie, I want to talk about something that you have been avoiding, but it's a subject we really need to get out in the open," Brie said, pausing for her sister's reaction.

When Sophie didn't respond, she continued.

"We need to talk about God."

Staring at Sabrina, Sophie fired darts with her eyes.

"Oh, no you don't, I'm not sitting here and having a conversation about God. If that's what you want to talk about forget it, I'm going to bed," Sophie announced, standing up from the sofa.

Brie grabbed her wrist pulling her back. Sophie plopped down appalled her sister would do such a thing. Sitting in defiance, she crossed her arms. Now she was mad.

"This is the very thing we need to talk to about. With every mention of God, you shut down, or get defensive. I want to have this conversation and for you to tell me why you do that," Brie said, cornering her.

Sophie was silent, and Brie could tell she had momentarily zoned out. She didn't know what her sister was thinking, but desperately wanted to find out.

"Please, Sophie, let's talk about this. I need to know why you feel this way. I sensed it back when we were dealing with Aunt Millie's legacy, but I had no idea how strong your aversion was. It's important."

"Why would it be important? Nothing concerning God is important to me, and that is all I care to say on the subject."

"Everything concerning God should be important. Obviously, something happened to make you feel this way, what was it?"

Sophie hesitated. Brie had been pushing this conversation on her for months now. She knew talking about it was going to make her feel worse, but Brie wouldn't back down this time. If she didn't have this discussion, their relationship would become estranged, and she couldn't handle being completely alienated.

"Alright, let's get this over with once and for all. You want to know why I have distrust in God. He took our parents away from us, and he has now given me a child with a potentially fatal condition. That's certainly enough to despise someone who would do such a thing. So now you know, are you happy? Does that satisfy your curiosity?"

Brie didn't know what to expect, but this certainly wasn't it. She never knew, all these years, her sister held God responsible for their parent's death. Thinking back to when they were in college and told the news their parents had been killed in a boating accident was devastating. The pain was excruciating, but with the help of Aunt Millie, they managed to forge through it. Perhaps because their upbringing wasn't based on a solid foundation and understanding of God, Sophie wasn't spiritually prepared to cope. However, neither was Sabrina, yet, she never thought to blame God. Unknowingly, she let her sister down.

"I had no idea you felt this way. Why didn't you share your feelings with me when they died? You've kept this to yourself all these years. Now I understand. Oh, Sophie, I should have been there for you. I'm so sorry."

"This isn't your fault. You didn't know because I chose to not tell you."

"Why didn't you? We always said we'll be there for each other, and yet, we haven't. It's very sad to think about you dealing with those feelings alone."

"Everyone sometimes holds their emotions private in certain situations. You've done that too, Brie. You admitted you withheld some sort of epiphany concerning the legacy, *Passionate Promises*. You have yet to share it with me. So perhaps, unintentionally, we do keep secrets from each other not meaning to burden. We were only nineteen, teenagers. How is someone so young supposed to deal with losing both of their parents?"

"That's what I see you doing with Faith. It's what brought me to Florida this weekend. You've withdrawn. Do you see this situation with Faith the same way? Do you think God is controlling what happens to her?"

"Of course, He carries the ultimate power to do as He

pleases. What did I do that He would take away our parents and now dangle my baby's life in front of me? I don't know how to rectify my past to make Him change the course we are on with Faith."

"Do you really believe God took our parents from us?"

"Yes."

"And He gave this heart condition to Faith?"

"Yes."

The impact of how Sophie viewed God was unimaginable, that she could think something so unkind of Him. The one who loves us so much would turn against His own children was unthinkable to Brie. How was she ever going to get Sophie to open her heart and comprehend what she was about to tell her?

"I'm sorry you were hurt so deeply by our parent's death, and I wasn't there to help you, but blaming God is not the right direction you should pursue. Sophie, He didn't do these things you hold Him responsible for. Our parent's death was an accident. He has nothing to do with Faith's heart condition."

"You're wrong, Brie. He took them away from us."

"Why would He do that? What would be His reason for such a terrible act of unkindness toward two teenagers? He is a God of love and mercy, so it doesn't make sense."

"I don't know. I'm in a quandary over this, but I must have done something to displease Him because He's doing it again."

"Oh no, Sophie, you have a terrible misconception of God. He is the creator of life and everything that is good. He is love. We are His children, and He loves us and wants the very best for each one of us. How can a being of love do the bad things you think He has done?"

"Well, He can if He wants to."

"What is His motive?"

"I think it's a way to keep us in line, make us tow-the-mark, and if we don't, zap," she said, snapping her fingers in mid-air.

"How long have you felt this way?"

"I'm not sure exactly, perhaps when mom and dad died. I

suppose I didn't have a reason before then."

"Sophie, you are so wrong. You have developed a misguided concept of God. Maybe the pain of their death caused you to need someone to blame. Sometimes when we can't deal with an emotional crisis, it makes us feel better to place a fault with someone else. But God isn't the one who is raining bad things down upon your life because of something you didn't do right. He doesn't work that way. Haven't you ever thought perhaps it's the other spiritual being that is causing all the bad things to happen? Realistically, there is another spiritual being."

"Why would I think that?"

"That's my point. You aren't considering any other alternative to the *cause* of your problem with Faith. You automatically place the blame on God without evidence to support your belief. I think you have made a critical error in judgment against Him based on your suffering with our parent's death. That is unfair and unrealistic, but I don't expect you to see it that way at the moment. It seems we can conveniently turn to God when things are going well in our lives and give Him the appropriate praise, but when something bad or unpleasant comes along, we fault Him just as easily. How can we do that? Why would we hold Him accountable for both the good and the bad that happens? For me, it would make me question Him being a loving God if He presented sometimes good events and other times bad. If He loves me as much as I know He does, after all, He is *love*, then why would He want to hurt me, too? Do you see what I'm trying to say?"

Sabrina paused to allow her words to register. She hoped to break through the barrier her sister held onto so tightly to understand the true nature and character of their heavenly Father, as one who loves her. When she didn't speak, Brie continued.

"There are two spiritual forces. You are concentrating on only one, placing all that happens good or bad on God, and not even considering that the other just might be the culprit. In all that thinking you have been doing, did you ever stop to turn it around and look at the situation from a different prospective?"

Sophie sat silent. She had never seen Brie so passionate about anything, not even her photography. *When did she get so fired up for God,* she wondered.

"How long have you felt this way about God? Obviously, you hold very strong beliefs, just as I have mine against Him. Somewhere along the way, I missed that in you."

"Truthfully, two years ago with Aunt Millie's legacy. Until then, I didn't see a need for God, nor had a true appreciation of Him. But now my life has been redirected, and I'm so blessed, you just can't imagine. I want the same for you."

Sophie didn't have an immediate response to that remark. They were so far apart in their individual relationship with God, she didn't think she could ever be where Sabrina was, nor did she want to be. It must have been something extremely miraculous for Brie to feel so strongly, and yet, it wasn't for her.

"How ironic we should have such different viewpoints. This may be one that we'll have to call a truce and accept our differences," Sophie stated, firmly.

"I hope you will do some soul-searching before you draw a final conclusion, but it is your decision. We are individually responsible for a relationship with Him."

"It is my choice what I believe. You want me to accept God isn't orchestrating anything bad, and all the ugly things come from the devil. I do believe in an evil force, but since God is in charge of His creation, I would think He would be overseeing Satan as well."

"Because we are dealing with two spiritual beings, that's where God has allowed us to make a choice of whom we will trust. If we truly believe God to be of love, kindness, mercy, and grace, then again, why would He put in our lives, or allow anything so painful?"

"To teach us, I suppose."

"Teach us what? You think God is using destructive things,

like mom and dad's death or Faith's heart murmur to teach you something? What happens if you don't understand whatever your lesson may be?"

"That's the part I'm scared about. I don't know what I'm supposed to be learning, and time is running out for me. What will happen to Faith if I don't discover what God wants? I'm so terrified He will take her from me. I just don't know what to do," she said, bursting into tears.

Sabrina scooted across the sofa reaching for her sister, pulling her into her arms. It broke her heart to witness the turmoil within her twin. Sophie seriously blamed God for her predicament with Faith, and honestly believed there was a restitution required of her to appease a God of wrath. *Oh my goodness, how could this have happened?* she thought. Silently holding Sophie while she cried, Brie prayed for words of wisdom to help Sophie overcome the fear and anger she held in her heart. As Sophie regained her composure, she withdrew from her sister wiping her eyes with the sleeve of her blouse.

"I didn't mean to break down like that," she said, embarrassed.

"I never knew you held so much pain in your heart. But you are also holding onto fear and anger, as well, that you need to let go of. It's misplaced, and I believe it is part of the *root* to the problem you are dealing with. Sophie, God isn't holding anything over your head waiting for you to perform, and if you don't, He'll take away something you hold precious as punishment. You are a parent who loves her babies, protecting them. God is a parent too, and loves His children and provides us protection. If you can see it from that perspective, perhaps you will understand God doesn't want anything bad to happen to Faith."

"Then why do I feel He is the one doing this?"

"You have misunderstood God, but you are right about one thing, He is waiting. However not for a performance, but rather you coming to Him wanting a relationship with Him, one whereby you trust in Him because He is your heavenly Father.

That's when we come under His umbrella of protection as His child. Do you understand what I am telling you?"

"I hear your words, but how do I know you're correct? Maybe, I have it right, and you're wrong. Have *you* thought about that?" Sophie countered.

"When we turn to God asking for forgiveness and repenting of our sins, we have made a decision to believe in Him and put our faith in His Word. He tells us over and over again through His Word in the Bible how much He loves us, and because He does, we have His grace and promises. He only wants good things for us, always. You need to communicate with God, pray and He will answer."

"So if what you are saying is true, where does that leave me with Faith? You're saying God didn't give Faith a bad heart."

"The blame should be placed where it rightfully belongs."

"So why hasn't God come along with all His goodness and corrected the problem?"

"He has."

"No, Faith still has a heart condition."

"If you can understand and believe that God didn't give Faith a heart problem, then you will also know it doesn't exist with Him. He sees Faith as one of His perfect creations. God gave His only Son to die on the cross for our sins, so that we may have salvation and eternal life in heaven one day. But Christ's death was also for our sickness and diseases. He bore all things that we might have a relationship with God when we give our life to Him. We should trust our heavenly Father that we may receive His blessings. He is our parent."

"What do you mean? That doesn't make any sense."

"It makes perfect sense if you understand God's character and His nature of love and goodness. If we accept God as our Father and turn our life toward Him, living for Him under His grace, He will take care of us, His children. It is not His will that Faith is ill. That is not His desire for her."

Where did she get such nonsense, Sophie questioned. How

can anyone not see that God is the Almighty and in charge of everything that happens?

"When did you learn about God? I know when we were kids we didn't go to church that much, just on those special occasions when our parents thought it was required of them to attend. Remember, we went for Easter and Christmas, weddings and times like that, so I know you didn't acquire this kind of knowledge from mom and dad."

"Truthfully, after the impact Aunt Millie's legacy had on my life, I had a burning desire to know all I could about my heavenly Father. I wanted desperately to have a personal relationship with Him, so I studied the Bible."

Sophie was at a loss for words. Seeing the passion in her sister and hearing her confession about God seemed so outlandish and absurd, but then, was it? She just didn't know. Brie couldn't be right, it was too simple.

"And you really believe that?" Sophie asked, still skeptical.

Sabrina could tell her sister wasn't grasping what she was telling her. For someone with so much mistrust and blame, she knew Sophie wouldn't be very receptive to the truth. After all, it would destroy the foundation of what she has held onto for years. Brie never knew they had such vastly different opinions on faith, and God's role in their individual lives.

"Yes, Sophie, I do, and I hope some day you will also. Until you do, where are you going to find the answers you are seeking for Faith? Who else can deal with a problem of this magnitude?"

"Like I said, this is His fault, so there isn't anything that can be done to help Faith, unless He changes His mind, and I don't see that happening. I really don't."

"If you continue to blame Him for something He is not responsible for, the outcome may not be what you want."

Sabrina was dismayed to hear the finality in her twin's voice knowing what was at stake, but there was nothing more to be said. If Sophie didn't open her heart and accept the truth, she couldn't force it upon her. It saddened her deeply to realize her words didn't have the impact she hoped for.

"What do you mean?"

"Who do you think is stealing Faith away from you right under your eyes, and you are so blind to it. While you sit around blaming God, your daughter is in a crisis. Have you given any thought to the reason she is in limbo?"

"She's not in limbo."

Now the conversation was going nowhere.

"Sophie, at least humor me and think about everything we've talked about. I hope you come to understand that God didn't have anything to do with our parent's death, and He isn't the one allowing Faith to be in harms way. You keep forgetting there are two forces at work here. You are so hung up on blaming God and can't see what's really transpiring."

"That's a thoughtless thing to say to me."

Once she made the statement, Sophie wished she could retract her words. After all, she had witnessed Brie's connection with her daughters. To witness her sister defending God so profoundly was disturbing, and yet, she couldn't deny there was something between them. It showed in the ardent way she spoke of Him.

Sabrina knew there was nothing else to be said and was dissatisfied their conversation would end on such a distrusting note. With nothing to add, she remained silent as Sophie was getting defensive again. Knowing the position her sister had taken against God, it would take a mighty change in her beliefs, and Brie could only pray that it occurred for her sake and Faith's.

"I appreciate your concern, and thank you for making the trip down this weekend. I've listened to what you had to say, but this is going to be a subject we will have to agree to disagree, and leave it alone. I will say this, you paint a very nice picture of God, one that is too good to actually be true. I know you believe in Him and that's great for you, but I don't agree with you," she paused to catch her breath, and continued.

"It was probably bound to happen, eventually, that we would take separate sides on an issue. What are the odds of us agreeing on everything for the rest of our lives? I'm sorry, Brie. I don't mean to disappoint you, but I can't accept your beliefs. I hope you understand," Sophie told her, wanting to end the conversation.

Sabrina knew her sister needed to do some serious meditating with a willingness to release the fear, anger and blame; however, Sophie wasn't ready to do that. Other than pressing her point, there was nothing more for Brie to say. She had an answer to her sister's aversion to God, and how it came about, and did her best to correct a misguided belief. Everything hinged on Sophie changing her heart.

"Alright, we'll call it a truce," Brie said, disappointed.

They sat quietly, each in thought, before Sophie got up to check on the twins. Brie followed, and they said goodnight in the hallway before disappearing into separate bedrooms. Apparently, David had retired for the night because the guest room was empty when Brie walked in. Though she was disturbed with the conversation, Brie also knew Sophie would give it some thought, or so she hoped.

Chapter 43

The next morning, Brie had nearly three hours exclusively with her nieces. Leaving them alone in the living room, Sophie made the excuse of cleaning the girls' room, and David disappeared to the computer. Brie sat with them on a large blanket spread out on the floor. Grace, lying on her back, wanted to show Auntie Brie her aerobatic abilities by attempting to grab her outstretched legs while making sweet baby sounds. Brie lifted her niece high in the air swinging her around before putting Grace back on the blanket to rest.

Then she gently took Faith in her arms and holding her upright on her lap, Faith focused on her aunt's face. The connection between them was powerfully felt as Sabrina spoke to her.

"Hello, my sweet Faith," Brie said softly, placing a kiss on her forehead.

It was important for Sabrina to hold Faith and personally identify how she was doing. Though Faith was aware of her Auntie Brie, she showed slowness in her movements, unlike before. Sabrina gave more attention to Faith, without ignoring Grace, as she continued to play and talk to the girls until interrupted by Sophie. Hearing them, she came to investigate.

"What's all this commotion? Sounds like someone is having fun," Sophie said, picking up Grace.

"We're playing," Brie said, hugging Faith close.

"I could hear you from down the hall."

With Faith in her arms, Sabrina went to sit on the sofa knowing soon she would have to say goodbye. It was hard to leave her sister when she was so unhappy, accepting her visit didn't alleviate Sophie's despairing frame of mind. In fact, their recent conversation may have worsened her condition, but Sabrina believed it was a needed discussion.

"Will you be okay?"

"No, not as long as we're dealing with the surgery."

"I'm expecting to hear from you every day or so just like always. If I don't, I'm flying back down."

"You don't have to keep tabs on me."

"I'm always here for you."

"I know you are."

Sabrina sensed her sister would fall back into a semi-depressive state as soon as she walked out the door, but staying indefinitely wouldn't help, either. She hoped Sophie would come to accept a relationship with their heavenly Father and overcome the negativism she had been harboring. Everything that needed to be spoken between them had now been said. It was up to Sophie.

Giving Faith a hug and whispering words of love, Brie slipped her into a swing and then kissed Grace's cheek telling her the same. Sophie placed Grace in the matching seat while Brie went to the guest bedroom to find David and say goodbye.

He followed her back to the living room gathering her suitcase by the front door and placing it in the trunk of the rental car. Standing outside the doorway, Brie hugged David and then turned to her sister, holding tightly as tears filled their eyes. It was an emotional departing; neither wanting to let go, but finally Sabrina pulled away from the embrace as she couldn't linger any longer.

"I'll call you when I get home," Brie yelled from the car window as she backed out of the driveway.

Sophie waved before stepping into the house. She went directly to sit on the sofa, needing a few minutes to gain her composure.

"Did you have a good visit with Brie?" David asked, taking the chair across from her.

David saw the instant metaphoric change as though someone had thrown a veil of despair over his wife. He hated to see her this way and hoped Sabrina's visit helped, but perhaps not.

"We had a good time," she replied, without conviction.

Getting his wife to hold a conversation was a challenge. Perhaps he could persuade her to expound on some of the topics she and Brie had discussed.

"What did you talk about?"

"Wedding dresses, her friends, our parents. Stuff like that."

"Does she have everything under control for her wedding?"

"She's all set. A few minor details left to do, but the major things are done."

"That's good."

There would never be a good time to bring up the subject of Faith's surgery, but they needed to discuss it. It was going to happen, and it was imperative they be on the same page before he rescheduled the appointment. He had learned from the first mistake.

"Honey, we need to talk about Faith's surgery," he said, carefully.

"I don't want to talk about it. You know my position."

Sophie was being bombarded by both Brie and David. She just had an unpleasant conversation with her sister over God, and now David wants to discuss the surgery. *When will they stop?* she questioned.

"We can't keep avoiding it."

"Yes, I can."

"You know what we need to do. Whatever occurs because of the surgery couldn't be worse than her heart slowly failing her. We'll have to deal with things, if and when they happen and hope everything will turn out alright. We need to decide on a date and get this over with. What do you suggest we do?"

"I don't know."

"That's not a solution. You can keep saying that, but it's not helping Faith," he said a bit too sharply.

Sophie stared at David not believing he actually accused her of being indifferent to their problem. Surely, he should know if she had an answer, she would have voiced it by now.

"Do you really believe I've detached myself because I can't give you another option?" she asked, appalled David would think such a thing of her.

"I'm not sure anymore. We need a resolution and since you can't come up with a different one, we have to do the surgery. I understand your fears but without another remedy, we need to move forward with the one we have."

"Are you saying you would do this without my agreement?"

David didn't want to oppose his wife, and especially over their baby, but he was fearful, himself, to continue postponing the inevitable. He felt torn between two people he loved with all his heart.

"No, I did that once. I'm not insensitive, but time is slipping away."

"I keep envisioning Faith lying on a table with her chest cut open. I can't express in words how much I hate this situation," she told him, raising her voice.

"Sophie, you need to come to terms with the surgery and find the means within yourself to cope with it. Doing nothing isn't reality. Take a few days to get a grip, so we can make the appointment," David said in finality to the conversation.

As usual, they weren't any closer to agreeing, and it wasn't doing any good to continue hashing out their differences. David felt no other choice but to push Sophie.

"That sounds like an ultimatum."

"It's not meant to be, but you are the one holding up Faith's progress. The sooner we do this, and put it behind us, she'll be on a path of recovery. Let's move forward," he said with a gentler tone.

There wasn't anything else she could say without breaking into an argument. It was disturbing that they would take such opposite sides. As harsh as some of her words had been toward David, she couldn't blame him for having a few of his own.

"I'll think about it."

David studied his wife for a moment. They needed to do this and he refused to make another appointment without her consent. Until she gave her agreement, he was stuck. Sophie knew deep within her heart she could never say the words her husband wanted to hear. They were at a crossroad.

Chapter 44

Sabrina arrived home with bittersweet thoughts of her nieces. She longed to hold Faith again believing she needed her. Brie knew the visit didn't helped Sophie, and it grieved her to witness the turmoil and conflict created between her sister and David.

She called Ben and they talked briefly bringing him up-to-date on matters; however, because he was unable to break away to stop by the house, they agreed to meet for breakfast in the morning. Next, she phoned Sophie as promised.

"Hi, Sophie, I'm home."

"Good. No problems with the flight?"

"None, it was right on schedule. How are you?"

"I know you want me to tell you I'm okay, but I'm not. David and I talked after you left, and he wants to proceed with the surgery and for me to come to terms with it. He thinks I'm not being realistic."

"What will you do?"

"I have a few days to think about it, but we both know nothing is going to change. Parents put their children through surgeries every day, but I can't bring myself to do it. I'm not made of stern stuff."

"Sis, you are made of a much stronger countenance than you give yourself credit for. You've never had to exercise it before, that's all."

"I certainly don't feel it."

"It's there, and when the time comes, you'll be able to rely on your inner strength."

"I sure hope you're right because I'll need every bit to get through this. What if something happens to Faith and the doctors aren't able to undo it? There are so many risks."

"What does your heart say?"

"I wish I knew. I feel so empty and terrified of the future."

"You'll know what to do. The answer will be there for you."

"Unless you know something I don't, that doesn't seem to be happening."

"Pray and the answer will come to you. Trust me, it's there."

Silence swelled between them for it was up to Sophie to accept or deny the recommendation, for she knew what her sister was implying. *Here we go again,* Sophie thought.

"I'll think about it," she replied flippantly, having no intention of doing so.

Fleetingly, Brie thought of talking with David, but not knowing his relationship with God left her at another disadvantage, so she dismissed the idea. Not that she and David would gang-up on Sophie, but perhaps between them, they could help her get past the anger. They concluded the conversation agreeing to talk the next day. Brie could only pray that her sister would turn to God and correct her relationship with Him.

After hanging up the phone, Brie pulled out her wedding planner and reviewed the lists making sure nothing was overlooked. Even though it would take place in formal surroundings, she wasn't adhering to a stringent, traditional wedding with someone walking her down the isle. The only person to consider would be David, and in lieu of asking him, she truly preferred to walk single and saw no reason why she shouldn't.

The invitations had arrived and would be mailed in mid-October, and Bella had taken over the assignment of the floral arrangements. Dresses were ordered and everything was falling into place. Sabrina's friends could help with any last minute issues, and even Joe, her assistant, would be flying in early making it possible to show them around Asheville before the wedding.

The next morning, Brie met Ben for their usual breakfast. He arrived first and was enjoying a conversation with a local customer when she walked in.

"Here's my bride," he announced with a smile, watching Sabrina approach him.

She walked up to Ben standing at a nearby table and right into his open arms, having no problem showing their affection in public.

"I haven't seen her for the past few days, so I'm overdue," he remarked, kissing her.

Sabrina wrapped her right arm around his neck pulling him closer, not caring who saw their performance. She had missed him, too. Everyone in the diner, knowing Ben for years, broke out in applause, whistling, and cheering them on.

Pulling apart, he turned to his audience and bowed from the waist while simultaneously swinging his right arm outward, in acceptance of their affections. Grabbing Brie's hand, they walked the length of restaurant to a back table and sat down opposite each other. A waitress followed carrying two cups of coffee and took their order.

"Tell me about your trip. How are Sophie and the girls?"

"Sophie is feeling the stress, but that is to be expected under the circumstances."

"How is Faith doing?"

"She isn't in harms way, and that's important to know."

"You sound so sure about that."

"I'm confident all is well with Faith and will be also for my sister."

"That's a very positive attitude. If I were you, I would hold onto that thought."

"That's what I'm doing."

"Your sister will get through this tough time," Ben told her, encouragingly.

"Yes, I believe she will."

Changing the subject, Brie asked about his business and Ben mentioned some upcoming changes he was planning in preparation for the holiday season. Likewise, he inquired about her photography assignments, each enjoying discussing their current projects and bouncing ideas off one another. When they were ready to leave, he pulled out a folded piece of paper from his shirt pocket and handed it to her.

"This is the invitation list from our side of the family. I told Mom to keep it short, but she still came up with about seventy-five names."

"Not a problem. She can invite whomever she wants."

"I think she has covered the important people."

"I'll combine her list with the one I've already started because the invitations need to go out soon."

Ben placed money on the table to cover the check with a hefty tip before leaving the restaurant. He was headed into town to pick up supplies and then back to the farm.

Before her afternoon photo shoot, Sabrina thought of visiting with her friend, Bella for awhile.

Chapter 45

Sophie couldn't prevent herself from slipping back down the despondent black abyss where hope did not prevail. She spent all her waking time thinking of a solution but continued to draw a blank. So terrified of the mere thought of surgery, it was becoming a monster in her psyche that she wasn't equipped to destroy. *How silly,* she thought, to think of this situation in such a metaphoric manner, but that was how she viewed it, and there was no one to help her slay this beast that had invaded her life. It seemed to grow stronger each day causing her more anguish and mounting fear.

Nothing had changed since Brie's visit. She and David had their routines, and she waited on pins and needles expecting him to want an agreement from her. He had not mentioned the surgery, but it was inevitable he would set the date, figuring he had given her ample time to come to terms with it. It wasn't fair. Coerced and unwilling, she had discussed it with her husband and sister, neither giving her a resolution that was acceptable. Brie wanted her to turn to God, and David wanted her to turn to the doctors. *Some choices,* she thought.

David waited patiently. He felt badly that she was having such a difficult time and was at a loss how to comfort her. Each day he came home to see a little more of his beautiful wife chiseled away into a sullen individual he hardly knew. This couldn't go on much longer, things had to change for the better because his family was falling apart.

Two weeks since their conversation, David was intent on taking charge after first mentioning his thoughts to Sophie. Apparently, she wasn't coming around of her own accord, and he needed to take the necessary action. Returning from work, he stepped into the house first walking down the hallway into the girls' room addressing them before searching for Sophie. He found her in the master bedroom lying on the bed on her side with her back to the door. Not wanting to disturb her, he quietly tiptoed into the room and peered over her shoulder to see her eyes were closed, and tears sliding down her cheeks. *Oh, Sophie, my love,* he thought.

Seeing his wife crying in private pained him. Still leaning over her, he turned his head toward the nightstand when he heard a noise coming from the baby monitor. It was Grace babbling, enjoying the sound of her own voice. Looking back down at his wife who hadn't moved, he gently tapped her on the shoulder whispering her name, but she didn't budge. If she was aware of his presence, she showed no acknowledgement. This wasn't good.

"Sophie, honey, look at me," he pleaded, rubbing his hand up and down her arm.

She still didn't move, but he noticed more tears flowing down her cheeks. She wept silently in death-grip stillness. It was disturbing to witness. David scooted her over enough to sit on the edge of the bed and lifted her onto his lap. She was suffering, and he had not been cognitive of the extent of her heartache. *Was he to blame for this,* he questioned. He knew he had failed Sophie. She was looking at this from a mother's point-of-view being protective of her babies. How could he expect anything less?

It was his responsibility to protect and keep her safe as he was trying to do for their daughter. He had concentrated so much on Faith; he neglected supporting his wife. If anything, he probed her about unrealistic expectations and not acting in reality. David chastised himself. Had he truly been there for

Sophie, would she be in this emotional condition? As much as the truth stung, David thought himself a negligent husband believing his wife would not be this way had he paid more attention to her. It was a hard blow.

He made no attempt to begin a conversation. Words were not what she needed from him at the moment. Eventually, her tears ceased as she wiped both cheeks with her finger tips. Pushing away in an attempt to remove herself from his lap, David held tighter not releasing his hold.

"Let me go, David."

"I will if you stay with me and not walk away."

She nodded her head, not looking at him, feeling the release of pressure from his arms. Sophie slid off his lap onto the side of the bed beside him, staring at the floor. She had nothing to say. David reached over and gently took her hand and held it.

"I'm sorry."

"For what?"

"I'm sorry I haven't been the best husband to you."

"What are you talking about? You are a good man, David."

"I haven't been if I let my wife become so despondent. I should have been more attentive toward your needs. I'm sorry I didn't do that."

Hearing the dejected tone in David's voice, Sophie turned to see the worry etched on his face. The sadness in her husband's eyes pulled at her heartstrings.

"I've never thought of you as any less of a husband, and you haven't let me down. We may not agree on how to handle this crisis, but you are not the one I blame."

"But I am responsible."

"You aren't the one who is making me unhappy."

"Then who would you blame, if not me? As your husband, I should make sure you are taken care of, and I failed."

"That's not true, and I don't want you thinking that way."

Before he could reply, an unfamiliar sound came from the monitor. David jumped up racing down the hall into the twins' room, leaving Sophie sitting on the edge of the bed.

Chapter 46

David looked at Grace thinking she was merely exercising her vocal cords, but it wasn't Grace who made the unusual sound. Hearing it again, he turned to check on Faith and gasped when he saw the purplish coloring of her skin and lips, noticing a wheezing noise with each breath she inhaled.

"Sophie, get in here quick," he yelled, instinctively knowing she would hear him through the monitor.

She flew into the room taking one look at David's ashen face before looking down into Faith's crib to see her baby struggling to breathe. Sophie panicked.

"Oh my gosh, oh my gosh, oh my gosh," she repeated, staring at Faith not knowing what to do.

"Keep an eye on her while I grab a phone. I'm calling 911," he commanded, running out of the room.

With the phone to his ear, he answered questions from the emergency person as he locked in on Faith. Discovering it would take approximately fifteen minutes for an ambulance to arrive, he abruptly disconnected the call throwing the phone on the rocking chair seat. He couldn't wait. A lot could happen in fifteen minutes, and his baby needed help now.

"Get Grace, we're taking Faith to the hospital," he ordered as he reached down carefully lifting his daughter, mindful of her breathing. He had never been more scared in his life operating on pure adrenaline. All David knew was that he had to save his baby girl.

They ran out of the house placing the twins in their car carriers. Sophie hopped into the front seat closing the door as David peeled out of the driveway, speeding through the neighborhood, vaguely remembering to put the emergency blinkers on before thrusting into traffic. Sophie remained focused on Faith. David took a quick glance noticing his wife had gone completely pale to the point of concern she might faint.

"Sophie, are you okay?"

"No," she answered, petrified.

"How is Faith doing?"

"I'm not sure, but she's breathing. How much longer?"

"Two more lights."

David expected a police officer would patrol them to the hospital, noticing a speeding vehicle; however, none appeared as he managed to hit every green light pulling into *Florida Hospital's* emergency entrance, parked and grabbed the carrier with Faith in it. Appearing through the automatic sliding doors, he yelled for a doctor as Sophie followed carrying Grace. A nurse approached, seeing an infant was the patient, and immediately ushered them past the registration desk down a short corridor into a private room, instructing David to place the carrier on the examination table.

The nurse took one look at Faith's coloring and pressed an oversized button protruding from the wall, and immediately, hospital personnel stormed the room pushing David and Sophie away from the table. A short, slightly plump man with a thinning hairline wearing round-rimmed glasses ushered through the gathering and unlatched the carrier buckles, lifting Faith and set her on the table. An oxygen mask was placed over her tiny nose and mouth before he reached for the stethoscope from around his neck and listened. Simultaneously, a nurse worked from the opposite side taking Faith's temperature with an ear thermometer and wrapped an infant blood pressure cuff around the calf of her right leg.

Having placed an oximetry clip on Faith's big toe to check

the oxygen level in her blood, the monitor showed seventy-five percentile, and as long as it didn't drop lower, she was out of the critical stage. The pure oxygen through the mask would bring that number up as the nurse spoke aloud, informing the parents of her condition while rhythmically attending to Faith.

David and Sophie had been pushed against a wall making it almost impossible to see what the doctor was doing, yet straining to hear the nurse's comments. David couldn't take his eyes away from the scene, though through his peripheral vision, he saw Sophie silently weeping. Fearful she might drop the carrier holding Grace, he reached for the handle relieving her grip. Rotating Grace to his left hand, he put his right arm around her shoulder holding her close as they waited in that position for what seemed like eternity, until the short man in authority searched them out.

"Your baby is stable for the moment. I need to get her medical history. First, how old is she and then tell me what happened? And by the way, I'm Gary Underwood, the emergency room staff doctor," he said in a monotone voice.

"Her name is Faith, and she is three months old. She is an identical twin. This is her sister, Grace," David replied, lifting the carrier slightly to show Grace to the doctor before continuing.

"Faith has a hole in her heart and is under the care of Dr. Phillip Whalton, a pediatric cardiologist. Her pediatrician is Dr. Tracy Smitherton. We brought her here when we noticed she was struggling to breathe," David said, succinctly.

"I know Dr. Whalton. I'll call his office to let him know I have his patient here. Let's see what he has to say and take it from there. You can stay with your daughter while I go make that call."

He walked away without waiting for a response. They noticed that everyone but one nurse had left the room. David spotted a chair in the far corner and pulled it beside the exam table for Sophie.

"Sophie come sit down," he instructed, gently taking her

hand and leading her to where Faith slept with a clear plastic mask over her face. It was heartbreaking to see her baby so small and helpless lying on a huge gurney under exposing strobe lights. She desperately wanted to pick her up and run out of the emergency room back to their haven where all was safe.

It was cold in the room, so the nurse took a thin print blanket from a closet, and gently placed it over Faith tucking in the sides around her tiny body. Still standing by the gurney, Sophie looked up at the young nurse who smiled at her, such a contrast to how she felt.

"I'm Amelia, and I'll be with your baby while you're here," she said in such a melodious voice, Sophie just stared at her without responding.

Sophie sat down in the chair while David stood next to her with Grace. Approximately forty-five minutes later, Dr. Underwood returned with the news that Dr. Whalton would like Faith to be ambulance transported to the *Thornton Pediatric Diagnostic Center.* They were told it could take as long as an hour to obtain an available ambulance, and in the meantime, there was paperwork requiring David's attention for the hospital's records. A medical staff member from the reception area came in with a mountain of forms on a clipboard and handed it to him.

"Why can't we take Faith home? She's fine now, you said she was stable. I want to take her home instead of to Dr. Whalton's office," Sophie said, speaking up for the first time since they arrived.

"Dr. Whalton needs to examine your daughter to ascertain there has been no change in her condition. It will be up to him whether she goes home. It's out of my hands, at this point, as she is under his care," Dr. Underwood answered, matter-of-fact.

"But if she is alright now, isn't that a decision we make as her parents?" Sophie pushed her point.

"I wish I could grant your wish, but again, it isn't my place to counter a colleague."

"Honey, let's follow the protocol and go see him. It might be for the best," David interjected.

Sophie looked at her husband with disdain. Was he really siding with the doctor? Logically, she knew it made sense to have Faith evaluated by Dr. Whalton before taking her home, but she didn't want to be logical. She wanted to gather her babies and leave, and it didn't help that David wasn't thinking the same thing.

Dr. Underwood left the room, and David continued filling out the forms. Sophie looked down at Grace lying in her carrier nearby and then at Faith asleep with the mask covering most of her face. *Why was this happening?* she asked herself for the umpteenth time.

Chapter 47

The ambulance took Faith with Sophie to the *Thornton Pediatric Diagnostic Center* across town while David and Grace followed behind. It was dusk when they arrived and were ushered into an examination room. No sooner had they sat down, Dr. Whalton came briskly walking in holding a facsimile report from the emergency room.

"I heard we had a little scare today," he began, glancing at Faith in the stroller.

Her coloring had returned to normal thanks to the oxygen supplied a few hours ago. He asked for details.

"Tell me what happened."

"We heard a strange sound through the baby monitor and went into the girls' room to check on them. I arrived first and noticed Faith was making a noise each time she inhaled, and her lips were a funny shade of blue with her over-all coloring off. I called 9ll but couldn't wait for an ambulance, so we gathered the girls and broke every speeding record to get to *Florida Hospital.* It's the closest to our house," David explained.

"What did they do there?"

"We went through the emergency entrance and were immediately taken to an exam room. They put an oxygen mask on Faith and checked her over. Dr. Underwood made the call to you, and now here we are."

"Let's have a look at Faith," Dr. Whalton said, walking to the sink to wash his hands.

David placed Faith on the examination table while Sophie joined her husband, watching the doctor remove the stethoscope from around his neck. Listening carefully for several minutes, he gently rolled Faith to her side and listened from the back.

"I don't hear anything alarming, but I would like to have a chest x-ray done to rule out pneumonia. Sometimes infants and young children can have pneumonia with no outward signs. Her lungs sound clear, but I want to be absolutely sure. We don't want to miss anything, and an x-ray is quick and easy for some peace of mind."

Dr. Whalton looked at Sophie accepting her unhappiness with his insistence of a test being performed. After the experience with the unexplainable coma, he could appreciate her position.

"Faith will be fine, Mrs. McKinley," he told her, attempting to alleviate her fears.

Sophie looked at him without responding. She tried to muster a smile but couldn't bring herself to do that. What was there to smile about, anyway? This was not a happy situation, or a pleasant place to be. David spoke on their behalf.

"We'll do the x-ray if you think it is necessary."

"It's precautionary, and I lean toward always being cautious."

"We understand."

"Good, it takes only minutes. I'll look at the x-ray, and we'll take it from there. In fact, I suggest we do an ultrasound of her heart as well, again, just for precaution. I'll go make the arrangements," he said, without giving them an opportunity to respond.

"I don't like this," Sophie spoke the minute the door closed.

"It's just a couple of tests and will take a load off our mind before we go home. I would feel better knowing, and I'm sure

228

you would also."

"Of course, but I'm not comfortable in this place. Faith shouldn't be anyone's patient. This whole thing isn't right, David," she said with more grit than she had shown in the past several weeks.

"I agree."

Before David could continue, the door opened and Dr. Whalton walked in handing two scripts to him.

"Take these to the third floor. When you're done come back and check in with the receptionist. It might take an hour or longer depending on how busy they are. I phoned the radiology department, so they are expecting you and requested STAT, but sometimes that doesn't get things done any faster. I'll see you later," he said, before leaving the room.

Sophie picked up Faith and held her close. Why won't they leave her baby alone? *More tests*, she thought. But at least they would be quick, painless and require no anesthesia which she wouldn't allow anyway as she consoled herself to the situation.

They went upstairs to the third floor and checked in with the receptionist, a familiar face, and sat waiting their turn. Approximately thirty minutes later, they were escorted to a small room for the ultrasound which was performed, un-eventfully, and then sent to x-ray down the hall. Walking down a long corridor, they were met by a technician and led to a large, dark room illuminated by only a lamp with oversized equipment hanging from the ceiling. It was a bit scary seeing the huge metal machines sprawled around a long, narrow table. The extended arms from the piece situated directly over the table appeared as though it would gobble up anything placed in its path. Sophie thought it was downright creepy. Apparently her expression revealed her thoughts because the technician looked at her with sympathy.

"Don't look so worried. We aren't using that machine. I'm using a much smaller one that I'll roll over here to the table. In fact, I'll show you, nothing to be concerned about," the young male told her.

Sophie watched as he went to a corner of the room and wheeled over a boxed piece of equipment. He spoke the truth for it wasn't nearly as intimidating as the monster machine overhead.

"This is the one for the x-ray. They called down with the details, but I do need that script from you for our records."

David slipped it out of his shirt pocket and handed it to him.

"By the way, my name is Bruce, and I'll be taking care of our Miss Faith. If you'll place her in the middle of the table, I'll put an extra sheet down to insulate Faith from the chill coming through the stainless steel. I know its cold in here, but we have to keep the temperature low for the equipment. Okay, which one of you wants to stay with her, the other has to wait outside the door."

"I will," they both said, simultaneously.

David and Sophie looked at each other, but David quickly relented. He took Grace to wait just outside in the hallway. The technician followed him closing the door, and upon returning, grabbed a heavy drape-like coat handing it to Sophie.

"Put this on in front and secure it to protect you of any radiation from the x-ray," he instructed.

Doing as she was told, Sophie thought about all the radiation they would be shooting into her baby's body. What about Faith's protection? In deep concentration, she missed the actual x-ray being taken.

"Now see, that wasn't so bad."

Sophie glanced at the technician without saying a word while taking off the heavy drape and handing it to him. She gathered her baby and practically ran out of the room without a backward glance. It might have appeared rude, but she couldn't help herself.

Before going to Dr. Whalton's office and waiting for the results, they went to the cafeteria for dinner. Having food and supplies readily available in the twins' diaper bag, Sophie was thankful she remembered to grab it on their quick exit. Now she could relax, somewhat, to feed her babies. Sophie wasn't breastfeeding as much since they were sampling baby cereals, so formula was kept available. She prepared the bottles while David went to stand in line. Surprisingly, neither of the twins had complained about being hungry.

David brought a tray with two sandwiches, fruit salads, chips and iced teas. While Sophie held Faith feeding her a bottle, David placed the tray on the table and took Grace holding her in his lap doing the same. They didn't speak, each consumed by their own somber thoughts, and their attention devoted to their girls.

With the twins fed, freshened up and back in the stroller, David and Sophie ate their simple meal. He noticed Sophie wasn't speaking and wondered if she was angry at him. Eating in silence was unnerving as they had spent the past several hours emotionally depleted and with no opportunity to discuss anything. David couldn't wait until this dreadful day was over and he had his family home.

Chapter 48

They were directed to wait in the doctor's office for the results. David reached over and took Sophie's hand, and held it firmly in his. She looked down at their entwined fingers and was about to say something when Dr. Whalton walked in with an x-ray and papers in his hand. Just like before, he sat in a smaller chair in front of them making direct eye contact. Sophie was getting a real bad feeling because this was his same pose when he told them about Faith's heart.

"I'm going to give it to you straight up. The good news is no pneumonia, her lungs are clear. However, the ultrasound shows some rather disturbing changes in her heart," he said, pausing for this news to sink in.

"What do mean?" David asked, alarmed.

"The hole has perforated; there is a tear."

"Wait a minute. You're saying the hole is torn, ripped. How could that possibly happen?"

"That's a good question, but I don't have an answer for you. These things occur, and we don't always know why. What I do know is that it is causing her heart to work harder to pump the blood. It needs to be repaired, and there is no longer an option to wait."

"Is this why she was laboring to breathe and turned purple?" David asked, ignoring the implication of immediate surgery.

"Yes, whenever she gets excited, she breathes deeper, and

that was probably the sound you heard. Being quiet, her breathing is shallow and appears fine. It's when Faith becomes excited that she pulls more air through her lungs, and this works against her heart."

No way! This is not happening, Sophie chanted in her head. *No way, no way, no way!* She was trying to block out the sound of the doctor's voice and the words he spoke, but it was only partially effective. Sophie kept the chant going letting her own inner voice rise louder in her mind, skipping over the exterior volume. It was all just a regurgitated hum to her now.

"I strongly suggest we admit her to our surgical wing and schedule the surgery."

"Is there really a need to rush? She seems fine now," David asked.

"It is never an easy decision to make when surgery is the only option for a child. However, in Faith's case and especially with this latest development, it has already become detrimental to her wellbeing. Not attended to could be fatal," he said, pressing his point that they not take this situation lightly.

Sophie couldn't block the word *fatal*. It jolted her back to reality. David took a quick glance at her seeing she was white as a bleached sheet. He was still holding tightly to her hand and felt her go stone cold.

"Could we go home for a couple of days?" David asked.

"That is not an option. Faith should be admitted. Since we don't know what has caused this tear in her heart, I'm concerned it will continue to perforate causing blood to pool in a chamber and not be properly pumped through the heart. Time is really not on our side at the moment. I can't stress enough the severity of the situation. I'm sorry. I wish it didn't have to be this way, but we have to do what is necessary to save Faith's life."

Sophie just died. Her own heart had stopped beating the precise second she heard the finality of Dr. Whalton's voice when he said, *save Faith's life*. Those three words echoed in her ears as the room spun into blackness. This was the end as she felt her body spiraling downward.

Chapter 49

David felt the release of pressure from Sophie's hand a split second before she went limp, sliding off the edge of the sofa, catching her body just before she hit the floor. Pulling his wife back and laying her on the sofa, Dr. Whalton stepped beside David ushering him to the side so he could attend to her, lifting her eyelids and flashing a pencil-sharp light into her eyes.

"I'm terribly sorry the news caused your wife such distress. I'll get a nurse in here," he said absently, walking toward his desk and picking up the phone.

David thought there must be a code used for emergencies because a nurse appeared in the room before the phone was back in its cradle. She glanced toward Sophie and then at the doctor.

"Bring some smelling salts. She'll be alright, she just fainted," Dr. Whalton told the nurse when she looked, again, toward the sofa.

David had never seen Sophie faint before and hoped he never had to witness it again. It took the life right out of him. Seeing the panicked look on David's face, Dr. Whalton felt uneasy to cause them both such stress. Giving people unpleasant news was the part of his job he disliked. On days like this, he was grateful he wasn't a family man.

The nurse rushed in handing a small, narrow foiled envelope to the doctor. He peeled the flaps at one end and waved the ammonia strip under Sophie's nose, causing her to turn her face away from the offensive odor. Upon opening her eyes, she saw three pairs staring down at her. *Who were these people and why are they looking at me so strangely?* she wondered. Then she recognized her husband and focused on him as the realization that she had fainted bore through her foggy mental state. She had never fainted in her life. Sophie watched as David squatted down next to her face.

"Are you okay?" he asked, gently smoothing her hair from her face.

"I don't know."

"Do you think you can sit up?"

"I'll try."

David took her arms helping Sophie to a sitting position, and then sat down next to her putting his arm around her shoulder. She leaned into him resting her head on his chest still feeling slightly dizzy.

"Would you like a glass of water?" Dr. Whalton asked, sympathetic to her plight.

"Yes, thank you," she replied, without looking at him.

The nurse left the room and returned with a clear, plastic cup of water. Sophie didn't like being the focal point of attention as she became more cognizant to her surroundings. She sought out her babies, and they were both in the stroller just as she had last seen them.

"I want to go home," she said to her husband.

"So do I, honey, but I don't think we can leave just yet," he said, looking at the doctor.

"David, I want to take our girls and go home, now," she stated more emphatically.

"I know."

Sophie attempted to get up from the sofa, but David held her back. His arm was still draped over her shoulder.

"Let go, David. I want to get up."

He removed his arm.

"We can't take Faith home right now, Sophie. We have to

stay here and get her checked into a room."

Sophie looked at him as though he had slapped her. Ignoring her husband, she turned to Dr. Whalton with the same determination.

"I appreciate your concern, Dr. Whalton, but I'm taking my babies and going home," she told him, standing up.

She swayed struggling to gain her balance as her equilibrium was affected by the blackout. Sophie stood still for a moment hoping it would soon pass because she had to get out of this place.

"Mrs. McKinley, there isn't anything I would like better than for you to do just that, but I can't agree to Faith leaving," he told her, trying to be as empathic as possible.

"You can't stop me. I'm their mother, and if I want to take my babies home, I will," she said, raising her voice.

Placing her hands on the stroller handle in an attempt to leave the room, she was stopped by her husband. Rising from the sofa and standing next to her, he put his hand on her shoulder.

"Honey, we can't," he said, gently.

"Maybe you can't, but I can," she told him, shrugging her shoulder to dislodge his hand.

"Sophie, no. Neither you, nor I can take the girls home. Faith has to stay. We would be putting her life in danger if we did. I know you don't want to do that."

"David, I can't do this. You know I can't. It would kill me to have her cut open. And look what we went through with the anesthesia. What if she ends up in a permanent coma, or worse for it?"

"I feel the same way you do, but if we take her home and something happens, I could never forgive myself."

David needed Sophie to be realistic and see the severity of the situation, but before they continued any further, Dr. Whalton interrupted.

"It isn't a choice any longer. As Faith's physician, I can not allow either of you to remove her from the premises in this condition. I would be liable should I permit you to leave with Faith. The responsibility defaults to me," he said, getting back to business.

He turned to the nurse, who remained in the room for further instructions, and dictated a list of things for her to do. First, she was to call over to the south wing, their surgical center, and make sure a room was available for Faith and get her on the schedule for first thing in the morning. This latest development with the perforation worried him. Time may be running out for this little girl.

Sophie gripped the handlebar of the stroller so tightly her knuckles turned white. Not feeling her best at the moment, she was appalled by Dr. Whalton's directness. He was actually forbidding her to remove her babies from the premises. Isn't there some law against holding someone against their will? He can't make her do this. She had rights, they are her children.

"You can't keep us here against our will. What if I don't agree with your medical advice?"

Sophie pushed back.

"Then you are welcome to switch her care to another physician."

"Okay, that's what I want to do."

"That is acceptable to me. I can have one of my colleagues take over her care."

"That won't be necessary. I'll find a doctor myself," she replied, attempting to push the stroller past him, but he didn't budge.

"Mrs. McKinley, I still cannot allow you to leave with Faith. She is too sick. If you choose to bring in another specialist, I will be glad to relinquish her medical records, however, she still must remain at the center," he told her with as much compassion as he could muster.

He knew she was acting on fear. The coma experience was still fresh, and the images running through her mind of her baby having heart surgery could only be a nightmare. He understood her position, but she also had to come to terms with his.

David didn't know what to say as Sophie battled with the doctor. He didn't like the situation but was able to accept the news far better than his wife. She was going to have to find a way to live with it. The perforation in Faith's heart was enlarging and only surgery would correct it, unless of course, you believed in miracles. Surgery was inevitable.

Chapter 50

Dr. Whalton escorted them to the surgical wing. Catching the elevator near his office, they rode up to the fifth floor and continued trekking through winding corridors until they reached unmarked double doors. Stepping ahead, he pressed a few numbered buttons on a small panel recessed in the wall, and the doors automatically swung open into a hospital environment.

David was pushing the stroller and Sophie, reluctantly, walked by his side attempting to maintain her composure. She didn't want Dr. Whalton, or his staff, to witness the extent of her unstable emotions. They wouldn't understand the devastation that consumed her piercing the very core of her soul, not wanting to be depicted as a distraught mother.

Intellectually, she rationalized that David didn't want this surgery for Faith anymore than she did; however, emotionally, it angered her that he was handling everything so calmly. He should be just as upset with Dr. Whalton for dictating what they do and taking away their parental rights. She had never felt so alone and betrayed as she did at this exact moment. Sophie accepted her viewpoint could be construed as irrational because children go through surgery all the time. So why was this affecting her so deeply? Fear consumed her.

She followed as they were led into a private room painted pale yellow with nursery rhyme appliqués on the walls. A crib was settled against the longest wall with a rocking chair angled in a corner. A small vinyl-covered sofa was situated under the window which unfolded into a daybed. Obviously, the attempt was to replicate a nursery because it didn't resemble a hospital room. There was no equipment visible to the eye, but they discovered it was quickly assessable from behind the flushed cabinet doors on the walls. Sophie had to give them credit for the décor.

Dr. Whalton instructed the nurse, who followed them into the room, to bring another crib for the convenience of Grace having her own bed. Sophie went to sit on the sofa while David spoke with the doctor. She had the stroller in front of her focused on the twins, intentionally blocking Dr. Whalton's voice, not wanting to hear anything else he had to say. Her attention went to Faith lying so peacefully. You would never know anything was wrong, and her precious Faith had no idea what she was facing.

Sophie could no longer control the tears as her thoughts roamed to the inevitable. David came to sit beside her when Dr. Whalton left the room and was heartbroken to see her crying. He reached for his wife's hand lying in her lap, but Sophie jerked it away. She didn't want to hold hands. That wasn't going to make her feel better. David didn't know what to say to get Sophie to accept their fate. It seemed she blamed him.

"Sophie, being angry with me isn't going to help our situation. Right now, we need to be together and support each other for Faith."

"Don't tell me what I need. You lost that privilege when you sided with the doctors. How could you do that, David?"

"I haven't done that," he replied, stunned by her remark.

"What about making the surgery appointment behind my back?"

"This is not the time for us to be in opposition. Dr. Whalton wants to do the surgery in the morning. The nurse will be in later to give us the instructions for the night. You will have to find a way to accept this. It will be behind us by tomorrow evening, so try to look far enough ahead, and think about it being over within hours from now."

That was not a comforting thought for Sophie.

"That's what you said to me over the procedure and look where that got us. Faith went into a coma. Things could be a lot worse in a few hours. Neither you nor the doctor are privy to know what may happen."

"We've had this conversation before, but I'll ask again. What other choice do we have? Give me something else to consider, and I'll be more than glad to agree to another option. There isn't one. We can't take Faith home, we can't do a thing but what the doctor tells us to do. I don't like this anymore than you do, but frankly, I'm glad the decision has been taken out of our hands and something is getting done. No more delays and if that hurts your feelings, I'm sorry."

"See, I knew all long you sided with the doctors. You just proved it. You really don't care how I feel, or what could happen to our baby," she said, lowering her head.

"I care very much, and that is a low blow to say I don't. I love you and our daughters and would do anything for you, anything. I can't produce a miracle, and right now, we both know that is what our daughter needs. I'm just as scared as you are for what may happen when she is on the operating table, but I'm trying hard not to think about it."

Sophie couldn't deal with this conversation any longer, not wanting to hear David's statements of proclamation. She knew better than to question his love for her, that wasn't the issue. Logically, she accepted David was right about them being supportive toward each other during this critical time, but she couldn't bring herself to get past the pain she felt.

Without saying a word, she reached into the stroller and picked up Faith. Holding her against her breast, she clung tightly as she swayed back and forth humming a lullaby. Her baby would be sliced open in the morning, and she wasn't able to get the image out of her mind. How long would they make the incision? Would it be down to her cute little belly button? Would her body be all black and blue with bruises? How much pain would she have to endure and for how long before she cried no more? Sophie truly didn't think she was going to survive. Everything was closing in fast, and she had no say in the matter.

Tears silently slid down her cheeks as she whispered into her baby's ear. Sophie didn't even know what she was saying, but she wanted Faith to hear her voice and know that mommy loved her. Oh, the agony. The pain was cutting deep like a two-edged sword. With her eyes closed, unaware of her surroundings, she engulfed them into an invisible cocoon. It was the movement of David leaving her side that caused Sophie to open her eyes.

Accepting the conversation had ended, David lifted Grace from the stroller and placed her in one of the cribs with a soft toy. He stood watching Grace and wondered, as an identical twin, how much did she sense wrong with her sister? Through the years, he had witnessed the closeness between Sophie and Sabrina with their innate ability to tune-in to the other. Did Grace and Faith have that same kind of connection?

Sophie couldn't release Faith to her crib. She continued to hold her baby, perhaps unconsciously guarding her young as best she knew, daring anyone to come and take Faith from her. She didn't try to analyze it. She was trapped with no one to help her, and no where to go, and time was running out. In the early morning hours, Dr. Whalton would request Faith to be brought to the operating room. David encouraged her to look beyond the surgery to when it would be over, but she couldn't bring herself to do that. Thinking ahead wouldn't help her get through this.

The door to their room was closed blocking outside corridor noises which made the room very quiet. Sophie wanted to scream at David for the betrayal she felt, but what good would that do? He asked her to give him another resolution, and she wanted desperately to do that and put an end to this insane ordeal. They were barely speaking to one another, and when they did, there was no better restitution for

243

it. *How much more alone could she possibly feel?* she silently cried.

Fleetingly, she thought of Brie, and knew she should call and let her know what was happening. How strange that her first thought when they were checked into the surgical wing wasn't to contact her twin. Typically, her sister would be the one person she would want by her side for support and especially since she and David weren't close at the moment. Brie would be upset for the postponement in contacting her.

Sophie decided to phone when the girls were settled for the night, knowing Brie would take the first flight out of Asheville. However, there was no rush unless her sister could perform a miracle, for surely that was the only saving grace for Faith.

Chapter 51

David felt helpless and terrified for what was ahead. He and Sophie should be together supporting each other and here they were barely speaking to one another. He didn't know how it got to this point, and wished he could wipe away the pain he saw reflected in her eyes. The estrangement and his own misery were consuming him, and David feared after the surgery things may never be the same between them.

Without saying a word, he walked out of the room needing time to think and rode the elevator down to the first floor. Stepping outside, David walked around the building to a small, private garden with wrought-iron benches and sat. Alone, he bent forward placing his elbows on his knees, holding his head in open hands. Covering his face, David wept. He was desperate, but who could help him? Who could erase the heartache they both felt, and most of all, who could repair Faith's heart and make everything right? As ineffectual as he believed it to be, he prayed.

David knew Sophie blamed him for everything that was happening, and he couldn't hold it against her. From her perspective, it would appear he was supporting the doctor's decision for the surgery, but truthfully, the idea made him sick. Though he couldn't seem to convey his true feelings to her, he hated the entrapment.

He remained in this position as tears flowed down his

cheeks. It was the first time he had outwardly expressed his own emotional suffering. He didn't want Sophie to see the severity of his distress, believing it would only add to her despair. David leaned back on the bench, pulling out a handkerchief wiping the remnants of his pain, while staring blankly at the ground. What could he say to Sophie that would make her realize he wasn't the bad guy in this situation?

He thought of his sister-in-law and wondered if Sophie had called Brie in his absence. *Surely she has by now,* he thought, opting to talk to her as there was no one else to share the situation but Sabrina. Pulling out the cell phone from his shirt pocket, he pressed the speed-dial button and waited. Brie answered on the third ring, noticing the caller was David.

"David, what's wrong?" she asked, knowing something wasn't right for him to be calling her.

"We're at *Thornton Pediatric Diagnostic Center.* The doctor wants to do surgery in the morning," he blurted out as tears slid down his face.

"Tell me what happened," she insisted.

"Faith wasn't breathing right, so we rushed her to the emergency room, and they transferred her here by ambulance a little while ago. Dr. Whalton says she has a perforation at the area of the hole in her heart that could rapidly become a life-threatening matter," David explained as matter-of-fact as possible.

"Oh, David, I'm so sorry. How is Sophie handling this?"

"You mean she hasn't called you."

"No, I haven't heard from her. I'll get there as soon as I can, but it may be very late when I arrive. Give me your room number, and I'll find you. And David, please don't say anything about my arriving. Let me deal with Sophie when I get there. For her not to call, speaks volumes to me."

"Alright, if you think that is the best way. I don't know the right words to say to her anymore," he confided.

"I know you're upset, but trust me when I tell you every-thing will turn out okay."

"You sound so confident. If you only knew how much I want you to be right."

"We're going to get through this unfortunate situation. There is a rainbow at the end of this gloomy cloud. I promise you, David."

"I sure hope you're correct. I need to get back to the room. See you soon and thanks, Brie."

"I'll be there in a few hours, hang in there," she said, before ending the call.

Under different circumstances, Sabrina might take offense to her sister's lack of a courtesy phone call. However, considering the magnitude of what Sophie was dealing with, Brie didn't take it personally. This was going to be extremely hard for Sophie if she doesn't have a change of heart and soon, Brie thought. She could only pray that her twin came to that realization.

Chapter 52

David had one more call to make. Pressing the button on the cell phone to the automated school line, he left a message of his unavailability for the next several days, explaining that one of his daughters was in the hospital. At the moment, he wasn't concerned who taught his students. The school personnel would make the necessary arrangements.

He returned to the room to find Sophie just as he had left her holding Faith, but she had moved to the chair rocking their baby. Sophie's eyes were closed. David noticed Grace was awake, yet quiet. Not wanting to disturb them, he went to the sofa and sat down.

Observing the mother of his babies sitting in this sterile environment caused more anguish. It was only a few months ago when the twins were born, and they were the happiest parents taking their newborns home. Now, they sit in a hospital room. He felt alienated from his wife. Tears welled up in his eyes again.

There was nothing he could do for Faith to prevent what was about to happen, and apparently, nothing to be said to help his wife deal with it. *What kind of a husband and father am I if I can't take care of my family?* he chastised himself. The emotional pain ripped through his heart as though it was about to explode. Never in his life had David encountered such sorrow. He must have made a sound because Sophie opened her eyes looking directly at him. Suddenly, he felt foolish sitting there crying, never meaning for her to see him this way. David quickly wiped his face across his sleeve and looked away.

Sophie knew this would be just as hard on David, though she didn't give it much thought because of her own inward grief. After all, he was the one in compliance with the surgery, so surely he wouldn't be overly distraught about the matter. However, seeing his tears, something she had never witnessed before, made her deeply saddened. She didn't know what to say. It wasn't right to blame him for the circumstances of Faith's surgery, yet deep down, that is exactly what she was doing. She needed a scapegoat and he was her target. It didn't make her feel better for it, especially when she saw the vulnerability in him. Intellectually, it wasn't fair to David; however, emotionally she needed the crutch. *What do they do now?* she wondered.

David turned his attention back to his wife waiting for her to speak first, but when she didn't say anything, he knew he should make the attempt to reconcile their differences. He had to at least do that, he thought. Not planning what to say, he simply spoke from his heart and hoped it would be enough. What else could he do?

"Sophie, I'm so sorry we're here with Faith's life hanging in the balance. I never imagined we would ever be facing something so serious, and I know these past few months, you somehow think I approve of the surgery. But if you only knew how much I detest this. Inasmuch as I worry for Faith, it grieves me even more that you are suffering. To see the pain in your eyes, and to think that somehow I am responsible for it, tears me apart, and I don't know how to make things right. I'm at a loss what to say to convince you how much I love you, and the girls, and that I hate what we are going through and what it has done to us. I'm so sorry for everything," he said solemnly, bending his head down.

There was a part of Sophie that wanted to say the words David needed to hear from her, but she couldn't seem to speak them. It was selfish to withhold comfort, but her anger over the situation was overriding her compassion, she held back. She loved David and knew it wasn't right to hold him captive with her harsh behavior, but she just couldn't seem to help herself.

David looked at her anticipating a response, but when she sat silent and staring, it cut deep. It was truly at this moment he accepted the magnitude of her indifference and wondered if she even loved him anymore. Had it come to that? He had to know.

"Sophie, do you love me?"

She never expected he would question her love for him. Sophie would not have David thinking otherwise, so she spoke the truth. No matter what their differences to issues in their marriage, she positively would not have him believing she didn't love him. That would be cruel.

"I do love you, David. Please, don't doubt that. You know this is hard for me. I abhor it to the core of my being, but it doesn't change how I feel about you. I love you," she told him.

"That makes me feel better. At least, I haven't lost your love. We love each other, and we will get through this," David said, more confident than he felt.

Before Sophie could reply, a nurse entered with instructions of NPO after midnight for Faith. Sophie looked over at David, and their eyes locked, but neither spoke. It was the first official order of many to come. No food or substance for Faith after midnight. It had begun.

Chapter 53

They silently prepared the twins for bed with a quick sponge bath, fresh clothes, feeding and spending time playing with them later than their usual bedtime. As the clock slowly ticked away the hours, Sophie's apprehension grew by leaps and bounds. One wrong word spoken to her and she would lose that last remaining emotional thread.

When they couldn't delay any longer settling the girls for the night, Sophie took Grace first and rocked her for awhile holding her close. Once Grace fell asleep, she settled her in the middle of the mattress placing a thin blanket over her. Then she took Faith from David and went to the rocking chair. Holding her baby girl knowing what was to come was killing her. Was she the only mother to feel this way? *Surely not,* she thought.

Sophie wasn't certain which she feared more, the anesthesia or the knife as both were horrid to her. The previous experience with the anesthesia had her in a panic, flooding her mind with unacceptable conclusions. She continually whispered sweet love words to her baby, until reluctantly, laid a sleeping Faith in her crib. Not able to bring herself to leave Faith's side, David approached putting his arm around Sophie's shoulder. She didn't pull away but rather stood perfectly still fighting the tears that pooled in her eyes.

"I'm going down to the cafeteria to get us something to eat. You need to keep up your strength. I won't be gone long.

Will you be okay?" he asked when he saw tears sliding down her cheeks.

She merely nodded her head and watched him walk out of the room closing the door quietly behind him. Sophie stood all alone in the illuminated room with only a nightlight glowing from a built-in wall unit near the baseboard. She focused her attention on Faith thinking back to the beginning when they were first told of the hole in her heart. Nothing has been the same since.

Her thoughts fast-forwarded to what tomorrow might bring, and her heart began to race in her chest. The fear was so exact and absolute it engulfed her. Each time her thoughts drifted to the unknown in the hours ahead, she felt the panic rise within her. Sophie didn't know how to control her emotions, but she had to find a way before morning. *Why am I having such a hard time with this?* she questioned herself.

Feeling isolated and alone with no hope in sight, Sophie broke down and wept. This time she didn't hold back. Every negative emotion came spewing out of her with each tear that slid down her cheek dripping onto her baby's blanket, spotting a wet section. Without knowing she had spoken the words aloud, she cursed God. Words of anger were ripped from her soul, relinquished like a burning whip, slapping at the one she blamed. This was His fault, and she wanted Him to know exactly how she felt. Pain seared her heart as she cried out in agony.

She felt no concern for waking her babies. Sophie wanted to strike out and cause the same kind of torture she was enduring, but it didn't make her feel any better. Weakened from the ordeal, she slowly slid to the floor. This was how Sabrina found her when she opened the door to glance inside the room before entering. Sophie's head was bent forward, so she didn't see her sister walk past her to the sofa.

Brie sat quietly without making a sound and waited. She heard enough of Sophie's accusations toward God, condemning Him with every word spoken. When Sophie finally spoke again, there was such despair in her voice, it broke Brie's heart to hear it.

"Why, God? Why are you doing this to me? I don't understand what I have done that was so terrible you would do this to my baby. I know you are doing this, but I don't know how to fix whatever I did wrong. What do I need to say to convince you to stop? I just don't know anything, anymore," she pleaded, unsure of how to get God's attention. Sophie was willing to do whatever it took to save her baby, even approach the one she held responsible.

The desolation she felt was beyond anything she had ever experienced, even the death of her parents. Nothing compares when it's your own child. Sophie wasn't sure God was listening to her. After all, she had lived many years without His presence in her life. Knowing logically, He was the only one with the power to change the events that were unfolding with Faith, she wasn't sure she knew how to reach Him. Would He accept her plea for help when she had treated Him so badly? She didn't know, but He was her last hope. How ironic, she thought, to have to go to the very one she blamed.

Sophie sat quietly for a few minutes with her head downward as tears flowed from her eyes dripping into her lap. The excruciating pain in her heart was so sharp she thought it would cut her in half leaving her for dead at that very spot. This was the only way to save Faith from her predicted fate. It was a hard lesson to learn, and as much as she wanted it to be otherwise, Sophie was smart enough to know there was only one person with the power to change the circumstances. It was imperative she accept that only God could help her; if He would. She had to try again, and began to pray. She didn't know what else to do. She was willing to beg.

"God, I don't know how to pray, but I will try and hope you are listening. I'm sorry for the words I spoke earlier toward you. I'm so angry and hurt that I wanted to strike out. I've blamed you for a long time for a lot of things. I've always believed you controlled the good and the bad that happens to

us, and maybe that is the way you work. I don't understand that part. But I know you can heal Faith's heart. You are the only one who can make this right. That is, if you will. I do believe that, now. Can you look past my mistakes and forgive me for the wrongful things I have said and done? God, please, please heal my baby's heart. She just can't go through surgery. Please God, not for me but do it for Faith. She's just an innocent baby," she said through unrestrained tears.

David walked in carrying a tray loaded with food. He took one look at his wife on the floor, and Brie sitting on the small sofa, and stopped in his tracks. Brie quickly placed her right index finger over her mouth indicating that Sophie wasn't aware of her presence. Sophie looked up to see David place the tray on a nearby table. Catching a movement in her peripheral vision, she turned toward the sofa to see her sister. Standing up, embarrassed that anyone would have witnessed her behavior, her first words were curt.

"How long have you been sitting there?"

"Not long. I didn't want to disturb you, and by the way, why didn't you call me, immediately?" Brie asked, deflecting the embarrassment her sister felt.

"Well, I can see David took care of that," Sophie replied, sharply.

"He called assuming you already had. So what's with that?" Brie asked, ignoring her sister's tone.

David walked over giving Brie a hug.

"Thanks for coming. We need you to be here with us. Why don't you both sit down and eat this food before it gets cold, and I'll go back down to the cafeteria and get another plate for myself," he instructed.

Before exiting, he stopped and turned toward Sophie.

"Honey, are you okay?"

"No, but go and get your dinner."

Brie walked over to Sophie, still standing by the crib, and put her arms around her sister. It took Sophie a moment to warm into the embrace. Finally relaxing her stance, she held tightly to Brie for a few seconds before letting go.

"Everything is going to be alright," Brie spoke softly, while looking at Faith.

"You heard me, didn't you?"

"Some."

"I'm sorry I didn't call you right away. I was going to later tonight. I knew you would want to get here as soon as you could, but there's nothing you can do."

"Come over here and let's eat," Brie told her, taking the tray and arranging it carefully on the sofa.

There would be plenty of time to discuss things later. Brie sat down taking a plate of meatloaf, mashed potatoes and green beans. Sophie took one look at all that food and it turned her stomach. She had no appetite and didn't think she could eat. Seeing Sophie staring at her plate, Brie encouraged her.

"Sophie, you have to eat something. You need to keep up your strength."

"I'll try," she said, picking up the fork and pushing the food around on the plate.

She took small bites of the mashed potatoes, but it wasn't sitting well on her stomach, so she put the fork down.

David reappeared with his own meal and noticed Sophie had not eaten.

"Honey, you need to eat."

"I can't eat this."

"Can you try the mashed potatoes, or the dinner roll?"

"I tried a couple bites of the potatoes. Maybe I can eat the bread," she replied, reaching for the roll on her plate.

She just couldn't do it. Even the smell of the food was making her sick. The mood was solemn as David and Sabrina ate their meal in silence in the dimly lit room. Conversation was not needed.

Chapter 54

David excused himself to return the plates to the cafeteria and informed them he was taking a short walk outside, leaving them alone for awhile. Sabrina quietly walked over to the cribs to see Grace and Faith asleep. Brie gently touched Grace's back, and she stirred with barely a detectable movement of her lips which was gone in a fraction of a second. Placing her hand on Faith's tiny chest right over her heart got minimal response. Brie knew Faith had weakened considerably. Sophie slipped up beside her sister.

"What are you doing?" she asked, watching Sabrina touch her girls.

"I'm saying hello to them," Brie said, easily.

They don't know you're here. You're going to wake them if you keep doing that," she scolded.

"First, I'm not going to wake them, and secondly, they do know that I'm here. I'll prove it to you. Watch closely."

It was time to openly expose to Sophie a revelation that soon would be expounded on. They stepped over to Grace's crib and observed her sleeping. Sabrina gently laid her right hand on the middle of Grace's back. Not only did she move, but a tiny smile appeared on her lips. Sophie witnessed it.

"You are disturbing her."

"No, I'm not. She is aware of my presence and letting me know."

"That's absurd."

"Alright, you try it."

Sophie looked down at Grace, and then at Brie, and couldn't ignore the dare. She did the same as Brie, but Grace didn't budge. She did it again, but this time with a little pressure to make sure Grace felt the hand on her back, nothing. Feeling slighted, Sophie practically urged Brie to do it again, believing it wouldn't happen. This time Brie laid her hand on Grace's arm, and she squirmed letting out a soft sigh. Without a word, Sophie did the same. Grace didn't even flinch for being touched on her bare arm by her mother. Stepping away from the crib, Sophie stared at her sister not wanting to believe there was a special bond between Brie and her nieces, yet Sophie's eyes told her the truth just as before.

"I don't understand it, but then, I always knew there was something between you and the twins the moment they were born. I remember in the hospital how they responded to you, and no newborn has that capability. I saw it and will admit to being jealous and should be now, but instead, I'm finding myself more curious than upset. Don't you think it is time to share this with me?" Sophie asked, putting her sister on the spot.

"Yes, and I will soon."

"Why not right now? We have the time, no one is going anywhere."

"I would rather concentrate on Faith. She is the reason we're here, and the one in need of our help."

"I don't know what to do. I want more than anything for this to go away and take her home where she belongs."

"Will you let me help you with Faith?" Brie asked.

"If you remember, I asked you once for your help, and you said you couldn't. We both know this will take a miracle."

"This is true; however, you wanted me to provide that miracle for you. You have not forgotten who gives miracles, but were so unjustly angry with God, you didn't want to ask Him for it."

Sophie looked at the serious expression on her sister's face as her words hit a nerve, but strangely, she wasn't compelled to argue her position. Perhaps, unconsciously, it was easier to approach her sister having witnessed some kind of phenomena with her babies, hoping Sabrina could supernaturally promote a healing of Faith's heart. Now she accepted that, unintentionally, she had placed an unspoken burden on her sister. It was misguided anger she held against her twin when Brie didn't accommodate.

"I'm sorry, Brie. I didn't realize how much pressure I had placed on you for a resolution. I became distant and angry when you wouldn't comply with my demands the way I wanted you to, and admit I fought your way, to turn to God. I'm so sorry," Sophie told her, getting teary-eyed again.

"Oh, Sophie, what is important is that you have turned to our heavenly Father. I heard your prayer, but most importantly, He heard it. You can't imagine how that makes me feel. I am so blessed right now for your sake. Do you understand what I'm saying to you?"

"Yes, I actually think I do."

The disdain she once felt when Brie spoke of God seemed to have vanished. In its place, she felt an urgent need to believe in someone; no, not just someone, but in God. She needed to believe again in God and turn to Him.

"I've already asked for His help, but I don't think He will want to give me a miracle for my baby. I said some nasty things to Him earlier."

"Don't you believe He has forgiven you?"

"Yes, I do think that works for some people, but I've held a grudge against God for a long time. I have years of actually hating Him. He's not going to find me worthy of forgiving any time soon."

"You have to know that God didn't take our parents from us, and once you pray and ask Him to forgive you, it is forgotten; erased. You are the one holding these thoughts against yourself, and it's time to let go. You need His help right now for Faith. Trust Him; it's the only way, Sophie. If you really want to save Faith from the surgery, you must accept God wants to do this for you even more than you want it."

"If you heard me earlier, then you know I was pleading with Him. I don't see anything any different going on here, so I guess He didn't feel I was worth the trouble."

"I really hope, for Faith's sake, you don't believe what you just said. Certainly you aren't still depicting God as an unforgiving, merciless Father."

"Perhaps not merciless but maybe unforgiving at times, like now."

"Do you believe He would want to give Faith a miracle?" Brie asked, pressing her point.

"Yes, I believe He would want to heal her, but I don't think He will because of me."

"Ask Him again, and this time put your whole heart and soul into the prayer. Your miracle is there. Who do you think gave me my special abilities?"

Sophie stood frozen by that statement as though she was suddenly smacked in the forehead. What was Brie saying? Did God give her something special, and if so, would He do the same for her? Is that what this is all about, her innate ability to communicate with her nieces? Could she get a miracle, after all? *No, that wasn't possible,* she argued with herself.

"What are you saying? Are you telling me God gave you something?"

"Yes, Sophie, God gave me something very special."

"Why would He do that for you?"

"Only God knows the reason for what He does."

She had to think about this. If God can give her sister something phenomenal, would He be willing to do the same for her?

"I think that is truly wonderful for you, but I don't see it happening for me. I haven't been worthy of anything from God."

"Sophie, if you believe God loves you and that He forgives, then you have to know He wants only good things for

His children. You and I, David and the twins, we are all His children and no matter what we may have done in the past, if we say we're sorry, He does forgive."

"I prayed after I cursed Him. He may not have thought I meant it after the terrible things I said to Him."

"God is looking at your heart, and not so much the words you say to Him. Speak the right words from the heart and He will surely answer. Are you expecting an answer?"

"I don't know what I expect anymore. I know you mean well and trying to help, but I'm sure there is something I will need to do to get back into His good graces, and it will take time, time I don't have."

"No, that's not true. You have such a dismal picture of God. I didn't know your emotional scars were so deep. He is our Father. If we can't trust Him, then who can we believe in? Have the faith in what He is willing to do for you because He loves you, and you are His daughter."

"But I told Him I hated Him. When our parents were killed, I told God I would have nothing to do with Him ever again. He's not going to forgive that."

"Have you asked Him?"

"Yes, I did earlier."

"Okay, it's done and forgotten by God."

"No, I don't think so."

"Sophie, you are forgiven now move on. Don't you think God wants to help Faith?"

"Of course, but will He do it for me. That's the question."

"He already has."

"What do you mean?"

"His own Son shed His blood and died, so that we may partake in all the good things our Father has for us. He didn't just die for our sins so that we may have salvation, but just as importantly, that we may also have God's blessings which include miracles. You need a miracle, and through Christ, it is available to you. Ask God."

"I did ask for Faith's sake."

"Then believe it."

She was confused. Her sister made it all sound so easy. Just pray and believe, trust and expect, and there would be a miracle for Faith. Somehow that was too simple from her understanding. Though she admits to not having a relationship with God in many years, and faulting Him severely, it just didn't seem praying would get her what she needed. Surely she had to make restitution for her wrongful attitude, even if Christ's death did encompass miracles.

"I need to think. Can we just sit quietly for a minute?"

"Sure."

They both sat down on the sofa. Sabrina leaned her head back, closing her eyes and silently prayed. Sophie glanced her way and then stood up walking over to Faith's crib.

"I'm so sorry, sweetheart. Mommy doesn't know how to protect you, but I'm trying," she spoke softly.

Brie listened to her sister's confession. There was nothing more to be said between them. Sophie was on her own in seeking God for a resolution. Sabrina knew God's position and was hopeful of Sophie's.

Chapter 55

It was late and David had yet to return, so Sabrina thought to go looking for him, perhaps he needed some companionship. Without disturbing Sophie, Brie left the room. Sophie turned to see the door close. It was as though Brie understood she wanted this time with Faith. In a few short hours, they would be taking Faith away and who knew what condition she would return in.

She stood near her baby pondering on the conversation with Brie. Would God really forgive and forget? Does He love her in spite of herself? Would He bless Faith with a healed heart? She was desperate for Faith, desperate enough to want to believe. It had to be God. She knew that, finally. It was Him, or no one. There was no man who could give her what she wanted. If God had truly forgiven her for past sins, then would he give her an answered prayer? As though a light bulb suddenly went off in her head, Sophie clearly understood. *Oh my gosh,* she thought. Faith, she must have faith!

Falling to her knees, Sophie put her hands together, closed her eyes and prayed like she had never done before in her entire life for the forgiveness of things she said to God, to David, to her sister, and for the anger she held in her heart. She purged her soul of all the wrongful thoughts and emotions, and found herself pleading with Him to take her back as His child. She was begging.

With tears streaming down her face, Sophie prayed for her

baby Faith's heart remembering what Brie said, finally under-standing words were not enough. She must believe it to be the truth. She had to trust God if she wanted a miracle for Faith, and hold tightly to faith and belief. Rising to sit in the rocking chair as though waiting for an answer, she continued to pray.

"I do believe, I believe with all my heart, I believe Faith's heart is healed. I know God has forgiven me."

David and Sabrina entered the room witnessing Sophie chanting something they couldn't hear from the doorway. As they approached, she opened her eyes.

"How are you doing?" David asked, squatting down in front of her.

Sophie shrugged. He saw her tear-streaked face and the strain in her bloodshot eyes, and wanted to gather her in his arms.

"Come sit on the sofa with me," he said, holding out his right hand.

She stared at it for a second and looked into his eyes before flinging herself at him, practically knocking them both to the floor. Wrapping her arms around his neck and holding on tightly, Sophie cried. She felt so ashamed. Sabrina knew they needed to be alone, and left the room heading for the cafeteria for three cups of coffee, knowing she wouldn't be missed.

David noticed Brie leaving. He stood pulling Sophie up from the chair and with his arm around her shoulder, led her to the sofa. When they sat down, he snuggled her close to his side. It felt good to be holding his wife again.

"Tell me what you were saying to yourself earlier when we walked in."

Reluctant to share her thoughts, and yet, compelled to explain to David, she responded.

"I was believing Faith's heart is healed."

That was absolutely the last thing he expected to hear her say. Where did this come from?

"What do you mean?"

"I haven't been a very nice person. Not just lately, but in

general. I blamed God for a lot of things in my life, not trying to understand. I've learned it wasn't God, but me that was wrong, holding onto anger. My negative feelings carried over into this situation with Faith. It hurt to hear you agreeing with the doctors and not considering how I felt. I blamed you for not caring, but that isn't true. I know you care very much. I still don't agree that we are doing the right thing, but I'm not holding it against you anymore. I'm really sorry."

Taken off-guard, he thought for a moment, cautious of what to say before speaking.

"I'm not in agreement with the surgery. As much as it may appear that way to you, I detest this as much as you do. We find ourselves trapped and can't leave. I want to be a good husband and father. I never meant to cause you any unhappiness, but I have and for that, I'm truly sorry."

The moment was solemn as they confessed and shared the experience of the past few months. The strain it had created in their relationship made Sophie feel even worse. She knew her thoughtless behavior toward David wasn't right, and saying she was sorry didn't seem like enough. She got up and went to Faith, drawn to her baby.

David followed standing alongside her, and together they watched their daughter sleep, uncertain for what the future held. He reached for his wife's left hand slipping it within his, and entwined their fingers as tears filled their eyes. Sophie squeezed David's hand and whispered.

"You've told me many times, if I could give you another solution, you would willingly consider it. I know what it is now. The answer is God."

David turned his attention from Faith and focused on Sophie's face. The seriousness and sincerity of her words slid deep into his psyche. There was something almost tangible in the way she spoke them. What happened in his absence that changed his wife? It was all so surreal.

"You now believe God is the source of healing Faith's heart. Alright, I'm not going to reject that idea," he told her, not fully comprehending what was going on.

"Yes, pray with me, but first, put your other hand on Faith," she said, not explaining further.

They each placed a hand on Faith and held hands with their other making a complete connection, and with closed eyes, both prayed silently for a moment. Then Sophie spoke softly, aloud.

"God, David and I come to you praying for our baby. We ask your forgiveness for our sins and to heal Faith's heart. You see our hearts and know our plea. Our trust is in you for the miracle we need. Please hear our prayer, Amen."

David didn't know what to say. He had never heard such a poetically spoken prayer, and it came from his wife.

"That was a beautiful prayer. If I were God, I would want to grant it, and I'm not saying that to be funny. It really moved me."

"I've been angry with God for a long time. It was Brie who helped me release the anger and other negative emotions that I was carrying. I never had a reason to before now, but Faith brought out the desire in me to believe again, to have faith. She told me that Faith would live up to her name, and I didn't know, at the time, what she meant. Now I do."

Their conversation was interrupted when Brie walked in with a tray of three coffees and condiments. Placing it on the table, she had hoped her absence had been sufficient but noticed her reappearance had halted their discussion, and wondered if she should disappear again.

"If you both would like to be alone, I can take my coffee and go back downstairs to the cafeteria. I don't mind," Brie told them.

"No, we don't want you to leave, and thanks for the coffee. I could use that right now," Sophie spoke up.

"Are you sure? David may prefer to have some time alone with you."

"We aren't talking about anything you can't be privy to," David told her.

"I don't want to be in the way."

"You're never in the way. We're family," he said, reaching for a cup.

It was almost midnight and coffee would surely keep them awake for hours, but no one was ready to call it a night nor was there interest in conversation. Faith was on their minds. Unexpectedly and without announcement, they held a silent prayer vigil.

Chapter 56

A couple hours later with the caffeine buzz worn off, David thought it best that Sophie try to get some sleep. He pulled out the sofa into a daybed, and with the supplies brought in earlier by a nurse, made a comfortable place for her and Brie to rest. Sophie took one end and Brie the other. It was cramped, but they managed to make the best of it; however, neither was expecting to sleep. David sat in the rocking chair with a pillow. They had been informed that someone would be coming for Faith around six, and surgery was scheduled for seven in the morning. Only a few hours remained until the nightmare began.

It was impossible to think she could sleep, and Sophie didn't try. She lay perfectly still silently praying for the miracle she now believed was imminent. In less than twenty-four hours, she had made a monumental change in her relationship with God. She prayed her faith was adequate for Him to give her the resolution she sought, and held steadfast in her heart to believing it was forthcoming.

She must have slipped into a light sleep because just around five in the morning Sophie suddenly awakened, believing someone had touched her. Opening her eyes, she expected to see a nurse tapping her on the shoulder, but there was no one there, and the room was quiet with everyone asleep. Yet, she instinctively knew someone had disturbed her.

Without waking Brie, she slowly got up and walked to Grace's crib taking a quick glance before stepping over to Faith. She found Faith lying on her back with her eyes wide open.

Sophie placed her left hand on Faith's heart, and with her right, took her baby's tiny fingers gently rubbing them with her thumb. She stood staring at her daughter as their eyes locked, without blinking. Almost faltering in her stance, Sophie was shocked by a sharp awareness of wisdom she witnessed in the depth of her daughter's beautiful blue eyes. *Not impossible*, she thought. She stayed focused on Faith. The message was unmistakable. So peacefully was the answer laid upon her heart that tears filled her eyes. Silently, she thanked God and picked up Faith holding her close, while whispering joyful words of praise in her ear as tears flowed down her cheeks.

"My precious, little Faith; you are well and you know it. He loves you, and I love you, my sweet, sweet baby."

Hugging her close, she kissed her baby's face, smiling. The commotion woke David and Brie. He saw the look on Sophie's face and wondered why she was smiling when they would be coming for Faith in less than an hour.

"What's going on?" he asked, still groggy from sleep.

"She is well, David. Her heart is healed."

He glared at her for a moment not knowing what to say. Had the stress taken Sophie over the edge, literally? She saw the worried expression on his face and laughed.

"It's true, and I'll prove it to you. I want an ultrasound done, and you'll see there is no hole. God healed Faith's heart last night."

David saw the seriousness of her belief and knew he was in no position to question her words. With his entire being, he wanted Sophie to be right.

"Alright, we'll tell them to run the test before they do anything else."

"It won't be before they do anything else. There will be no need for surgery. I promise you that."

Sophie spoke with such confidence and authority, something he had not witnessed in her, and wondered where it was coming from. Could this be because of her newfound faith in God? He truly hoped so. Brie sat up and listened. This was the moment she had been waiting for in her attempt to encourage Sophie. She was thankful to see her sister make the right decision, to forgive and trust in God.

Grace awoke from the noise in the room and now that everyone was up, Brie took charge of changing Grace while Sophie did the same for Faith. Sabrina took Grace and sat in the rocking chair with a fresh bottle that David had prepared. Sophie requested one for Faith.

"You can't feed her. Remember, she can't have anything," David stated in alarm.

"Yes, she can. I'm not letting her go all morning without something in her tummy," Sophie replied, defying David to counter her decision.

"Sophie, I don't think it is a good idea to feed her until we know for sure what will take place this morning," he stated, again.

"David, if I believe what I know to be the truth, I'm holding to that truth and nothing is going to change that. You need to trust. Please fix Faith a bottle."

He wasn't about to argue when he saw the determination on her face. Obviously, something was happening here he didn't understand. It was nearing six when a nurse stepped into the room seeing both women feeding the twins and gasped when she saw Faith being fed.

"No, she can't have that. This is going to mess up her surgery time," the nurse exclaimed.

"I want a test done on her heart," Sophie spoke her request, ignoring the nurse's statement.

"All the necessary tests have been done. She is ready for surgery or was until now," the nurse informed her.

"You're not hearing me. I want an ultrasound on her heart done as soon as it can be arranged this morning," Sophie told her, reiterating her point.

"I'll have the doctor come in and talk to you," the nurse stammered, leaving the room.

David hoped Sophie wasn't merely attempting to delay the surgery, but quickly dismissed the thought as he recalled her earnest belief that God had healed Faith's heart. He sat down close to her on the sofa and watched Faith sucking on the nipple of the bottle. A tiny trail of milk was flowing down the corner of her mouth and pooling in the bib she wore. Quietly, he bent his head and prayed. Sophie had turned Faith around and was burping her when Dr. Whalton walked into the room with a stern expression, showing off the furrow between his brows. He didn't look happy.

"Nurse Betty informs me we have a problem this morning. Please tell me you haven't given Faith any liquids," he said, seeing the empty bottle.

"You do realize this will set her surgery back by several hours and throws off the schedule for the entire day. This doesn't just affect Faith's time slot, but other patients as well including the assisting doctors, anesthesiologist, nurses and everyone who makes up the surgical team. This is a thoughtless act you have done, Mrs. McKinley," Dr. Whalton continued, not holding back his wrath.

Ignoring his hostile attitude, Sophie spoke calmly dictating what she wanted.

"I may have caused you some grief, and I apologize for that, but once you see for yourself, then you will understand my actions. I want an ultrasound done on Faith's heart," Sophie told him, matter-of-fact.

"Mrs. McKinley, we have a current ultrasound, EEG, EKG, MRI and CAT Scan on Faith. Nothing needs to be repeated," he told her, holding his position as the physician.

"Yes, I know that, but I'm asking for another ultrasound. We both know it is non-invasive and only takes minutes to do. I want one," she said firmly, not backing down.

"What are you trying to prove? Nothing has changed from the last one. I can guarantee it."

"Let me put it to you this way. No ultrasound, no signature to perform the surgery, and we both know you must have that before you can do it. You may be able to keep us here, but you still can't do the surgery without our permission."

Dr. Whalton looked at David who merely shrugged his shoulders as if to say, *Don't look at me, I can't help you.* Focusing back on Sophie, believing her to be completely unreasonable, he backed down. He could see they were getting nowhere, and nothing was going to satisfy her until she had her way. She ruined his entire day.

"Alright, I'll put an order in for an ultrasound. In the meantime, don't feed her anything else while I switch a patient. We'll plan early afternoon for her surgery."

He turned and left the room not giving her an opportunity to respond. He was indeed perturbed.

"You have really gotten on Dr. Whalton's bad side. He wasn't happy," David spoke first.

"I'm only asking for one test, and I don't care about his happiness."

"It's more than doing a test. You've disrupted his entire surgical team."

"It couldn't be helped. I'm sure it isn't the first time things didn't go exactly as planned. I'm doing what I know to be right. Try to understand that, David. It would mean a lot to me if you did."

Events certainly had changed since they arrived at the center less than forty-eight hours ago. From being lethargic and depressed to this super confident woman was quite a transformation, and David was glad to see the spunky nature in his wife again. He still didn't know what to think of her reestablishing a relationship with God, not knowing until now how rocky it had been. Something had certainly come over her. Though they were never strongly dependent on Him, maybe it was time for that to change.

"Brie, you have been very quiet. Do you have anything to say?" Sophie asked.

"You said everything very nicely."

Their nonverbal communication spoke louder than words. David was used to it and took no offense at being left out of the loop. Sophie knew her sister was praying thanksgiving that she had finally come to terms with her anger and resentment.

"I'm going to the cafeteria for some coffee and breakfast. Either of you want anything in particular this morning?"

With them attending to the twins, David felt rather helpless.

"Coffee sounds wonderful. I'll take some scramble eggs and a muffin if they have it," Brie told him.

"That sounds good, same for me."

He stood in front of Sophie and leaned down giving her a quick kiss, and then planting one on Faith's forehead. Looking over at Brie, he winked before leaving the room. There was no doubt something miraculous just happened in this room, the atmosphere was charged.

"Sophie, do you mind if I switch and hold Faith?"

"Of course not, I need to give Grace equal attention."

They made the swap and Brie rocked Faith talking to her the whole time. Faith perked up wiggling in her aunt's arms. Holding her close, Sabrina silently prayed giving praise to God.

"What is it little one?" Brie asked of Faith.

"Yes, dear one, you are feeling good. I can see that."

She talked continuously to Faith and could hear Sophie doing the same with Grace. Twins being playful with twins was how Nurse Betty found them when she came in with the orders for Faith's ultrasound. A tech rolled in a wheelchair for Sophie and Faith to ride down to x-ray.

"I want to wait for my husband. He should be back soon."

The radiology technician was in no hurry and backed out of the room saying he would wait at the nurse's station. Minutes later, David walked in with a tray of food. Sophie explained that a technician was waiting to take them to x-ray. He suggested they eat their breakfast first, and then he would walk down with her while Brie stayed in the room with Grace. Sophie had her appetite back and ate quickly anxious to get this test done.

David stepped out to the nurse's station to fetch the technician and together they went to the third floor and were escorted straight into an x-ray room with no delays this time. Afterwards, they returned for the waited results. Sophie truly believed Faith's heart was healed and this would prove it. David could only pray that she was right.

Chapter 57

Approximately an hour later, Dr. Whalton entered the room with the ultrasound pictures in his right hand. He walked directly toward Sophie as she stood by the crib watching both her babies lying together. She didn't need to see his face to know the truth. It was for his benefit she requested the ultrasound because she knew it would be the only way to convince him the surgery was no longer necessary. After all, physicians relied on test results.

"What happened?" Dr. Whalton asked.

She looked at him and just as seriously answered.

"A miracle."

"I don't understand, though I can see with my own eyes there is no hole or perforation. There is absolutely nothing wrong with her heart. I rechecked all the previous tests, and there is no mistake she had a hole, but now she doesn't. This is beyond anything I have ever experienced. I'm at a loss for words," he said, perplexed.

"It's a miracle," Sophie repeated.

He stared at her for the longest time and could see she believed it, but couldn't dispute her words as much as he wanted to. There was no other explanation.

"This is one for the records. Absolutely unbelievable," he told her, shaking his head back and forth, still finding it hard to accept.

"No, Dr. Whalton, it's absolutely *believable*," Sophie said, correcting him.

"How did you know?"

"No offense to you, Dr. Whalton, but your method of healing Faith's heart isn't the same as God's, and I chose to put my faith in Him. I placed Faith in His care."

"Amazing, I don't know what to say, but that you're discharged to go home. There's nothing more we can do for you here. Wait till I tell my colleagues about this one. They won't believe it," he said, still bewildered.

"Maybe there are more people who believe in miracles than have confessed. You might just be surprised," Sophie told him.

"You may be right, Mrs. McKinley. These are for you, perhaps a souvenir."

He handed the ultrasound pictures to her and turned to shake David's hand, while nodding his head at Brie, before leaving the room. Sophie locked eyes with her sister and held a knowing glance before looking at David who had turned very pale.

"David, you don't look so good," Sophie told her husband.

"What happened here? Faith's heart is healed, there is no hole," David asked in amazement.

Sophie walked over to David grabbing him squarely by the shoulders and looked straight into his eyes.

"God gave Faith a miracle," she told him, not having yet registered herself the magnitude of what she was saying.

David stood completely still seeing the reflection of himself in his wife's eyes, and wrapping his arms around her, began to weep. She, too, broke down and cried. They were suddenly struck by the reality of what God had done, bringing them to their knees, literally. Sitting in a crumpled entanglement of limbs, they held onto each other unable to control their emotions. God had healed their baby's heart. What does someone say to something so unimaginably spectacular, so supernatural?

Brie stepped away leaving them to reconcile themselves to the majesty of God's power and went to the crib to watch the girls. Grace and Faith had their own celebration going on as they uttered baby sounds, continuously. It was a joyful moment in the lives of the McKinley's. Gaining some sense of composure, they got up off the floor, and Sophie hugged Brie without saying a word. David joined in a hug also. He was still speechless.

"Let's give thanksgiving for our family has been truly blessed today," Brie said, knowing there would be no objections.

"I'll do it," Sophie said and began to pray aloud.

"God, thank you, for healing our baby's heart. And thank you for loving me enough to forgive my sinful ways. I've been wrong all these years, and yet, you forgave me. I am so grateful for what you have done for my baby and for me, Amen."

"I want to say something," David spoke up.

Feeling a bit uncertain how to express into words what he felt so deeply in his heart, David struggled.

"Dear God, I don't know how to say to you how much what you have done for my baby girl means to me, but I know you see my heart. Thank you for my family, Amen."

Sophie looked at her sister silently nudging her to pray if she so wished; however, Brie shook her head declining, accepting this was their moment and their miracle.

Sabrina stepped away leaving them alone. David and Sophie turned into an embrace holding tight without saying a word. Finally, wiping the tears from his eyes, David stepped outside to inform the nurse they were leaving. When he returned, the girls were already in their stroller and the few miscellaneous items had been packed in the diaper bag.

Nurse Betty came in with the discharge papers handing them to David who noticed Dr. Whalton had written across the form in large letters, *miracle.* Seeing the word written on paper brought tears to his eyes once again. His family had been blessed.

Chapter 58

There was little conversation returning home with the twins. Knowing Faith was healed by God humbled them, to say the least. It almost seemed too sacred a topic to discuss, and yet, they believed the miracle their baby received was worthy of continual acknowledgement, and thanksgiving to God. They didn't know how to relate to each other over the miraculous event, so the atmosphere in the house was quiet reverence. They respected the fact that their lives would never be the same.

After bathing and feeding the girls, Sophie and Brie placed them in their new swings in the living room. David made a quick lunch of sandwiches with iced tea and brought the plates on individual trays, one at a time, so they could eat and watch the twins. The transformation in Faith was dramatic. She was happy and energetic, just like her sister, kicking her feet out and moving her arms in the air each time the swing went back and forth. They listened to the continual one-syllable stream of babbling coming from her and easily accepted it as her singing praises. Brie reached over tickling her tummy, and she squealed with delight.

Sophie observed closely the behavior of Faith, and tears filled her eyes, thinking of how close she came to not receiving her miracle. She watched the playfulness between her and daughters and sister accepting the bond which was practically tangible, each time Brie was with them. Sophie wasn't envious of what she was witnessing, suddenly it seemed so natural. Sabrina noticed in her peripheral vision her sister's concentration on them, and purposefully, made eye contact with a knowing wink and smile. Sophie smiled back.

David wanted to ask his wife how and when did she know Faith's heart was healed but decided not to press the issue, knowing she would share it with him when she was ready. So he sat quietly watching the interaction between his girls and their aunt. He couldn't take his eyes off of Faith. She was a completely different child.

"I've never witnessed anything like this in my entire life, but I now know what it is like to be a receiver of God's promises," David spoke aloud his thoughts.

"God is good, and He takes care of His children. We need to learn to trust in Him because He wants the best for us, always," Brie replied.

"Yes, I have learned that lesson for sure. This family is a recipient of His blessings, and I will forever be thankful more than words can convey," David said, getting a little choked up again.

"Of the three of us, I'm the one who held a grudge against God, but He forgave me and answered my prayer. How do I thank Him properly for what He has done for me?" Sophie asked, rhetorically.

"Love Him with all your heart by including Him in every aspect of your life. Live for Him first, and He will always be there to take care of your needs," Brie told her.

"Nothing will ever compare to what I have just experienced, and I can do no less than turn my life and my children's lives over to Him. I now understand He was always there. It was me who turned away, but He took me back. You made this happen, Brie. If it weren't for your persistence, we may not be sitting here with our happy ending," Sophie confessed, tears pooling in her eyes.

"You were always His child, you just didn't believe it.

Now you do, and praise God for His grace and mercy."

"This is a day that will go down in the history of this family that will be told to our children. They will grow up not just knowing of God, but living their life purposefully for Him," David said, voicing his own commitment.

"This is what you were trying to get me to understand all along, but I kept fighting you," Sophie told her sister.

"Yes, I wanted you to know the truth."

"Will you now tell me about your special talent?"

"Let's just say I'm an ambassador for God."

"What does that mean, exactly?"

"It means that I am always seeking to do His will to help others, wherever I am needed."

"So I was one of those that you felt a need to help?"

"I'm your sister and will forever be by your side. I was hoping you would come to trust in God for the answers you were seeking, but you needed to do this on your own. I was merely giving you guidance."

"It must have been very frustrating for you trying to get me to accept Him in my life again."

"I believed in you. A relationship with God is not something that can be coerced on someone."

"What is the connection you have to your nieces? It's as though you talk to one another with your own language. I've witnessed it several times. They know you and respond."

"They do know me, spiritually."

"Explain it to me."

"What we share is through our spirit."

"How can that be possible? I know God is a spirit, but how can people do that?"

"I don't know the details. What I do know is that I have the ability to know what is in a child's heart, and they seem to be able to *feel* my presence."

"Are you saying that you have this connection with other children? How can that be?"

"It is my gift."

"So if children are drawn to you, what is the purpose? What do they come to you for, and how do you respond?"

"Young children have such pure hearts and seem to gather close to me when I am around them. It must have something to do with an invisible aura, or again, a spiritual awareness."

"I still don't know how this works for you. You haven't had this *gift* your entire life, so when did you acquire it and why?"

"It came about through our aunt's legacy."

"What are you saying? This has to do with *Passionate Promises*. You weren't going to tell me, were you? It took this situation with Faith and my seeing for myself, otherwise, you didn't plan to let me know," Sophie said, hurt by that knowledge.

"That's not true. I was going to tell you, but didn't know when a good time would be. And then the situation came up with Faith's heart, and it wasn't the first thing on my mind. Like you, I was focused on Faith."

"But I asked you, and you brushed me off. You had several opportunities. Besides, if this had to do with Aunt Millie's legacy, that was two years ago. You've kept this to yourself all this time. I want to know what happened."

"Remember all those strange occurrences. There was a reason for them. It was to get my attention to take over the legacy. When I finally became aware I was being chosen for a purpose, I just didn't feel it was something I could immediately share with anyone, not even with Ben. And besides, at that time, you showed no interest in *Passionate Promises*, and I didn't believe you were ready to accept anything I had to say about it."

"It still took me asking. You hadn't mentioned it on your own."

"It takes awhile to understand the manifestation of something so powerful, let alone wanting to share the experience. It wasn't deliberate on my part to withhold anything from you, but I was learning what it meant in my life. It was overwhelming at first."

"I can relate, somewhat, having just received a miracle. I'm trying to comprehend something so intimate, and you're right, I have no desire to share with others right now."

"Knowing the anger you held in your heart, you would not have been receptive to what I have told you. So perhaps, it was meant to be shared now because look where you are in your own relationship with God. It makes a difference," Brie said, trying to explain.

Sabrina didn't want her sister to feel slighted by her not exposing something so monumentally important in her life. Sophie knew Brie spoke the truth. Had she been told this news two years ago, she would have rebuked it as nonsense. After all, there was no evidence for Brie to prove her point. However, seeing for herself the transformation in her daughters when they are around their aunt, she can't deny something has transpired within her sister. She has witnessed it.

"You're right, Brie. Had you told me, I wouldn't have believed you. I would have tried because you are my sister. I am glad you have something very special with Faith and Grace. As they get older, your relationship with them will be extraordinary, and I truly am happy about that."

They stretched across the sofa and embraced. David sat in the chair across the room and watched the entire scene unfold. He had yet to express a single word. Most women sit and talk about their husbands, children, recipes, and the latest fashion trend, but the women in his life talk about being anointed with supernatural gifts. This was definitely one conversation he had no intention of repeating because no one would believe him.

Chapter 59

While Sophie and David took care of getting the girls ready for bed, Sabrina booked a flight out the next morning. She thought of extending her stay a few days, but considering the emotional rollercoaster Sophie and David had been on, it was best to leave them to their family. She also called Ben to give him the news that the crisis with Faith was over and everyone was home. Not wanting to stay on the phone, she promised the details when she returned. There was much to tell him.

After the twins were tucked in securely for the night, David brewed coffee handing one to Brie and also to Sophie when she joined them. They sat quietly for a moment enjoying the hot drink. David was the first to speak.

"Honey, I wasn't going to press you, but how did you know Faith's heart was healed?"

David couldn't wait any longer to know what happened.

"I felt a tap on my shoulder. Someone or something had awakened me, and it wasn't from a sound. The room was completely quiet. I got up to check on the girls, and I saw that Faith was awake just lying in her crib perfectly still. It was when I looked into her eyes, she spoke to me. That's the only way I know how to say it. There was something in her eyes that communicated to my heart and I just knew. There was no doubt."

"You mean, Faith told you she was healed."

"Yes, in a manner-of-speaking, she did."

"Amazing. Do you think anyone would believe us if we told them?" David asked.

"I don't care to tell anyone, at least not at this time. It doesn't feel right. There may be a circumstance when we are compelled to share our experience, but it isn't now," Sophie told him.

"I agree. I'm not ready, either."

Brie listened without contributing. Her thoughts were on Sophie accepting such life-altering changes in her belief, and quickly, because everything hinged on her trust and faithfulness. It was a huge leap for her to overcome the negative she harbored, but she did it.

"Did you thank him for me, too?" Sophie asked, knowing the answer.

Sophie knew her sister was silently praying.

"Absolutely," Brie replied with a smile.

"When are you returning home?"

"I booked a flight out in the morning. I'll leave for the airport around eleven."

"I wish you would stay a few days, but I understand you need to get back to your business."

"It isn't my business that is drawing me home. You and David need this time alone without company in the house. This has been a sacred experience that you both need to share alone. Besides, I will see you in a couple of months."

"Brie, you don't have to leave so soon. Please stay as long as you want too. You know we love having you here," David interjected.

"Thank you, David, but I have to go home sometime."

"Your wedding is going to be so beautiful. I can't wait to see you walking down the isle. It will be perfect," Sophie said, changing the subject.

Sophie felt very emotional with everything she had personally experienced and wasn't ready for her sister to leave just yet. She didn't want the feelings to fade away. It was all so fresh in her heart.

"That's why Ben and I decided to postpone our honeymoon until the spring. Being with family is important to both of us. With his family living nearby, it is a great occasion for everyone to be together, our wedding and the holidays."

"I'm glad Ben doesn't object to us spending Christmas with the two of you, especially when you'll be newlyweds. There's going to be a lot of activity in your house. Are you sure he won't mind?" Sophie asked.

"Truthfully, I think he is looking forward to it more than I am, and you know how much it means to me. I don't know which I want more, my wedding, or the holidays with family. It's a real toss up," Brie said, laughing.

"Oh, I think the wedding takes precedence."

David listened to them chatting and laughing as though nothing miraculous had occurred in the previous hours. It felt good. There was no heartache but rather peace had settled back into their home, and it was a beautiful sight to see his wife happy again.

On a serious note, Sabrina changed the subject. There was something she wished to express to her sister before leaving in the morning.

"Sophie, I'm so proud of you. It was hard to place your trust in someone you never intended to ever trust again. Discovering how much you had drifted away from God makes it that much more astounding you turned to Him."

"It was for Faith. Had it not been for her, I probably never would have."

"The important thing is you did. It was for your sake and Faith's."

"Thank you, Brie, for not giving up on me."

Brie smiled as no further words were necessary. Realizing they were going to settle into girl talk, David left the room. Rather than doing school work, he went to the guest room in search of the Bible he knew was on the bookshelf. With his cup of coffee, he relaxed on the sofa and read while they talked late into the night.

The next morning, David prepared a large breakfast of eggs and pancakes while Sabrina played with the twins in their room. They had her undivided attention as she held them close, repeatedly voicing how much she loved them, especially whispering blessings in Faith's ear. They were very responsive to their aunt's presence. Brie was saddened to leave but knew she would hold them again soon. Faith and Grace had stolen her heart the moment they were born, and each time she was with them only intensified her love for them.

After a hearty meal and two cups of coffee, Brie couldn't delay departing any longer. She hugged Faith and Grace, one final time, and gave David a quick embrace before he put the suitcase in the trunk of the rental car. Brie lingered in the doorway holding Sophie tightly before stepping outside. Seeing the tears in her sister's eyes made it difficult to not cry, especially this time, but it was necessary she return home. It was time to have a serious talk with Ben.

Chapter 60

Arriving home mid-afternoon, Brie phoned Sophie as she always did letting her know she made it safely. Deciding to wait to call Ben knowing he would be busy, she took the time to unpack, check her mail, phone messages, and the appointment schedule for the upcoming week. She needed time to think about how to explain something, like Sophie, she should have shared before now, and especially before they married. Brie wasn't sure how Ben would react but because he was a good-natured man, she believed he would take it in stride as he did life in general.

Once settled, she called and invited him to dinner expecting him around six, allowing enough time to prepare a chicken casserole from David's recipe and put it in the oven to bake. She made a salad and brewed a fresh pitcher of iced tea to complete the meal.

He arrived promptly and when she opened the door, Ben lifted Sabrina off her feet swinging her around until she was dizzy. Settling Brie back down, he kissed her passionately as she melted in his arms. Oh, how she loved this man. What a fool she had been to procrastinate marrying him. *We could have children running around this big house right now,* she thought.

"I'm not sure which one of us missed the other more," she told him, reluctantly slipping from the firm hold he had on her.

"Oh, I missed you more," he said, teasingly.

"Maybe not."

He followed her toward the kitchen as she went straight to the oven, and pulled out the casserole placing it on a trivet in the center of the table. Everything else was ready to eat.

"Something smells mighty good, and I'm famished."

"I'm glad to hear that."

Ben went to the kitchen sink washing his hands and took a seat. As they enjoyed dinner together, she brought him up-to-date on Faith. Ben was astonished to hear the details. Though he never discounted miracles happen, he had not known of one personally. The fact that it was his fiancé's niece was amazing to him. He thought it was an awesome thing, though he didn't understand the semantics of how people received miracles. Was there divine intervention for everyone who prayed for a miracle? It was a subject he knew nothing about, yet was awed by the revelation with Faith.

"This must be quite an astounding experience for them as parents? How is Sophie doing?"

"Very well, considering the many obstacles she had to overcome."

"I don't think anyone could forget something so super-natural. And Faith is perfectly fine, the hole completely gone."

"Yes, gone as though it never existed."

"Wow, what a story she has to tell."

"True, but at the moment she's holding it close to her heart, and thankful to have Faith home and healed. She knows she has been blessed, and that is all she wanted."

"Absolutely profound."

"Yes, it is."

They ate in silence for a moment before changing the subject to talking about work on the farm and upcoming projects Ben had planned. Getting ready for the holiday season was a year around effort. Most consumers weren't thoughtful to the workings behind the scene. They bought a tree when needed, decorated and threw it on the curb a few weeks later with no interest of what went on the eleven months prior. That was Ben's job to care for the trees and provide his customers with the best Douglas Fir available.

After they finished dinner and shared the chore of cleaning the kitchen, Brie made a fresh pot of coffee taking their cups to the den. While sitting across from Ben in her favorite chair, Brie considered how to approach the subject she wanted to discuss with him, but before she could muster the words the doorbell rang.

Surprised to have a visitor that late in the evening, she answered to see Lindsey and her mother standing at the front door. As she invited them into the foyer, Lindsey rushed up putting her arms around Sabrina and holding tight. Brie held her close while looking at Lindsey's mother understanding the reason for the visit.

"I'm sorry to bother you this late, but Lindsey insisted I bring her to see you right away. She got very upset when I told her we should wait until tomorrow," she said, apologetically.

"Oh, no problem. I'm happy to see you both," Brie said, pulling Lindsey away and kneeling down to eye level. Before she could say anything, Lindsey spoke first.

"You saved my mommy. I had to come see you. She had a test done and found out today that she is all better. You saved her, and I wanted to tell you."

Lindsey flung her small arms around Sabrina's neck as Brie looked upward at her mother.

"It's true. My cancer is completely gone. I had a large, malignant tumor on my left ovary, and they where going to surgically remove it, possibly a hysterectomy, and then I would start a regiment of chemotherapy. The doctor scheduled a routine MRI a few days prior to surgery and couldn't find a trace of cancer. He was stunned, just as I am. I don't know what happened, but I'm grateful beyond words," she said, pausing to gain her composure before continuing.

"Lindsey told me about her talk with you in the park that day you took our family portrait. She kept telling me that I wasn't sick anymore. I don't doubt she has overheard conversations, and I thought all this medical talk was scaring her so much she was denying that I was ill. But she spoke with such assuredness and confidence, it was almost alarming coming from a five year old. I don't know what has happened here. One day I have cancer, and the next I don't. To top that, Lindsey seems to believe you are the person responsible for my miraculous healing."

After hearing such a confession, Brie focused her full attention on Lindsey. Before she could say anything, Lindsey reached up and placed her tiny hands on either side of Brie's face, pressing into her cheeks. Deliberately looking Sabrina squarely in the eyes, she spoke with a knowledge Brie understood.

"You did it. You made my mommy well again. You know its true," she said, challenging Sabrina to deny it.

"Lindsey, honey, I didn't do it, but you know in your heart who really healed your mommy," she told her gently, brushing a soft curl of hair from her forehead.

"Yes, I know God saved my Mommy, but it was because you told him to," she insisted.

"Sweetheart, I don't think anyone can tell God what to do. We can ask Him for help, and we know He will give us the very best we ask. I appreciate that you think I had something to do with your mother's recovery, but we have to give the thanks to the one who really did all the work. It is important that we do. I want you to understand what I am saying," she explained, knowing Lindsey accepted the truth.

Lindsey nodded her head up and down vigorously, smiling at Brie. She hugged Brie again and whispered thank you in Sabrina's ear. Brie told her she was very glad her mother was well and to remember to thank God when she said her prayers that night.

"I will," Lindsey replied, solemnly.

Sabrina stood holding onto Lindsey's hand.

"I don't know what has occurred between you and my daughter, but thank you. Thank you for caring," she said, tears filling her eyes.

Stepping forward, she embraced Sabrina.

"Come on Lindsey, let's not take anymore of Sabrina's time this evening," she said, placing her hand on her daughter's shoulder.

"Lindsey, I am so glad you came by to tell me this wonderful news," Brie told her, giving her a final hug.

Lindsey took her mother's hand and walked away toward their car, turning around with a knowing smile and waved. Brie threw up her hand watching until they had backed out of the driveway. Closing the door, she turned to see Ben with his arms crossed over his chest leaning against the wall not far behind her, obviously witnessing the conversation. Walking up to him, he looked her directly in the eyes and asked the obvious question.

"What was that all about? That little girl believes you had something to do with her mother overcoming cancer. Now that's very interesting since we just had a miracle of our own. Would you care to tell me what is going on?"

She stepped past him into the den and retrieved her mug to make a fresh cup of coffee. Without a word, he did the same and they resettled back into their original positions in the den. Sabrina had yet to give him an answer.

"You know, I have all night, and I'm not tempted to leave until you explain what the deal is here. I learn of two miracles in one day which has to be an absolute record of some kind," he proclaimed, getting annoyed that she had not spoken a word since the little girl left.

Brie looked directly at him and smiled. Taking a sip of her hot coffee, she was pondering how to explain these events.

"Miracles happen all the time, Ben. We just don't have the privilege of always being on the receiving end. You got lucky."

"It would appear these two miracles somehow revolve around you. How is that?"

"First, I didn't have anything to do with Lindsey's mother learning she is cancer free."

"Then why did her daughter believe you had something to do with it?"

"I can connect with children."

"That's good to know. It means you'll be an exceptional mother, but then I never doubted your maternal instincts; however, that doesn't really explain your involvement with the miracles."

"There is a special communication, spiritually, between children and myself. It is like a language that only we understand."

"What do you mean, spiritually?"

"We *talk* to each other through an understanding that resonates from our heart. I haven't always been able to understand a child's heart. It came about with my aunt's legacy," she said, carefully.

"Brie, honey, I'm a little slow tonight. You are going to have to spell it out for me."

"Remember when I told you of my Aunt Millie's legacy, *Passionate Promises*. I discovered it had a significant meaning with responsibilities and desired to carry on in my aunt's footsteps. In doing so, there were special privileges bestowed upon me. The first time a child came to me and spoke with a pleading request, I realized I could understand what was in their heart even before they said the words aloud. It was the most powerful experience, and I knew it to be a spiritual connection specific to the pure hearts of children."

"What is the purpose of this spiritual awareness?"

"I try to help in whatever capacity I feel led. Most of the time, I give them guidance and hope."

"So a child, like this little girl, comes to you because she somehow feels a connection with you, already believing you have the ability to cure her mother. Where does she get that awareness to come to you?"

"Children are drawn to me through their heart and not with their eyes."

"So there is more to you than meets the eye," he said with

a little pun intended.

There was a pause in the conversation as he absorbed her words.

"Why did you keep this from me? I find this news a bit disturbing when we have been together long enough for you to confide in me, and not once did you trust me with this part of yourself. We had many conversations about your aunt's legacy when you first came to Asheville. So when did you discover this ability?"

"There was a lot going on in my life shortly after my aunt died that centered on her legacy which was the reason for my return trips. I was searching for the meaning behind *Passionate Promises*. It was shortly after I decided to make this my permanent residence that the revelation unveiled."

"So that is why you relocated. And here I thought it had to do with wanting to be closer to me. Do you have any other secrets I should know about?" he asked, annoyed.

It didn't settle comfortably with him that she withhold something of this significance. It was a true paradigm shift in her life, and Brie chose to remain silent about it. *What other things would she keep to herself?* he questioned.

"No, I haven't any secrets, and I don't look at this as keeping a secret. It was very personal and intimate. Sometimes, there are occurrences or events in our life that we aren't compelled to express. This was one for me, just as Sophie's miracle is for her right now. It isn't something you go around bragging about, and besides, people would think it nonsense."

"But I'm not just anybody. I've been your fiancé, and soon-to-be husband, and believe I have a right to know about things in your life, especially when it affects our relationship. This is a huge deal, and yet, you took no thought to share it with me. I find out, it seems, by accident."

Learning about this, put Ben on edge.

"I'm happy for your spirituality, but you have to admit, it's a bit strange. I don't know what to think at the moment."

"What is there to think about? I've just told you I have a

gift for understanding the hearts of children. There isn't anything wrong with that. And I was planning to discuss this with you tonight before we were interrupted by Lindsey's visit," she told him, not understanding his attitude.

"It's not a matter of being wrong, but it's not the norm. That's an easy save for yourself, saying you were going to tell me tonight, but it didn't happened that way."

Ben was disappointed Sabrina would deliberately keep this from him, two miracles centered on her. He wondered how much of Faith's healing was Brie responsible for. It was weird to think she had anything to do with miracles, from any aspect, because everyone knew miracles came from God. How could she possibly have that kind of a connection to Him? What did all of this mean? Feeling at odds and strangely hurt by this news, he needed time to think.

He got up to leave, and Brie was stunned he hadn't responded with compassion. This wasn't the reaction she expected. She didn't know what was on his mind as he wasn't telling her his thoughts. How did their conversation escalate to where Ben wasn't accepting her explanation?

"Don't you want to talk about it?"

"No, not tonight. It's late, and I need to get home," he told her, abruptly.

Brie followed him through the foyer, and he turned before leaving giving her a quick kiss and said he would talk to her tomorrow. Closing and locking the door, she stood there for a moment, leaning against it, wondering why Ben was acting so out of character. She went back into the den and sat down replaying the conversation. *What just happened here?* she questioned. Was he upset that she had this special ability, or that she didn't share it with him? Sabrina wasn't sure, and it bothered her that Ben may not be as forgiving as she assumed.

It wasn't too late to call Sophie.

"Hi, sis, got a minute?"

"Why are you calling at this hour? Is something wrong?" Sophie asked.

"Ben came over for dinner, and I explained my spiritual connection with children; however, he didn't take the news well. I'm not exactly sure what is upsetting him because all he said was he needed time to think about it."

"I wouldn't worry. It's not your typical dinner conversational material, and I imagine it was a shock but he'll come around. He adores you and nothing will ever change that. Remember, this is the man that has patiently waited for you to marry him."

"You're right. I just needed to hear you tell me that. I've never seen Ben get upset about anything. He always deals with situations without becoming distraught, or angry. I don't know what he's thinking. Thanks for the talk. I'll call you tomorrow."

"For all the sound advice you've given me, it feels good to reciprocate. Talk to you later."

Their brief conversation ended on a peaceful note. Brie took the coffee mugs into the kitchen and went upstairs to prepare for bed. She wasn't going to be concerned about something until there was a reason, and hoped there wouldn't be one. It would be the first with Ben.

Chapter 61

Ben did not call the next day, nor the next or the one after that. Three days and Brie had not heard from him. That was a record and as much as she wanted to phone him, she didn't. Why was he acting this way? From her point of view, there was no logical explanation for his behavior. Brie wished he would contact her, but she wasn't going to push. Apparently, he needed time and she intended to respect that.

Setting her mind on other things, she pulled out her wedding planner and went down the list triple checking that everything was taken care of. It was a matter of waiting for their special day. She thought of Ben living in her house and moving his belongings in the week prior to their wedding. They had decided to live in hers as it was the larger of the two and her business was located on the first floor. Ben had already made arrangements to rent his house to one of their long-standing employees.

Focusing attention to her photography, Sabrina followed up on phone messages with one being to her assistant, Joe, to confirm the details of a scheduled two-day photo assignment in Atlanta. She had not mentioned this trip to Ben and wanted him to know she would not be home over the weekend. If she didn't hear from him soon, she would leave him a voice message.

Another call to her sister soothed Sabrina's roaming thoughts about Ben. Typically, it was Brie giving advice to

Sophie in crisis, so to be on the receiving end was different. There was a new depth to their sisterhood having grown closer with the recent experience with Faith.

Switching the conversation to the McKinley household, everything was back to normal. Sophie's world was perfect again. She had her family as it should be and began each day with praise and thanksgiving. When she held and played with her daughters, Sophie was forever talking to them about God and what He did for Faith. Even at such a tender age, she wanted them to hear the words often to plant the seed of truth in their spirit.

David came home each day to a happy family. He knew life would never be the same, and he had changed in ways he could feel deep in his soul. It had never been a priority before, but now they talked about establishing themselves in a church so when the girls were of age, they could attend Bible study. Neither believed it was a requirement of God that they present themselves in such surroundings; however, it would be a good beginning for worship. Each night after the girls were put to bed, they took their Bibles and sat in the living room studying together. There was so much they wanted to learn.

Sabrina phoned Ben leaving a brief message. She wasn't comfortable with the separation she felt from him and wanted it to come to an end, even if it required her to take the initiative. She had only one day before leaving for Atlanta and hoped he would call.

She went to visit with Bella to bring her up-to-date on Faith's healing. Brie carefully chose her words to explain the miracle, deliberately leaving out pertinent details. Though Bella was her friend, Brie wasn't privy to knowing her beliefs. You never know how someone may react to such proclamations, either an acceptance or a rebuttal. It remained for many a touchy topic. In this case, Bella appeared to accept the miracle for what it was having no problem believing it happened.

"That is the most wonderful thing I have ever heard in my

lifetime. You read about such things, but honestly, I've never known anyone who actually received a miracle from God. I sit here in total awe," Bella proclaimed.

"That's how Sophie and David felt."

"Amazing, absolutely amazing," she repeated, pausing for a moment to think about it.

"And how is this affecting you, Sabrina?"

"It's incredible, and I'm completely thrilled for Sophie," she replied, giving a simplified version of her thoughts.

They didn't dwell on the subject, and the remainder of their conversation paled in comparison to this exceptional news. Instead, they turned the discussion to the wedding arrangements and incidental things in Bella's life before Brie left. It was a short visit in comparison to other times.

When she returned home, Brie was deciding what to have for supper when the house phone rang. It was Ben.

"Want to meet me at the diner?" he asked, without any preliminary words.

"Well, hello to you too. I haven't heard from you in four days, and you call to invite me to dinner. Why don't you come over here?"

"I've just arrived back in town and haven't had a chance to clean up first. It would be easier to meet there. So do you want to?"

"Okay, what time?"

"Can you be there in thirty minutes?"

"Sure."

"Good," he said, ending the call.

Sabrina ran upstairs to freshen up her makeup and hair. If she left now, she would be there before Ben and could save them a table.

Sitting at their favorite booth near the back, she watched him coming through the front door making his way toward her. The sight of him made her heart skip a beat. Whatever was going on with Ben, she was determined to straighten it out right now, whatever it took.

As he got closer, she saw fatigue in his eyes and his mannerism slowed. What had he been doing these past few days that made him look so haggard? He approached leaning in to kiss her briefly before sliding onto the opposite bench. A waitress came over with two iced teas knowing it to be their usual, and they placed an order for the special of stuffed peppers, mashed potatoes and carrots. Ben reached across the table claiming her hands linking their fingers together. It sent a chill down her spine. Sabrina asked the question that was on her mind.

"Why haven't you called me?"

"I didn't know what to say."

"You've never been without words. Tell me what's going on with you."

"It's not a matter of what is going on with me, but what is happening to you. You are different, and I'm trying to figure out what that entails."

"That's not true. I'm the same person I've always been."

"Maybe you see yourself that way, but from where I am sitting, there is a distinct difference when I learn you can produce miracles," he said, lowering his voice.

Exasperated he would hold anything against her was unbelievable. Of all the things to be at odds over, this wasn't one she predicted, and didn't know how to convince him otherwise. It seemed his mind was set.

"First, I do not produce miracles. Get that straight, and secondly, how do you see me?"

"Look, I think it is great you have this gift, or talent, or whatever you call it. However, if it affects your life it will also affect mine when we are married."

"Ben, you are making too much out of this. Nothing is going to interfere in our marriage."

"Will you be keeping more secrets from me? Things you don't feel a need to share."

She didn't see that one coming. It was a low blow. Brie leaned back in her seat withdrawing her hands, placing them in her lap. She couldn't believe she was having this conversation with Ben. Taking a deep breath and slowly letting it out, she replied.

"If it's any consolation, Sophie didn't know, either. I just told her before leaving to return home from this last trip. She suspected something when she saw how the twins responded when I was with them, but at least she didn't give me the grief you are. I don't know what to tell you that will change how you view this. I have a special gift that I'm not ashamed of and chose to keep it to myself for personal reasons. When circumstances came about that made it obvious there was something between my nieces and me is when I needed to tell Sophie, and now I've told you. I'm not going to defend my decision, and if you or anyone else has a problem with that, then it is your problem, not mine. You are the one who has to accept it, or not."

The silence between them grew thick. She stated her position, and now it was up to Ben. He thought for a long time over her declaration and knew she was right. She was entitled to her privacy, and though it stung she hadn't told him before now, it was her decision. If things were reversed, he would expect the same.

"You're right. It was something personal, and you had the right to decide if you wanted to share it. I have to respect that. I was offended you didn't want to tell me, but that is a selfish attitude on my part. This has nothing to do with me and everything to do with you, and I've been a real butt about it. I'm sorry, love."

There was a deliberate pause before she addressed his confession.

"So does this mean you'll still marry me?" she asked, teasing him the way he often did her.

"I'll think about it," he said, with a big grin on his face, knowing he was forgiven.

Brie kicked his shin under the table. Laughing was how the waitress found them when she brought a large tray of food to their table.

"Gosh, I've worked up an appetite," he said.

"Me too."

Ben raised his iced tea glass and Brie did the same tapping the brims in a toast, and without another word, enjoyed their meal. He knew their marriage would be different than most and in many ways was looking forward to the challenges. Living with Sabrina would never be dull. If anything, Ben wondered if he would be able to keep up with her. He had the rest of his life to find out.

Epilogue

Looking into the full-length mirror made her eyes teary. With her blonde hair in soft ringlets pulled away from her face, Sabrina studied her reflection. Was that really her in the mirror, or was she dreaming a fairy tale where she was the princess soon to be united with her prince. Alone, Brie stood still and in a split second saw the shadow of another standing beside her, the same one who appeared to her two years ago. There was a beautiful aura as Sabrina returned the smile before the form vanished again.

Brie was standing in a private room at the church when Sophie rushed in with her veil and carefully placed it on her head. It was short in front only covering half of her face and trailing longer in the back. While all this commotion was taking place, Bella sat in the front row of pews babysitting the twins in their stroller. David availed himself to helping the groom and his escorts.

Sophie, David, Grace, and Faith were the first to arrive at Brie's house just days prior. Two days later, her friends from the magazine pulled into the driveway in a rental car having flown together. Now Sophie was running back and forth from their room to Brie's helping everyone with last minute preparations. She even had to borrow a stapler to hem a dress that someone had torn with their high-heeled shoes. If she stopped to catch her breath, Sophie knew she would start to cry. As the maid-of-honor, she refused to walk down the isle with red-rimmed eyes.

"Oh, Brie, you look so beautiful. Mom would be proud if she were here."

"Yes, I agree. I never could have done this without you. Thank you so much, sis."

"It's my pleasure to help my sister get married."

"I almost forgot something borrowed and something blue. Sophie stepped over to a table and gathered two items. Here, this is the borrowed. It's the white-laced handkerchief from my wedding. Pin it under your hem for good luck. And the blue is a lacy garter I came across in a bridal shop. I meant it to be a surprise," Sophie told her, taking it out of the box and helping Brie slip it onto her left leg.

"That was something I completely forgot to put on my list. Good thing you remembered, or Ben wouldn't have anything to throw at the bachelors," Sabrina said, laughing.

Focusing intently on Brie's appearance with an eye for detail, Sophie took one last look to make sure everything was perfect from head to toe. Stepping back, she smiled.

"Okay, are you ready to become Mrs. Bennaird Cooper?"

"Yes, I am," Brie said, smiling.

"Then let's do it. I'll let them know you're ready. When you hear the music, stand outside this door while I get everyone in the lineup."

She gently hugged her sister and kissed Sabrina on the cheek before walking out of the room. Sabrina could hear someone playing a piano. Calmness washed over her as she opened the door and stood exactly where Sophie had instructed. The bridesmaids came up to where she waited, ready to begin. Sophie quickly returned and began getting the women matched with their escorts.

"Okay, here we go," she said as she signaled them to begin their walk toward the front of the church.

Just before it was Sophie's turn, she leaned into her sister and whispered.

"Next time we talk, you'll be Mrs. Cooper. I'm so happy

for you, Brie," she said, choking on the words.

One final hug and she got into position for her stroll taking the forearm of her escort, her husband, and they proceeded like pros. Sabrina didn't want an escort. Since her father was not alive to give her away properly, she chose to walk alone. It was now her turn and all eyes where focused on the back of the church as she began to walk down the isle. Sabrina kept a deliberately slow pace to commemorate to memory this incredible moment, her wedding.

Against the planned rehearsal, Ben couldn't wait for her to walk the length of the church to join him. He stepped down from the platform approaching her, focusing on the most beautiful woman he had ever seen. Their eyes locked when mid-way he stopped in front of her and smiled. The music ceased and everyone remained still, not a sound was heard throughout the church. Sabrina fleetingly wondered if they could hear the beating of her heart.

Ben reached down taking her hands in his and leaning forward whispered in her ear.

"From the moment I saw you, I knew I would marry an angel."

"How's my halo?"

Ben threw his head back and burst out laughing. Sabrina smiled at him with love in her heart.

Passionate Promises

A Legacy

Excerpt

She is young, beautiful and on a fast-track with a career as a photojournalist when Sabrina receives a phone call that, abruptly, jolts her life. Sudden and unexplainably, her beloved Aunt Millie, their last remaining relative, is found dead in her home. As she and twin sister, Sophie, return to their aunt's hometown of Asheville, North Carolina for the funeral, they are told of an inheritance. While dealing with the heartache, they further learn of a legacy bequeathed to them in *Passionate Promises, A Legacy*.

The twins are shocked to discover their aunt's well-hidden secret and question if there is a connection to her demise. Subsequent to the funeral, and upon returning home to Florida, Sabrina is plagued by a soft voice whispering messages in her ear and *feels* the presence of someone nearby, always with her. Then the dreams begin. She is being drawn into a whirlwind of strange encounters that make her question her sanity, but she can't let go of the feeling that someone is one step ahead leading her to an unknown destination. She is certain there is something she must do concerning the legacy and wants to find out what, and perhaps, who is behind *Passionate Promises, A Legacy*.

Deciding to take a brief sabbatical from her career, she returns to Asheville to investigate both her aunt's death and uncover the meaning of the legacy. As she remains a relentless sleuth, Sabrina discovers that unveiling the mystery of the legacy is profoundly changing her life forever.

During her stay, Sabrina encounters Bennaird Cooper, a local bachelor, who claims they are soul mates, but will she allow him into her well-guarded life? Is she willing to take a chance on love and does *Passionate Promises, A Legacy* have something to do with her decision?

About the Author

Patricia Marlett is dedicated to writing inspirational novels for both the adult and young reader genres. With a contemporary platform, she enjoys penning plots that reflect life experiences through drama, intrigue, suspense, humor, and love. Inspirational messages are subtly woven within the endearing themes of her stories lending to heartfelt expressions from laughter to tears and always with hope and joy.

Visit Patricia at her website, www.patriciamarlett.com, to learn of her passion for writing, view her books, and for contact information.

www.ingramcontent.com/pod-product-compliance
Lightning Source LLC
Chambersburg PA
CBHW051241260626
47162CB00002B/549